Nick Stokes had never seen anything like this dump job—not as an experienced criminalist for the Las Vegas police, not in his three years with the crime lab back in Dallas.

He moved past the detective and squatted over it with his digital camera. The victim's hard-core body mod was grotesque but masterfully intricate—his eyeballs dyed black around their irises, a large round monocle tattooed over one eye, the area from the middle of the brow up transformed into a gold crown. It curved around the front of the head from temple to temple, its five evenly spaced points raised above the hairline.

"Implants," Nick said.

"You mean the crown points?"

"They're subdermals." Nick took some snapshots. "Inserted under the skin, that is."

Dressed in a sport jacket and jeans, Louis Vartan stood with his arms crossed and an expression of weary horror on his face.

"The Tattoo Man strikes again," he said. "At least, the third case in as many months that fits the profile."

"Except none of the others left anyone dead."

Vartan expelled a breath. "True enough," he said, looking down at the vic. "His eyes . . . were they *inked* that color?"

Nick nodded and adjusted his lens for a close-up. "Eye tats have been around for a while," he said. "There're also legit medical proced— — — ing the eyes of peopl— — — — — — se, he'd never heard — — — — — — e's eyeballs solid blac— — — — — — le these days, especia—

Original novels in the CSI series:

CSI: Crime Scene Investigation

Double Dealer
Sin City
Cold Burn
Body of Evidence
Grave Matters
Binding Ties
Killing Game
Snake Eyes
In Extremis
Nevada Rose
Headhunter
Brass in Pocket
The Killing Jar
Blood Quantum
Dark Sundays
Skin Deep
Serial (graphic novel)

CSI: Miami

Florida Getaway
Heat Wave
Cult Following
Riptide
Harm for the Holidays: Misgivings
Harm for the Holidays: Heart Attack
Cut & Run
Right to Die

CSI: NY

Dead of Winter
Blood on the Sun
Deluge
Four Walls

CSI:

CRIME SCENE INVESTIGATION™

SKIN DEEP

a novel

Jerome Preisler

Based on the hit CBS series CSI: Crime Scene Investigation produced by CBS PRODUCTIONS, a business unit of CBS Broadcasting Inc.

Executive Producers: Jerry Bruckheimer, Carol Mendelsohn, Anthony E. Zuiker, Ann Donahue, Naren Shankar, Cynthia Chvatal, William Petersen, Jonathan Littman

Series created by: Anthony E. Zuiker

POCKET STAR BOOKS
New York   London   Toronto   Sydney

Pocket Star Books
A Division of Simon & Schuster, Inc.
1230 Avenue of the Americas
New York, NY 10020

This book is a work of fiction. Names, characters, places, and incidents either are products of the author's imagination or are used fictitiously. Any resemblance to actual events or locales or persons, living or dead, is entirely coincidental.

First Pocket Star Books paperback edition September 2010

POCKET STAR BOOKS and colophon are registered trademarks of Simon & Schuster, Inc.

For information about special discounts for bulk purchases, please contact Simon & Schuster Special Sales at 1-866-506-1949 or business@simonandschuster.com.

The Simon & Schuster Speakers Bureau can bring authors to your live event. For more information or to book an event contact the Simon & Schuster Speakers Bureau at 1-866-248-3049 or visit our website at www.simonspeakers.com.

Cover design and illustration by David Stevenson, based on a photograph © Vasily Smirnov/Shutterstock

Manufactured in the United States of America

10 9 8 7 6 5 4 3 2 1

ISBN 978-1-4391-6082-4
ISBN 978-1-4391-6929-2 (ebook)

For Kirby, who passed through as swiftly as life itself.
And always and again, for Suzanne.

We are as clouds that veil the midnight moon;
How restlessly they speed, and gleam, and quiver,
Streaking the darkness radiantly!—yet soon
Night closes round, and they are lost for ever:

Or like forgotten lyres, whose dissonant strings
Give various response to each varying blast,
To whose frail frame no second motion brings
One mood or modulation like the last.

We rest.—A dream has power to poison sleep;
We rise.—One wandering thought pollutes the day;
We feel, conceive or reason, laugh or weep;
Embrace fond woe, or cast our cares away:

It is the same!—For, be it joy or sorrow,
The path of its departure still is free:
Man's yesterday may ne'er be like his morrow;
Nought may endure but Mutability.

—*Mutability*, Percy Bysshe Shelley (1792–1822)

AUTHOR'S NOTE

For those with an obsession for continuity similar to my own, the events of *Skin Deep* occur during Season 10 of the *CSI: Crime Scene Investigation* television series, which is, of course, its driving inspiration.

While the narrative is entirely a work of fiction, I would like to acknowledge my debt to several people who helped give it some verisimilitude . . . in other words, let me pull off another one.

Thanks go to Victoria Ramone for her introductions and to Brian Decker, Joy Rumore, and master tattoo artist Logan Aguilar for their assistance with various aspects of my research—and their forbearance as I relentlessly picked their brains. My conversations with Brian and Logan resonated throughout the manuscript in ways that extended far beyond the technical to greatly deepen my understanding of—and respect for—the tattoo and body-modification community. They deserve all the credit for whatever I got right. The inevitable errors and inaccuracies are my responsibility alone.

Readers familiar with Nevada and Las Vegans in particular might notice that I've taken occasional geographic liberties to suit the needs of my story.

I wish that I could as easily shift places around in real life, but the world is ever quick to remind me that it does not exist at my convenience.

A very special word of appreciation goes to Ed Schlesinger, my editor at Pocket Star Books. I suspect he knows why. What he might not realize is the extent to which I value his humanity and decency.

PROLOGUE

THE GOOSENECK LAMPS cast a wide fluorescent oval around his surgeon's stool, making him feel afloat in the surrounding darkness, like some lost, forgotten castaway drifting on a remote sea of night.

Lost, forgotten . . . it suited him. And served him, no? He surely wasn't eager to be remembered at this late stage.

He put on a thin nitrile exam glove, snapped it at the wrist, and slipped a second glove over the fingers of his other hand. Then he rotated his stool toward the stainless-steel counter along the wall, where he had mounted the young swine's pink, fleshy head on the platform of an adjustable sculpting stand.

Rolling forward on silent castors, he swung a lamp directly over the head and then turned a handle to raise it several inches. *Better.* The light would sharply highlight the grain of the skin and allow him to sit up straighter as he worked. Bending forward for any length of time had become painful, even agonizing, as had many things he'd taken for granted in the past. He needed to avoid distractions and maintain a sure, steady hand.

Now he turned toward the equipment cart at his elbow and examined the implements and supplies on its upper tray—three ink caps, a disposable hypodermic syringe with a fine thirty-gauge needle, a set of surgical scalpels and graded circle elevators, and his silicone elastomer implants. Also on the tray was a row of glass sundry jars containing suture, cotton pads, bandages, and other medical supplies.

He swiveled back around and brought his face up close to the pig's head, studying it for a moment before beginning his work. With its large blue eyes and static grin, it had a humanlike appearance that once might have surprised him. He couldn't say for certain, not anymore, after so much had gone by. Experience bred familiarity—wasn't that the saying? Or was he confusing things?

He'd learned, regardless, that porcine and human flesh were close biological matches. They had nearly identical hair follicles and sweat glands and a layer of subcutaneous fat that distinguished them from other species. Their color, surface texture, and dermal absorption rates were comparable. And both had large bare, hairless areas. It was the reason pig skin was often used for plastic-surgery research . . . and why he had chosen the swine's head as a surrogate.

He would have ample negative space for his modifications.

Finding a blue-eyed specimen had been another bit of luck. He might have settled for one with brown pupils if nothing else had been available at the slaughterhouse. But it would have made it harder to notice ink bleeding from the sclera. If he pierced the cornea or pupil of a live subject and the color seeped through the eye's connective tissues, it could lead to complete blindness.

He didn't intend for that to happen. This would be a difficult, complicated piece of transformative art that would be ruined by the smallest mistake in preparation. He was determined that it be flawless.

"Manpig, pigman, we're going to show the world what's inside you," he said huskily into the silence, hardly realizing his lips had almost brushed the flap of the swine's ear. "The flesh follows the spirit."

He reached for the slender hypodermic syringe, took an ink cap from his cart, and inserted the needle into its rubber stopper. With the needle still inside it, he turned the bottle upside down, depressed the plunger to force any air from the shaft, and then lifted it back up to draw in the ink, filling it with double the amount he meant to use. Finally, he thumbed the plunger again as a further precaution against air bubbles, squirting out the excess before he withdrew the needle from the cap.

Ready now. Pulling the skin around the swine's eyeball taut with his gloved middle and index fingers, he slid the tip of the needle into its white and injected a small amount of ink. As he'd anticipated, a slight overflow bubbled up from its outer membrane, pooled at the corner of the socket, and then began draining out, spilling over its bottom lid like a runny black teardrop.

He took a cotton pad from his cart and dabbed the eyelid clean. Then he reached for the bottle of saline solution, flushed out the eye, and blotted the rest of the ink from the pig's face with another pad. A colored spot about the size of a small mole remained where his ink had penetrated the white.

It would take thirty to forty pricks of the needle to stain the eye completely. With a voluntary recipient, he would mix his color with liquid antibiotic and inject it in multiple sessions—two or three weeks apart—to prevent irritation, infection, and cysts. But he wouldn't have that luxury and was practicing for what would be relatively quick work.

When the blotch's edges stopped spreading out, he reinserted the syringe and squeezed another milliliter of ink into it. He repeated his injections twice more, dabbing after each of them. After a while, he wiped the syringe clean and laid it back on the tray, watching the ink spread across the eyeball's curvature.

He inhaled, exhaled, and flexed his neck, back, and shoulders to ease their tightness. There was no relief from the burning in his chest, and he'd expected none, but he had found meditations for when it became intolerable. In the Mirror Chamber, he could rise beyond pain.

He was ready to move ahead to the next step.

With the pencil grip of a fine-edged scalpel resting against his thumb, he wheeled back up to the swine's head and made his incision. Blood welled up in a thin line as he carefully ran the blade down and in across its brow. *Practice.* When he did his actual modifications, he would want to avoid nerve damage and, for aesthetic reasons, cause the least possible amount of scarring.

Satisfied with his cut, he set down the scalpel and took his dermal elevator from the cart by its narrow handle. Slipping the instrument's dull, round metal probe into the incision, he lifted away the skin to create a pocket between its subcutaneous layer and the thick fascial weave encasing the pig's skull. He was very careful to go no deeper than a centimeter down and stay within a single layer of skin.

After loosening up the adipose tissue inside the pocket, he scraped it out and used a towel to wipe the blood and tiny white gobbets of fat off his instrument. Then he reached for the elevator with the next-largest probe and inserted it to widen the pocket. The graduated method he had developed wouldn't be nearly as traumatic as one that utilized a single elevator. It hastened the healing process and would be especially important given his difficult working conditions.

Still gripping the elevator handle with his left hand, he picked up the first implant with his right and inspected it under his lamp. An inch wide and two inches high, it measured slightly less than the desired centimeter in thickness. The two others on his cart were perfect matches.

He wheeled himself closer to the head again, stretched the skin a little farther away from the fascia and bone with his elevator, and pushed the smooth silicone triangle between his fingers into the widened pocket. It went in easily. A soft, moist sound as he pulled the skin up over the implant, applying some mild pressure with his fingertips to tuck it down at the suture line.

He paused to briefly stare into the swine's unseeing eyes.

"Glory to the crown," he whispered, reaching for the needle and thread.

Alone, forgotten, attended only by darkness, he resumed his pressing and delicate work.

1

THE TOWN OF MIRIAM was some four hundred miles northwest of Las Vegas in the Virginia Mountains, a drive of less than seven hours when highway traffic was light and his radar detector showed the road to be clear of trolling state police. He had made the trip often in recent weeks and this time had set out late on a Wednesday night, pushing past the speed limit most of the way there. Because he'd taken a low dose of his painkiller, it had not made him drowsy, and he'd needed to stop only for gas.

At around a quarter past six on Thursday morning, he had parked on the residential street where the father and son lived and then sat fifteen or twenty yards down from their home to wait. The tall evergreen hedge bordering the sidewalk screened the yard from view but also gave him some convenient, well-situated cover. He would not stay long; his intention was simply to observe their patterns and routines. By late afternoon, he would be on his way back to Vegas, giving him a full day to recover from the trip and prepare for his after-dinner appointment with the judge.

The yellow school bus pulled up to the house at seven o'clock, flashing its lights and extending its stop sign. He had noted in his previous visits that it was always on schedule, and this morning was no different. The boy, too, was invariably prompt when it arrived—credit the father.

Sipping the coffee he'd picked up at a diner near the railway depot outside town, he watched the father and son come down the gravel path to the street. Something inside him snarled as they hugged and the boy jumped aboard the bus. But he had managed to keep its bite in check so far and knew he could do so until the right moment came.

Credit the man who once had been a father.

Now the stop sign folded back against the school bus, and it rumbled off. The father stood and watched its wide rear end for a moment before turning back to the house. He would typically leave for his job at the auto-repair shop forty-five minutes later.

Straightening, the man in the car put his coffee cup in the holder beside his seat. On previous days, he'd waited to follow the father. On others, he'd charted the son. He had not decided between them. Or, more properly, the decision had yet to be revealed to him.

After a minute or two, he drove on after the bus, remaining several car lengths behind. A few more pickups, and then it was out carrying the children over a local road that rolled west toward the edge of town, where the Catholic church and outbuildings stood between dun-colored mountain slopes to back defiantly on the sheer drop of the valley ridge. In Nevada, the desert wilderness always breathed close on civilization's neck. Its people understood this secret in their bones but would never share it with the tourists for fear of scaring them off. Every beast needed to be fed, and it was important to keep the swarm, with its money and giddy excess, lured by the tantalizing lights.

At the wrought-iron fence in front of the church grounds, the bus driver made a last stop to discharge his youthful passengers, idling at the gate as the students shouldered their bookbags and walked to the converted priory that served as their schoolhouse.

In his car behind the bus, the visitor again waited for its stop sign to be retracted. Once its operator drove off, he would move on past the church, wait a few minutes, and then circumspectly double back to resume his watch.

He never forced his inspirations and truly did not know whether it would be the father or the son. But time was growing short, that much was sure, and he felt confident the choice would present itself to him before long.

When it did, he meant to be ready.

Chinese food on Friday nights, Saturday mornings at the golf course, and Sundays out on the patio

snoozing with his face under an outspread copy
of the *Wall Street Journal*. Among the pleasures of
retirement, Quentin Dorset supposed he placed the
highest value on his leisurely, untroubled weekends.

He keyed the ignition of his Lexus SUV in the
parking area outside Wu Liang's, got the air going,
popped on his lights, and waved to the driver of the
Jaguar idling in the slot beside him. Joss Garland,
a regular in Dorset's dinner group, tapped his horn
in acknowledgment and pulled out with his two
passengers, Anthony Cervelli and Matt Pakonen. A
moment later, Dorset saw the retired bishop of the
Diocese of Las Vegas, Monsignor Sebastian Valder-
court, follow in his Honda.

Dorset had known the clergyman for twenty
years. And he went back even longer with Garland,
who had been among the Strip's most well-known
casino managers once upon a time. His boisterous
storytelling was peppered with names like Sinatra,
Presley, Newton, and Ann-Margret, who Dorset
still thought was the sexiest woman ever to kick up
her shapely legs onstage.

Yes, Joss had been a bona fide mover, and the
same could have been said about all of the members of the group. Cervelli had headed the Nevada
Gaming Commission throughout the 1980s. Pakonen was a celebrated defense attorney who'd represented mob boss Anthony Frattone at the height
of his unrivaled power in Vegas—and whom Dor-

set had ironically gotten to know on a social basis after presiding over an extortion-racketeering trial that sent Frattone to prison for a quarter-century.

But the diverse bunch included more than just former legal and political big wheels. Or, putting it another way, Dorset thought, recognizable but attention-starved old farts, *me paenitet*, Monsignor. Blake Weller was a bestselling novelist in his thirties, Sheldon Cranston an agent representing dozens of current entertainers, Lars Ullen a pre-eminent chef. Though he was onstage at the Sands tonight and only joined them on occasion, Jackie "Rob" Calston one of the group's relative newcomers, was half of Rob and Hood—pun obviously intended—the hottest illusionist act in town.

Surfacing from his thoughts, Dorset watched Garland's Jaguar leave the outdoor lot, passing under the ornamental Chinese arch. No sooner had it swung onto Spring Mountain Road than he heard a buzzing noise over to his left. He glanced around as Ullen, wearing a silver jet-style helmet, sped off on his little Italian scooter.

Dorset supposed he'd better get going as well. He would drive back to Vista Bella on his customary route, heading in the opposite direction of the Jag toward South Decatur, then taking the interstate and Summerlin out to his home off the gated community's eighteen-hole golf course. First, though, he'd make his usual stop at the gas station and Food Mart on the corner of West Charleston.

It was now a few minutes past nine o'clock. All told, he'd be in his living room mixing a Bitter Canadian by ten.

He backed out of his spot and drove under the arch to exit the plaza and merge with the evening traffic.

After stepping down from the district court, Dorset had second-guessed his decision on a host of occasions. He was in good health for a man of sixty-eight and felt he could have stayed on another five years, perhaps longer. But losing his wife had robbed him of something vital to the post. He didn't know what name to lay on it. Commitment? Focus? Really, he didn't know. He and Gilda had bought the Vista Bella house just three months before she was diagnosed with pancreatic cancer. They'd planned to spend their weekends shooting holes on the course, socializing at the club, easing into their senior years. It was never to be, though. They hadn't even had a chance to furnish the house when the pernicious disease took her from him.

And so he'd vacated the bench. The transition had been undeniably rough—rougher than he'd foreseen. And slower, too. There was boredom and loneliness and the long, sleepless nights of wondering if he'd made the right choice. But then, in eventual stages, almost before he knew it was happening, his doubts had eased off, and Dorset had found he'd settled into his lifestyle.

Approaching West Charleston now, he signaled, moved into the right lane, turned into the gas station, and pulled up to the pump. He got out, slid his credit card into the reader, and put the nozzle in his tank. He'd noted his fuel needle was halfway down and locked the handle before walking over to the grocery for his newspaper.

"*Señor Juez, cómo estás?*"

Dorset took out his wallet and smiled at the man behind the cash register. He always held a copy of the weekend *Journal* for him and had set it out on the counter beside cardboard displays of Easter candy and egg-decorating kits.

"I'm well, Enrique," he said, handing over a five. "I ordered a new dish tonight, the Mongolian beef. It was the chef's special."

"Ah. Is good?"

"Perfection," Dorset said. "You're welcome to join me one of these nights."

The vendor flapped a dismissive hand. "I not such an important person."

"Nonsense. Who am I but a subpar golfer with bad knees?" Dorset said. "Seriously. You should come to dinner some night, try that duck for yourself. My treat."

Enrique passed him his change. "*Gracias, Señor Juez.* Maybe one time, I surprise you."

"I hope you do," Dorset said. He tucked the paper under his arm. "*Buen fin de semana,* Enrique. Enjoy the weekend."

A nod. "*Tú también.*"

Dorset headed outside. It was a beautiful March

night in the valley, seasonally brisk, the moon a silver crescent above Mount Charleston, stars speckling the clear black sky. The chocolate Easter eggs and bunnies on Enrique's counter had reminded him that the holiday was right around the corner, although special occasions of that sort were admittedly when he thought most about Gilda, who'd always applied a festive touch to their home when they were coming up on the calendar.

Thought about her, yes. And *missed* her dearly.

He strode from the glow of the storefront window into the dark and crossed to the pump island with its lighted canopy. The gas nozzle had cut off when his tank was full, and he paused before going around to hang it back on the pump, opening his passenger door to toss in his *Wall Street Journal*.

"Excuse me, sir, I think this might be your wallet."

Momentarily startled, Dorset straightened with his door open, turned toward the sound of the voice, recovered at once. The man who'd come up to him under the canopy was smiling pleasantly, a brown leather billfold held out in his left hand. Thirtyish and clean-cut, he wore trendy thick-rimmed eyeglasses, a blue pullover Windbreaker with a kangaroo pocket and the Nike swoosh in front, and khaki trousers.

"I found it over there on the ground," he said in a friendly tone, nodding toward the Food Mart. "Figured you might've dropped it when you left."

Dorset didn't have to check his trouser pocket.

He could feel his billfold against his thigh, and the one in the young man's hand didn't resemble it at all. A gift from Gilda for some long-ago birthday, its worn tan leather was monogrammed in gold with his initials.

"It isn't mine, thanks." He smiled. "You're very decent wanting to return it . . . have you seen if there's identification inside?"

The man shook his head. "No," he said. "But look at this."

His right hand went into his kangaroo pocket and reappeared an instant later. Dorset's eyes widened in shock when he saw what was in it. The man was gripping a small black pistol, aiming it at him point-blank. He barely had time to wonder how he could have missed its outline against the jacket's thin nylon fabric before its snout was shoved hard against his side.

"Get in," the man said. His voice was harsh now. "Then slide behind the wheel."

He bodied up against Dorset, angling the weapon's muzzle up under his ribs, thrusting it into him as he forced him toward the SUV's door.

Dorset gasped as the air left his lungs, half stumbling, half falling into the passenger seat. The man was incredibly strong—far more powerful than he'd have guessed.

"Listen to me . . . you can have the vehicle," he said. "My money. Anything else. You don't need to do this."

"Shut up. Don't think I wouldn't put a bullet in you right now."

The man's eyes burned into Dorset from behind his glasses. He pushed him deeper into the vehicle, got in after him, and shoved him over the center console against his faltering resistance.

Dorset winced as his shoulder bashed painfully against the driver's-side door.

"Let's go," the man said from the passenger seat. The muscles of his jaw flexed. "You'll drive."

Dorset hesitated with the key in his hand, looking over at the man, struggling to keep his fear under control.

It proved impossible. Those eyes. They were boring into him. He felt as if he'd been pinned under the lens of a microscope.

"You have a wide forehead," the man said, his voice dropping to a low mutter. "I had to measure to scale from photographs."

Dorset looked at him in confusion. "What did you say?"

The man blinked as if startled from a momentary trance. Then Dorset felt the gun jab his side again.

"Never mind. Put your key in the ignition . . . hurry."

Dorset inserted it, turned it, felt the Lexus shiver to life. He looked out at the Food Mart's window and saw Enrique behind the counter.

"Do anything stupid, and you'll be dead before he can help."

Dorset's pulse roared in his ears. "What is it you

want?" he heard himself ask. His voice sounded distant and wavery. "Will you at least tell me that?"

The man was silent. His pistol still buried in Dorset's side, he slammed the passenger door shut. And only then gave his answer.

"I'm going to king you," he said.

"Okay. Stop."

"This place . . . why did we drive here?"

"You'll see."

"But—"

"Shut up and stop. I already told you what I want to do. You should be pleased."

Dorset braked, cut the motor. *I'm going to kill you,* he thought. He was sure they had been his words . . . *right*?

The pistol nudged his ribs. "Now, get out. Slowly. Remember, there's no one to hear me empty my gun into you."

Dorset shuddered. He was greasy with sweat under his shirt.

"What are you waiting for? Open your door."

Dorset reached for the handle and was reluctantly shifting around to leave the vehicle when he was struck under the back of his neck. It wasn't hard—a light, stinging slap. But then he felt a sudden numbness spreading from his shoulders down through his limbs.

Dorset's thoughts shrank into a cold point of terror. An instant later, darkness eddied around him, and he was swept away.

2

"JOSH, YOU'RE AN IIIDIOT."

"And you're wasted."

"A real iiidiot," Caitlyn slurred, ignoring him. "You don't believe me, jussht ask Mia and Owen."

Josh stared at her, standing there on the dark concrete median between the eastbound and westbound lanes on Koval about a mile from where they'd left the dance club—a place called Random, which was the third place they'd hit that night, after Flicker and that first club with the French name he couldn't pronounce. He was thinking that if Caitlyn the boozy birthday girl wasn't such a hot figure-eight in her bandage dress and heels, and if he didn't have maybe a seventy-thirty chance of rocking the mattress with her once she finally returned to their room and got over being pissed, and also if Owen wasn't her older brother, and especially if the muscle-bound lump wasn't twice his own size, he would tell her to keep her nasty, insulting mouth shut and show her what an idiot *really* was, leave her and her little posse stranded on this dark, miserable back road where there was nothing but trailer-truck depots, cheap all-night diners, and budget motels like the one they'd booked near the airport for their Vegas getaway. *Happy birthday, sweetie. It was nice banging—excuse me, hanging—with you while it lasted.*

All those things aside, Josh was still tempted to leave Caitlyn, her balloon-armed brother, and his twit of a fiancée right there. *Good riddance.* Meanwhile, he'd hike the mile or so back to where their cab had turned off the Strip at the monorail tracks and then cut onto Flamingo and grab a different taxi from the lines over at one of the resorts there, maybe with a driver who'd appreciate earning a buck in a day and age when half the people in America were unemployed and donating blood just to pay their electric bills.

Appreciate it, that was, in comparison with their last driver, the real culprit behind their getting dumped off like so much trash, no matter how Caitlyn was spinning things right now.

"Tell you something," he said. "If I'm an idiot, that cabbie was a douche."

"Gee, you sound soooo shhmart."

"Come on," Josh said. "Were we or weren't we supposed to be partying tonight?"

"Doesn't mean you had to get on that cabbie about the radio," Owen said.

"Who got on him? I *asked* the guy to turn it up."

"Told him's more like it," Mia chimed in.

"Whatever, I was respectful," Josh said defensively, thinking that all he needed was for *her* to start in on him, too, make it a perfect three. "Ain't my fault he was allergic to rap music."

"Dude don't got to turn it up 'cause you say so," Owen said.

"He wants his tip he does."

"No, he don't."

"That's the problem."

"What do you mean?"

"I mean, you're insisting on it's what got us kicked out."

"Look, I told him we're celebrating, right? Come all the way from Philly to celebrate your *sister's* birthday."

"Soooo shhmart," Caitlyn said.

Josh looked at her. "You hear me talking to you?"

"I heard you talking *about* me."

"So how about you don't chime in till I finish my point?" Josh frowned sulkily. Given how things were deteriorating between him and Caitlyn, he figured the odds of getting it on with her tonight—well, actually, this morning, since it was almost three A.M.—had already dwindled to fifty-fifty. They shrank any more, he was absolutely ditching out on her. "I want the radio cranked so we can sing along to that Rob Z track in the backseat, what's the major offense?"

"You got no right insisting that of him, is what," Owen said.

"For the second time, I didn't insist. Besides, what right does he have insisting we get the hell out?"

"You tell him he can forget about a tip he doesn't turn up the song, he's got the right," Mia said.

"It's the cabbie's cab," Owen agreed, nodding.

Josh gave Caitlyn a piercing look. He'd had his fill of taking crap from her gang of three here.

"It's the cabbie's cab," he parroted. "Now, that's what I call smart. Takes a genius to figure out it's the cabbie's cab."

"You inshhulting my brother?"

"Why not?" he said. Owen wanted to haul off on him, he could be his guest. "I *insist* to the cabbie, I *insult* your brother, I'm the biggest *idiot* on the planet—"

"Got *that* shhhtraight," Caitlyn said.

Josh kept glowering at her. Enough was enough. He was sick of being triple-teamed. Caitlyn could have their room to herself, assuming she ever made it back to the motel. He would get there ahead of her in taxi number two, have the driver wait while he packed his suitcase, and then bring him to another low-budget inn. There had to be a dozen near the airport with vacancies. More than a dozen, he bet. Once he checked in, he'd grab the phone book and order some takeout—preferably of the blond variety. Do some real Vegas-style celebrating.

"That's it," he said. "I'm going."

"Where?" Caitlyn said.

"None of your business."

"But it's, like, three miles to the motel," Owen said.

"Right."

"You get us tossed out of that cab, and you're cutting loose?"

"Right, genius."

Josh turned around quickly, figuring it was now or never as far as Owen smacking him one to preserve his drunken sister's honor . . . of which Josh had noticed little to none since they'd first hooked up in a bar maybe a month ago. When the blow upside his head didn't come, he figured he'd better get a move on before the dumb galoot changed his mind. Or had it changed for him.

"Kick hisssh assh, Owen," Caitlyn said behind him, trying her best to do just that.

"Screw him, he ain't worth it."

Breathing a sigh of relief, Josh hoped he would stay unworthy as far as Owen was concerned, if only long enough to disappear into the deep, dark night. He hustled across the eastbound lanes to the sidewalk and started backtracking toward the monorail, walking parallel to the chain-link security fence fronting an enormous truck lot to his left.

"Joshhh, you bashhhtard, shhhtop!"

Crap, he thought. Caitlyn had followed him across the road—he could hear her high heels unevenly scuffing on the pavement as she tried to catch up. Meanwhile, Owen and Mia were shouting her name even as she yelled *his* at the top of her lungs, creating the potential for a whole ugly scene to develop.

Josh wanted no part of it. Ignoring all three of them, he quickened his pace to a near trot.

"Joshhh, you ba—" Caitlyn suddenly broke off. "Omigod! *Omigod!*"

He barely had time to register the shock in her voice when a loud, wordless scream burst from her lips, tearing shrilly into the predawn silence along the deserted lane. He stopped cold and felt his blood rush into his legs.

Josh stood with his muscles locked. Caitlyn kept screaming. His heart beat twice, pounding hard against his chest, and he realized he'd turned to see what was happening. She was ten or twelve feet behind him, facing the truck depot, staring into it through the chain-link fence. Screaming, screaming, screaming, as Owen and Mia raced over to her from the median.

And then all three were gaping at something beyond the fence. Josh snapped his eyes in that direction. Saw the dark shape on the ground. It was just inside the linkage, visible at the outer rim of the glow from a lamp pole inside the lot. Caitlyn was still screaming hysterically, her eyes wide with fright and confusion, and now Mia was shrieking her head off, too.

Josh wouldn't recall running over. But the next thing he knew, he was there alongside them, peering through the fence.

"What?" he said. "What *is* it?"

None of them could answer.

"Nick, Detective Vartan, take a look."

Nick Stokes was already doing that. He had never seen anything like this dump job—not as an experienced criminalist for the Las Vegas police, not in his three years with the crime lab back in Dallas.

He moved past the detective and squatted over it with his digital camera. The victim's hard-core body mod was grotesque but masterfully intricate—his eyeballs dyed black around their irises, a large round monocle tattooed over one eye, the area from the middle of the brow up transformed into a gold crown. It curved around the front of the head from temple to temple, its five evenly spaced points raised above the hairline.

"Implants," Nick said.

"You mean the crown points?"

"They're subdermals." Nick took some snapshots. "Inserted under the skin, that is."

Dressed in a sport jacket and jeans, Louis Vartan stood with his arms crossed and an expression of weary horror on his face.

"The Tattoo Man strikes again," he said. "At least, the third case in as many months that fits the profile."

"Except none of the others left anyone dead."

Vartan expelled a breath. "True enough," he said, looking down at the vic. "His eyes . . . were they *inked* that color?"

Nick nodded and adjusted his lens for a close-up. "Eye tats have been around for a while," he said. "There're also legit medical procedures for tinting the eyes of people with visible defects." Of course, he'd never heard of a doctor who'd tattoo anyone's eyeballs solid black, though anything was possible these days, especially in this town.

Letting his camera hang from its neck strap, Nick ran his latex-gloved fingers over the points of the crown. A moment later, he noticed a circle of high-intensity white light to his left, turned in that direction, and saw Sara Sidle approaching from the periphery of the crime scene, where LVPD cops were busily working to secure it with barricades and yellow tape. Beyond them in the predawn dimness, row upon row of parked semi-trailers were lined up like a herd of somnolent dinosaurs.

"Find anything?" he asked her.

She doused the forensic lamp and offered a half shrug. "No footprints or tire marks," she said. "There are two places on Koval where the fencing's separated from the posts."

Making the lot easily accessible from the street. Nick could imagine how thrilled all the insurance companies covering the trailers for theft and damage would be over such airtight security. "Those openings close by?"

"The nearest one's about ten yards away toward Sands Avenue."

"And the other?"

"Fifteen or twenty yards farther along."

"Either of them wide enough for the body? And whoever brought it here?"

"I haven't taken measurements yet," she said. "My guess is that both would allow entry. But you'd have to push back the fencing to get through."

"Wouldn't be too hard for someone strong enough to carry more than two hundred pounds of dead weight," Nick said. Before becoming so much decomposing meat, fluid, and bone, their vic had been an older man, about six feet tall, and paunchy around the middle.

Sara stood regarding the corpse over Nick's broad shoulders. Her wedge-cut brown hair was tucked back behind her ears, and she had on a black crime-scene vest, a CSI ball cap, and matching slacks.

"The gaps in the fence aren't new," she said. "I didn't see the sort of clean, shiny edges you'd get from a chain cutter on the severed linkages."

"Vandalism?"

"Could be. But the loose panel closest to us buckles outward . . . like maybe a truck backed into the fence while it was pulling in or out."

Nick nodded his agreement. With giant rigs

maneuvering around the depot all day, he figured that would be a commonplace occurrence.

"He came, he saw, he ditched the corpse," he said. "Whether or not our killer scouted the depot ahead of time, it's probably just an opportune site."

"As opposed to one that has emotional or psychological significance."

"Right." Nick caught her hesitancy. "You disagree?"

She shrugged. "Why leave the body right along the sidewalk? It would have stayed hidden longer if he'd pulled it between the trailers."

"He might've had trouble carrying it. Or been in a hurry."

"Or wanted it on display."

Nick considered that as David Phillips, the assistant coroner, came ducking under the tape with his aluminum crime-scene kit, one hand on the small of his back. He acknowledged Vartan with a glance, knelt beside Nick, and set down his case. "Hail to the king," he said. "This man looks like he jumped off a deck of cards."

Now, there's an expert observation. Nick saw him rub his lower back again. "Something hurt, Dave?"

"Always." He shrugged. "The wife buys me new insoles for chronic backache. I'd get better relief if corpses would occasionally turn up where I don't have to bend or crawl to examine them."

Nick gave a slight smile. He unhooked his ultraviolet flash from his gear belt, flipped the amber goggles down from over his close-cropped brown hair, and shone the light on the dead man's head. "The incisions are well healed," he said, carefully running his finger over the points of the crown. "There's no bruising, very little swelling. And there aren't any scabs. My guess is the work was done a couple of weeks ago." He looked at Phillips. "You think whoever did this used dissolving sutures?"

"And gel bandages," Phillips said with a nod. "Basically the type applied to burn victims. They help prevent scar tissue from forming as the skin heals."

"A perfectionist," Sara said. "Our man's proud of his artistry."

"Yeah," Nick said slowly.

Phillips had opened his kit, taken a pair of gloves from it, and put them on. Now he lifted the dead man's eyelid with a fingertip, wobbled his jaw, and brought an arm off the ground to manipulate the wrist and elbow. "Rigor's at an early stage. There's considerable stiffness in the head, almost none in the extremities."

This indicated that the time of death fell within the past twelve hours. He'd lived to see what was done to him, Nick thought.

He noticed Phillips lowering the victim's arm and motioned for him to keep it raised. "Hang on a sec," he said, shining his flash on the back of the hand. "What do you make of this little red spot right here?"

Phillips peered down at the area in the circle of light. "A puncture wound over a dorsal vein." He ran a finger over it. "Looks as if he had a peripheral intravenous line running into him."

Nick considered that. After a moment, he turned off his flash, clipped it back onto his belt, and felt around in the corpse's pockets for identification. It didn't surprise him to find them empty.

"He's wearing a good suit," Sara said. "Very conservative but expensive."

Nick checked out the tag under the collar. *Brooks Brothers, sure enough.*

Her eyes narrowed. "He's clean-shaven. If he's been missing for a couple of weeks, wouldn't you expect to see stubble on his cheeks?"

Nick raised an eyebrow. "Somebody cleaned him up so he'd look his best."

"Or so the tattoos would."

Nick nodded silently and turned toward the group that had discovered the body. They were outside the taped-off crime-scene area, standing in the gray twilight with one of the cops who'd responded to their nine-eleven.

"What's their story?" he asked Vartan.

"They're out-of-town partyers," the detective said. "They pick up a cab outside a dance club, head back toward their motel outside McCarran. Then one of them hears a song on the radio, insists the driver crank up the music so they can sing to it."

"They think they're in some television commercial?"

"Everybody's got a Vegas fantasy," Vartan said

with a bemused shrug. "Anyway, the driver gets annoyed, boots them from his taxi about a half block up, takes off. They start arguing over who's to blame, our singer takes off in a snit, walks back in this direction to find another cab. His girlfriend follows him and finds the DB."

"That's it?"

"From their preliminary statement, right," Vartan said. "I don't think there'll be much more from them."

"How about witnesses to the body dump? Isn't there a guard booth?"

"Around the block on East Harmon." Vartan motioned across the lot with his head. "We had a hell of a time waking the night watchman up from his snooze."

Nick smiled thinly. "Anything else?"

"I'm running a missing-persons check on the vic," Vartan said. "I'll copy you once I have the list of possibles."

"I'd also appreciate any updates you might have on the other Tattoo Man case—Stacy Ebstein and Mitchell Noble. Whatever's in your files. Just to make sure the lab's current."

"They'll reach it before you do."

Nick was rubbing his chin thoughtfully. He continued to study the corpse for a few seconds, then rose from his crouch.

"I posted men at the fence openings," Sara said. "They're setting up floodlights. I didn't recover any contact evidence but thought you'd want a look."

Nick nodded to indicate he would. But Sara was too methodical to miss anything significant, and their killer seemed very thorough. That didn't leave him optimistic about his chances.

"I'll head over right now," he said, moving off toward the brilliance of the floods.

Forensic professionals weren't known for their sentimentality. The processing of evidence began not at the lab but at the crime scene, where the fluids, decompositions, and other untidy leftovers of murder were found and tabbed for analysis. Seen through scientific eyes, the butchery and carnage became a lush harvest there for the picking. You had to stick to that perspective.

Still, criminalists were human. It was empathy for the victims that got Nick Stokes through the long, dark hours of the night, when one door of inquiry usually led to another. *Who are you? Who did this? How?*

Sometimes the very emotions you'd taught yourself to contain reminded you why the work mattered. Sometimes it didn't hurt to bring them up for air.

Returning to his office from the Koval Lane trailer depot, Nick paused in the entrance and briefly saw it not as it was but as it had been. Such moments no longer took him by surprise, and he kind of liked rolling with them. The office had, after all, once belonged to Gil Grissom, who had been much more than just his mentor. Nick knew the day he couldn't feel his presence would probably be the day the human emotions in his tank had been depleted. If it ever reached that point, he would have to move on.

Grissom. The metal plaques visible outside the entry had identified him as the supervisor of the Clark County, Nevada, criminalistics bureau. As distinguished by another engraved plate on the wall, he was also an esteemed member of the Entomological Society of America. But those titles formed too small a suit for the substance of the man—his wide-ranging interests, his depth of insight, his probing, restless intellect. It was apt, then, that Grissom's meditative sanctuary within the criminalistics bureau had been a repository of jarred, bagged, mounted, and variously preserved taxonomic and histological specimens representing virtually every known kingdom, phylum, class, order, family, genus, and species of life on the planet.

Nick's memories of the collection crowded in on him now, filling his mind the way its contents had filled the room. Grissom had insisted he kept it ordered and catalogued, an assertion many held in doubt—though no one at the lab would admit to the widespread suspicion that he had long since forgotten about certain acquisitions and was hazy on others he'd stashed away. Here was a jar of cicadas, there the eyeballs somebody had once confused with Cerignola olives, as rumor had it, mistaking their pinkish, shriveled optic-nerve clusters for pimientos. On this shelf were reptiles and amphibians; on that larvae, grubs, and worms; on a third a fish tank holding only brittle aquatic plants Grissom had netted and dried with chemical desiccants. Behind the desk were his mounted butterflies, a South American tarantula displayed in clear acetate, and Peg-Boards covered with glassine envelopes full of tiny insects and crustaceans. In every available corner, reference books teetered against heavier volumes stacked ten or fifteen high, the texts crammed between Rolodexes and file folders, bottled organs, tissue samples, skulls, and freefloating appendages in odorless phenoxetols and Nipa esters. Some of the older biological specimens, acquired from dusty museum storerooms, hung pale and gray in formalin suspensions. Whenever Gris opened their bottles, it had conjured pungent associations of the mortuary and, for a few unwary visitors, had led to coughing, gagging, wheezing, and generalized skin rashes.

David Hodges, the trace tech, insisted he could still smell traces of formaldehyde in the office. But the CSIs took that with a larger handful of salt than Grissom's claims that he'd kept it organized according to his own mysterious scheme. Hodges had helped solve a murder a while back by sniffing out the bitter-almond scent of cyanide, a genetic ability shared by about forty percent of the population. It was nevertheless an open question whether his nose was as hypersensitive to other chemicals as he later claimed or if he was milking his moment of olfactory glory for all it was worth . . .

"Daydreaming?"

Nick turned with a mild start and found himself looking into the face of Jim Brass. It was a familiar one around the crime lab, and no wonder. Brass was captain of the homicide squad operating out of LVPD headquarters next door, his rank seemingly evidenced by the fact that his suits were always sharper and better tailored than those of the detectives under his command. The navy-blue cashmere he had on now was no exception.

"I usually wait till it's daytime." Nick showed him the dial of his wristwatch. "We've got a few hours to go."

Brass grunted out a chuckle from the corridor.

"What's up?" said Nick.

"You requested our updates on the Tattoo Man case, right?"

Nick nodded. He'd noticed the detective was holding several manila file folders against his side.

"Here's everything." Brass passed him the files. "Excluding tonight's report. It's still being completed."

Nick regarded him quietly. Brass was no errand runner. "I figured Williams would e-mail these to me."

"He would've." Brass shrugged. "I was coming

to see you anyway. Decided I might as well bring along the hard copies."

Nick waited. Brass nodded past him at the office.

"I just came from the morgue," he said. "We need to talk about the latest vic—it won't take long."

Nick moved aside to let him through the door and followed him in. Suddenly, Grissom's collection was cleared out, gone, or mostly gone, leaving only the room in its present functional incarnation. The walls of the so-called bullpen now shared by Nick, Greg, and Langston were bare, its shelves disassembled, the bulk of his things packed away in storage, and the rest shipped to Costa Rica, where he'd been conducting research of some kind or another in the tropical rain forest. All that was left was Gris's former mascot, the jarred fetal pig he'd said he used to test the effects of radiation on skin tissue. It had surprised everybody when Hodges, who'd seemed unaffected by Grissom's departure, revealed he'd held on to the pickled pig and returned it to the office, explaining that was its rightful place.

Nick hadn't given him an argument, and there it rested on a counter, immersed in its bath of preservative fluids, blindly greeting everyone who entered.

"Sidle here?" Brass asked.

"She's logging physical evidence," Nick said. "We haven't recovered much from the scene. Some hairs and fibers that might or might not be associated with the dead man. Nothing to identify him right off."

Brass was quiet. Nick dropped the case files onto his desk and gestured him toward a chair.

"No, thanks," Brass said, remaining where he stood. "Like I told you, I intend to make this quick."

Nick looked at the detective curiously. He wasn't positive what to make of his silence. But he had an inkling. "You have a name to go with our victim?" he said.

"Quentin Dorset," Brass said. "Ring a bell?"

Nick immediately realized it did. "The judge."

"*Retired* judge," Brass said. "There's been a four-eighteen out on him for a week."

Nick nodded. Four-eighteen was the LVPD radio code for a missing-persons report. "The body work on Dorset wasn't done overnight," he said. "It's almost healed."

"I noticed." Brass sighed. "Dorset's an acquaintance of mine. His wife died of cancer a couple of years back. Not long afterward, he stepped down from the bench."

"He lived alone?"

"Yeah." Brass reached into his pocket for a notepad, flipped it open, and scanned its pages. "Kept busy, though. Social functions, Chinese food with friends every Friday, Saturdays on the green, occasional travel . . . he got out of the house."

"How long since he was last seen?"

Brass was studying his notes. "Three weeks ago, Dorset said good night to his Friday dinner group at a restaurant called Wu Liang's. Drove home but didn't show up at the country club on Saturday. The weather's been on the cool side, so nobody there thought much of it. But when he missed his next Chinatown get-together without canceling with his pals, they became a little concerned."

"Just a little? Didn't you say this was a regular thing with them?"

"Dorset's the type who'd leave his cell phone in his jacket pocket, hang the jacket in a closet, and forget about it till the battery died," Brass said. "He also liked going on spur-of-the-moment jaunts. Nobody would've been too surprised to find out he'd left on an amateur fossil-hunting expedition or something."

Nick digested that. "Still seems odd that it was another seven days before the police were notified."

Brass gave him a jaundiced look. "Really? You know the stats on missing persons in Las Vegas?"

Nick frowned. Dropping out of sight wasn't a crime, and it so happened that this was America's voluntary-disappearance capital. A destination where visitors from every state, city, and town in the country came to run free with the mistress or the married boyfriend after jumping their white picket fences . . . or maybe spend the kid's hockey-lesson money on some exotic hired help. Two hundred people a month were reported, eighty percent of whom turned up okay except for a massive hangover and twisted undies.

"You're telling me it wouldn't have made a difference," he said.

Brass shrugged. "It's posted on the LVPD website—we all have the right to be left alone," he said. "Unless you're talking about a minor or someone with a record of convictions, there isn't much the missing-persons detail can do. They would've made some inquiries, seen if there was any evidence of foul play, entered Dorset's name into the SCOPE system."

"And nothing turned up?"

Brass was nodding his head. "When he skips out on his noodles and fortune cookies for a second week straight, his friends figure they should stop by his house. No answer, the SUV gone, they decide to knock on a couple of neighbors' doors. Nobody's seen him for a while, so they check at the golf course. When everybody there says *they've* been wondering where he might be, they start to worry something isn't kosher."

"Besides the roast pork," Nick said.

Brass expelled a deep breath. "Yeah."

Nick glanced down at the folders on his desk and tapped them with his fingertips. "Does anything in these files connect Dorset to the rest of the victims?"

"The body art was almost certainly done by the same person," Brass said. "But that isn't news to anyone."

Nick said nothing. He'd gotten a look at Dorset

and seen crime-lab and media photos of the others.

"Quentin Dorset was a good man," Brass said. "You ever testify in his courtroom?"

"No."

"I'm not sure how long I knew him. Close to a decade, I guess," Brass said. "He presided over a few cases I'd investigated and always got on my nerves."

Nick was quiet again. Brass's eyes remained on him, but their focus had moved off into the distance as he spoke.

"Defense teams loved him," he said. "Prosecutors knew he'd be a handful. A stickler for evidentiary rules. But I respected Dorset even though he annoyed me every time. He was fair, you know? Fair with his decisions, better telling dirty jokes in chambers."

Nick nodded slowly, a wan smile touching his lips. His mother a public defender, his father a Texas Supreme Court judge, he'd understood the push-me, pull-you of the court system early on. "For me," he said, "home was kind of like being in chambers."

Brass drew his gaze back in on him. "I forgot," he said. "It would have been, wouldn't it?"

"Yeah."

Silence.

"I had lunch with Dorset once or twice. It was after I started to spend more time at headquarters than in the field," Brass said finally. "When I heard another Tattoo Man vic had rolled into the morgue tonight, I never expected it would be the judge."

"The job has a way of doing that to us."

"Tag, you're it."

"Uh-huh."

Brass sighed heavily. "Quentin Dorset spent his whole life serving justice," he said. "I hope we can get some for him."

Nick looked at the detective, thinking he wanted to pay a visit of his own to the autopsy room.

"Me, too," he said.

He stood naked on a step stool in the Mirror Chamber, the shark hooks in his back, one behind each of his shoulders, another below his neck. The bends of the carbon-steel hooks went deep beneath his skin, their shanks protruding on one side, the points sticking out opposite the shanks. Fourteen inches long with five-inch gapes, they were the largest gauge hooks he'd been able to obtain. He took a slow, deep breath and moved barefoot toward the edge of the stool, the high chamber walls reflecting his image in multiplicity. Sweat glazed his forehead as the parachute cords running from the hooks to the suspension rig grew taut, pulling at his skin.

The rig had stood in readiness since he'd set it up weeks ago. But it had taken the judge's death to convince him *he* was ready.

Inhale, exhale. Slow, slow. Before inserting the

hooks, he'd marked off the areas where they would go with a surgical ruler and pen, wiped the skin with chlorhexidine disinfectant, then carefully guided a piercing needle through and under the colored guidelines. There wasn't much bleeding from the puncture wounds, just thin red dribbles like snail paths in the furrow between his shoulder blades.

Cold at first, the hooks now burned where they'd slipped into his body. Although he could feel his flesh stretching across the width of their gapes, it did not fold or bunch. The combined sensations were unpleasant but tolerable, and he knew the skin would be less likely to tear once it loosened up and gained some elasticity.

The tug of the lines pulling back the skin suggested a greater test of endurance lay ahead.

He had decided upon a basic three-point system. Anchored to an eyebolt in the floor, the 7/16 military surplus rappelling rope went straight up the wall to its juncture with the ceiling, ran through a swivel mount, and was then strung midway along the ceiling's width to a pulley he'd affixed to a structural crossbeam. He had bought a metal spreader bar, the parachute cord, and locking carabiners from an Internet vendor that specialized in mountain-climbing gear, also procuring the deep-water hooks online from a commercial fishing supplier in Seattle. Everything was shipped to an anonymous mail drop in Kingstown, on the

Caribbean island of St. Vincent, the same phantom address where he had his body-work supplies and equipment delivered and forwarded to the United States.

He'd had to remove the barbs from the fish-hooks, of course, and had done it easily with a power drill and a grinding bit. Then he'd painstak-ingly sharpened them with a hand file for smoother penetration. Each stainless-steel hook supported more than eighty pounds, a third more than he'd need to hold him aloft—he'd last weighed in at one hundred and fifty on his doctor's scale, hav-ing dropped twenty pounds in the past several months as his illness progressed. Finally, he'd put the hooks into his portable sterilizer to ensure they were rid of infectious bacteria and viruses and then tied them to the spreader bar with the parachute cord, aligning them so his weight would be evenly distributed.

He felt confident that the rig would be strong enough and had no hesitation or concerns about his decision. But his realization that the time was upon him had come in a sudden, unexpected rush of circumstances. He'd never meant to lose the King. The death had troubled him, made him feel internally eroded and depressed. At the same time, he had known the King was undeserving of life, and his remorse had gradually shrunk away. In the end, he had understood that the death had occurred for a reason. It had freed him to move toward a new state of being—and a power that was beyond pain and guilt.

It helped that he'd stayed as fit as possible. His body was failing him, but it had been a slow betrayal. He still did light daily exercises and maintained enough muscle tone and stamina to help him withstand the stresses of his Passage. In the last twenty-four hours, he'd taken further physical precautions, abstaining from solid food to cleanse his system and prevent nausea but staying hydrated with sports drinks that would replenish his electrolytes and carbohydrates and boost his level of endurance.

He shuffled forward again, bending his knees, his toes inching over the edge of the stool. The hooks plucked up his skin a little more, and he felt a sharp twinge. *Breathe in in in now exhaaaaale.* He stepped off and produced an involuntary groan—raw, inchoate, from his center, from the core of his pain and loneliness: *"AuugggghuhuuUUUH."*

His mouth agape, the volcanic release from within climbing up his throat, pouring out of him, an undulant wave sweeping over, through, and around his body. Looking down at his ankles above the concrete floor, he hung like a larval moth on lines of coarse spun thread, sweat sheeting from him now, oiling him, and the pain, the pain . . .

His head slung back, the veins in his neck blue and thick and bulging, his eyes rolled up under their lids, so only their whites reflected from the mirror in front of him. And suddenly—

He smelled sagebrush. Sweet, pungent, over-powering in the heat of a desert gully. The fragrant shrubs carpeting the hard, dusty rock as far as the eye could see . . .

"Oh," he heard himself say. "My boy. Yessss . . ."

The pain was gone, or almost gone, its remnants leaving him in shreds and tapers, flying off into a timeless, floating ecstasy.

He closed his eyes, lowered his chin, and crossed his arms over his chest, palms flat against his breast in an attitude of meditative rapture.

And hung in his chamber of mirrors, a dark chrysalis waiting to hatch from his shell.

3

THE CSIs COULD hear Dr. Albert Robbins's cane clacking dully against the tiled floor of the autopsy room. The sound, like his limp, was sometimes barely noticeable, but not so this early dawn. No one knew for certain what made the difference.

Nick had conjectured that it might have something to do with the long hours Robbins spent on his artificial legs. It was hard to tell. The chief coroner had groused about his knee joints sticking a time or two but otherwise never complained. He exercised on a treadmill in the lab and was fond of repeating a joke about being able to run all night without his legs growing tired.

Clack, clack, clack. Robbins moved around the dissection table, propped the cane against its edge, and leaned over to slice into the cadaver's upper brow with his scalpel.

"The implants are typically silicone or polytetrafluoroethylene," he said.

"Teflon?" Sara said.

"It's a cheap and highly biocompatible substance," Robbins said with a nod. "Almost frictionless, hypoallergenic, doesn't break down inside the body. The drawback's that an acid used in its production is a suspected carcinogen." He reached for his tweezers, worked them into the incision. "It appears whoever did this stayed neatly within a single channel of flesh. He could be a modern-day *feldscher*."

"Glad you're going to tell us what that means," Nick said.

Robbins's bearded cheeks lifted in the faintest grin. "The term goes back to medieval Europe," he said. "A *feldscher* was considered a poor man's surgeon, but that doesn't give the trade its due. The members of the Worshipful Company of Barber Surgeons were guildsmen who learned their profession outside the medical universities, usually on the cadavers of executed prisoners. Barbers made the best candidates for apprenticeship since they already handled cutting tools."

"You think the person responsible for this studied anatomy?"

"No doubt," Robbins said. "His skills are highly refined. My only question would be whether his education was formal or informal." He glanced up at Nick. "I'd challenge anyone to show me the line between certain accepted types of plastic surgery and body modification. Because in my opinion, it's gotten very blurred."

Nick watched Robbins's face but couldn't tell if he was being flippant. "I know I didn't hear you compare these body-mod artists to licensed doctors."

"There are plenty of unscrupulous quacks with medical degrees. You can see their handiwork walking around Beverly Hills."

"Doesn't answer my question."

"I wasn't sure you asked one." Robbins shrugged. "I'm able to afford a good plastic surgeon. Or for that matter, a dermatologist to remove an unsightly polyp from above my eyelid. You might want to save your inquiry for somebody who's stuck without comprehensive health insurance."

Nick said nothing as Robbins plucked a triangular object from under the skin with his tweezers.

"Okay, what've we got here?" the coroner said under his breath. He lowered his binocular forehead loupe over his eyes, switched on its optical lights, and studied the blood-slimed implant as a jeweler would a rare diamond. "Tattoo Man's material of choice is silicone after all. He must have carved it by hand—I can discern the minute scoring from his blade."

Sara shook her head. "As opposed to . . ."

"He could have opted for a molding-putty kit," Robbins said. "That would involve using CAD-CAM software to program his precision specs into a computerized lathe, then mixing and casting the silicone in a vacuum sterilization chamber."

"Sounds time-consuming."

"And expensive," Robbins said. "A vacuum sterilizer costs over a thousand dollars. A good desktop lathe several thousand more. The technique would be used for highly stylized, contoured implants. But the crown's design elements are perfectly geometrical, five triangular points spaced across the front of the head. It's easier to work from a stencil and cut them out of the solid, pre-sterilized block."

Nick was studying the body. "Did you see the needle mark on the back of his hand?"

"Yes," Robbins said. "Phillips made note of it."

"And you agree it's from an IV drip?"

"I can go one better and predict that his blood samples show trace amounts of Diprivan."

"The anesthetic given to Tattoo Man's earlier victims," Nick said, and looked at him. "You saw the case files."

"People are normally in the same condition as this fine gentleman when they reach my care," Robbins said. "It was refreshing to read about those who are still among the living."

Nick smiled with dismal amusement.

"About Diprivan," Robbins said. "Assuming for a minute we find it in Dorset's bloodstream . . . it breaks down very rapidly after it's administered. That means its concentration levels won't necessarily give us definitive results regarding overdose."

"In other words, he might have a low amount in his blood but still have OD'd," Sara said.

Robbins nodded. "There are other indicators, though. Concentrations in the urine can be more determinative, so I'll try to extract some from his bladder. And extended use can leave detectable traces in the hair follicles." He paused. "Another point. A rapid injection of Diprivan could lead to cardiorespiratory failure. That's why many anesthesiologists who use it for short outpatient procedures—gastroscopies and colonoscopies, say—prefer titrated infusion with Lactated Ringer's solution or a slow, guided intravenous drip in calibrated doses, rather than with an IV push."

"When a stronger dose is injected into an intravenous bag with a syringe," Nick said.

Robbins gave another nod. "You'd be more liable to see that under operating-room conditions, when a nurse with resuscitative training would be present."

Nick mulled that as another thought came to him. "About the ink," he said. "Shouldn't we compare the type used in Dorset's tattoos with the others?"

"A match would certainly help establish that all of the crimes were committed by a single individual. I just don't know if that would lead us in his direction."

"How's that?"

"Although tattoo inks are subject to the same FDA rules and approvals as cosmetics, the regulatory policies are limp," Robbins said. "The ingredients consist of a pigment and a carrier solution, but there's a wide range, and none of the outfits that produce, import, and export premixed inks has to label them." A shrug. "I'd be surprised if our man doesn't mix his own."

"So we'd probably have a helluva time tracing the ingredients to any one source."

"Or even multiple sources. I can't estimate how long it would take to list the over-the-counter dyes and chemicals used in different formulations."

Nick exhaled slowly through pursed lips. "It still seems worth a shot."

"I wouldn't argue," Robbins said. "I'll take excisions of the tattooed skin. You would need to get epithelial samples from the survivors to test for similarities."

Nick nodded. "Anything else jump out at you?"

"A couple of things," Robbins said. He snapped his magnifying lenses back over his head. "The victim shaved within a few hours of his death. Or was given a shave."

The criminalists exchanged glances.

"We caught that, too," Nick said. "Can you tell whether it was before or after?"

"Undeniably premortem." Robbins placed his fingers under the chin and tilted it up. "He scabbed where the razor nicked him. If he'd already been dead, the blood would have settled from his face."

Nick digested that. "Okay . . . what's the second thing?"

Robbins deposited the implant on a folded towel,

placed the tweezers in an autoclave sterilization tray. Then he rejoined Nick at the dissection table. "Care to help me turn him on his side?" he said.

Nick didn't hesitate. He grasped the body's shoulders and pushed his weight against it as Robbins supported the hips, peeling back the morgue sheet from below the waist.

Sara's eyes widened. She glanced at Nick, then back at the thick ruby-red lip tattoos smattering the bare, pale buttocks. "Lipstick kisses," she said, incredulous.

His hands still on the shoulder blades, Nick leaned slightly backward, angling his head to peer around Robbins at the tattoos. "Pucker up," he said.

Sara had turned to face him again. "I think that just might be the message," she said.

The last time Catherine Willows had visited the Basin Road Public Library had been years ago, when she'd driven her daughter there for a high school reading project. It was among the smaller branches in the Clark County–Las Vegas system, and the librarian had been a dowdy, gray-haired woman in her sixties wearing a simple plum-colored jacket-and-skirt suit. As she'd checked out Lindsey's books at the circulation desk, she offered each of them a chocolate fudge brownie from the batch a part-time volunteer had baked at home.

The librarian in the focus frames of Catherine's

camera was likewise on the short side. But she was about twenty pounds thinner, thirty years younger, a redhead, and wearing a long-sleeved psychedelic tunic blouse that hugged her narrow waist and flared out over her tights to accentuate her shapely figure. Sprawled faceup on the floor of the reserve room with her skull shattered by a bullet and the blouse's sleeve cut off above the elbow, she'd had her skin flayed almost to the bone from her right forearm to her wrist. Blood had hemorrhaged from her wounds in darkening, partially intermingled puddles, soaked through her clothes, and cast a gruesome mosaic of spatters and splashes into the surrounding bookshelves.

"Laurel Whitsen," Greg Sanders said. "She's thirty-one and lived out in Bracken."

He was studying the driver's license in a window wallet he'd retrieved from the dead woman's slouch bag. They'd found the bag behind the very front desk where Catherine and Lindsey had accepted a single brownie from the older librarian, reasoning that if they split it between them, it would only amount to halfway breaking their diets.

This morning, the CSIs had arrived to find the desk covered with blood, the slouch bag sitting open atop it, smeary red fingerprints all over its strap, outer and inner leather, and zipper pull.

"Does it look like anything was stolen from her bag?" Catherine asked.

Greg shook his head. "I found over sixty dollars in the billfold. Plus credit and debit cards and her driver's license. There are keys, a checkbook, a makeup compact . . . everything right where it belongs."

"And her smart phone? Where was that when you noticed it?"

"On the floor behind the desk," Greg said. "I think she might've gotten it out of the purse, made her call, and dropped it there."

"*After* she got shot in the head?"

He shrugged. "Don't forget skinned."

They traded perplexed glances.

"Libraries charge late fees and hold fund-raising events," Catherine said after a moment. "Did you see a register up front?"

"Just a wooden cash box under the counter that's straight out of Mayberry," he said. "The lock wasn't exactly high-security. I opened it with one of her keys and found thirty dollars and change, with calculator printouts matching the total amount of money." His face creased. "Plain vanilla holdup men don't carve out pieces of their victims, Cath."

She frowned, raised her camera, and circled the body to photograph it from every visible angle, careful to sidestep the copious blood spills and numbered, color-coded evidence markers all around it. Before she and Greg took their samples, Catherine would snap close-ups of each bloodstain relative to the body, the room's fixtures, and other stains, establishing their precise measurements and spacing with six-inch crime-scene rulers from her kit. Meanwhile, she had advised the antsy uniformed policemen who'd responded to Laurel Whitsen's baffling 911 call to get comfortable in the reading room. She hoped they would seek out long, thick novels with plenty of twists and turns, because she did not expect to finish her work anytime soon.

It was now a few minutes past nine o'clock on Saturday morning. Although the library's regular weekend hours did not begin until ten, Laurel must have arrived early to prepare for the day. The rest was as enigmatic as what she'd calmly told the emergency operator: "I've been shot in the head at the Basin Road library. Help me, please. I have to return Darwin's *Voyage of the Beagle* to the shelf before we open."

Minutes after she ended the call, the police arrived, found the library's door ajar, and went inside to investigate with their guns drawn. Besides finding the gory mess on the desk, they saw a confused trail of blood and bloody footprints running from the circulation desk to the research room, where they soon came upon Laurel Whitsen's gored and mutilated remains in the natural history aisle.

Catherine lowered her camera's viewfinder, studied the bloodstains between the dead woman and a shelf stack about ten feet to the left. There was a rolling cart piled with dozens of books over by the shelves, which she noted had some available spaces on them. A few more books were strewn around the cart.

She contemplated that for a moment, then brought her gaze up to the books lining the aisle at about eye level. They were drenched with blood, hair, and bits of scalp and brain tissue. One of them was protruding over the edge of the packed shelf. The title printed on its cover along the spine was *Voyage of the Beagle*.

Laurel Whitsen had been about Catherine's height. When the bullet tore through her head, the material would have burst out the exit wound and sprayed the shelves.

"She was putting away that book when the killer surprised her," Catherine said. "See those large drops of blood running from the stack?"

The oval drops on the floor, with their narrow leading edges throwing off spatters in the direction of the corpse, meant that Laurel Whitsen had been standing at the shelf when she was shot up close—and briefly remained standing before she went down. Catherine was thinking Laurel was slightly built and might have weighed a hundred and fifteen pounds. But that was still a lot of weight to support, and not many women possessed the strength. Most likely, her killer was a male.

Catherine continued to study the blood patterns. She'd noticed tiny red speckles around some of the parent drops, which told her that Laurel, or whoever was holding her upright, had paused long enough for blood to splash down into blood. From there, the blood smeared across the floor to where it widened out into a large, wet pool, as if that was where Laurel had been dragged and laid out . . . for a while.

She was now in a different puddle about six inches from that spot.

Catherine looked down at her body. *Shot up close.* That much was a sure thing. It was apparent from the charred edges of the bullet hole above Laurel's right eye and the star-shaped flaps of skin where the blowback gases from the gunshot escaped in an explosive rush.

Catherine imagined Laurel wheeling her book cart into the research room, stopping at a shelf, pulling a return from the cart. The Darwin book. Laurel had been handling it, trying to fit it onto the tight shelf, when something drew her attention. The sound of the killer's footsteps, maybe. Or he might have said something to make her turn and face him. The rest must have been a blur for her. The weapon in his grip or appearing suddenly from under a shirt or jacket, its muzzle rising, then pressing against her forehead, and finally the click of the trigger and the near-instantaneous blast of gunfire.

"The killer caught her off guard," she said. "Put a slug in her head, skinned her, left her there on the floor."

"And then what?" Greg said. "She gets up with

her head half gone and the flesh sliced off her arm to the bone. Goes over to the desk for her cell and calls the police. Then she comes back to finish putting away her book and finally drops dead." He scratched behind his ear. "I *might* not have a problem if this was some zombie movie."

Catherine shook her head, trying to reconstruct the sequence of events. Laurel Whitsen's killer might have lingered after closing time and found somewhere to lie in wait. Then snuck up on her while she was preoccupied, leaving her with no chance to react. Or could she have known him? Let him in early? It was possible he even arrived with her, accompanying her as she made her rounds. There was no sign that she'd struggled or tried to run.

Catherine stared at the book sticking partially out from the shelf and frowned. That was where the images stopped clipping across her mind's interior screen. Where they veered from any logical, orderly progression.

"Hey, Catherine, I found something." Greg had moved a foot or two down the aisle. He crouched inches from where she stood, picked a hollow brass cylinder up off the floor, and turned it in his fingers to inspect it. "It's a nine-mil . . . and look at the impression on the bottom."

She knelt as he showed her the brass. "Teardrop-shaped," she said.

Greg nodded as they exchanged glances. Most guns used circular strikers. When a shot was fired, the striker left a rounded indentation where it hit the primer cap. Except when the shot was fired from a gun that used a rectangular striker and consequently left a rectangular impression. Except, again, when that gun was a Glock, which used a *patented* rectangular striker, not to mention other unique design features. When the gun was a Glock, the recoil from the striker's percussion gave its barrel a slight downward tilt, and a small amount of the ignited primer flowed back out of the cap and distorted the rectangle, turning it into a teardrop-shaped identifying mark that forensics experts could recognize, if not a mile away, then without fail at the distance Greg was holding the spent brass shell from Catherine's eyes.

Of course, she thought, Glocks were among the most common pistols out on the streets of rootin', tootin' Las Vegas. There were probably hundreds, maybe thousands of them in unlicensed hands, making this discovery useful but nothing that would lead to her or Greg doing handstands between the rows of books. Still, it was one fewer question in the bundle.

Greg dropped the casing into an evidence bag. "The aisle's kind of cramped," he said, looking around. "He must have been practically right up against her when he pulled the trigger."

Which Catherine had already decided was a fair assumption.

She stood there silently looking over the smudged,

overlapping bloody shoe prints running to and from the aisle. They would need close analysis in the lab before Laurel's could be conclusively distinguished from her killer's. But they might help clear up several unknowns.

"One way or another, Laurel stays on her feet, or half on her feet, for maybe four, five steps. Then falls to the floor." Catherine pointed to where the drag marks began. "That's when she's pulled to where she is now, where whoever murdered and butchered her went to work . . . "

And where things stopped making sense.

Greg was looking attentively down at the body. "She's got tunnels," he said. "A tat on the side of her neck."

Catherine had already noticed the hollow metal plugs in Laurel's stretched ear piercings. But the tattoo was partly covered by a clump of bloodied hair. She knelt and plucked back the matted strands with latexed fingers. "Red stars and blue butterflies," she said. "Colorful."

Greg crouched beside Catherine as she took more snapshots. "See how the sleeve was clipped away from the arm he skinned?" he said. "No tears or loose threads anywhere . . . most likely, it was done with a good pair of scissors."

Sewing shears, she thought. Somebody had been painstakingly conscientious.

Greg was gesturing at the blouse's pleated left sleeve. "Mind if I pull it up?"

Catherine nodded, and he rolled it back above the wrist. A second later, he'd exposed a tattoo corsage of vibrant yellow, purple, and pink five-petaled blossoms.

"Plumeria," Catherine said. She caught Greg looking impressed. "Little boys know frogs, little girls flowers. In Hawaii, they symbolize birth and life."

"Too bad Laurel wasn't in Hawaii," he said.

She gave a small, morbid smile. "What do you think we've got here?"

Greg stared at the victim's arm with its missing flap of skin. "One insane robbery after all," he said.

LVPD undersheriff Conrad Ecklie was hardwired for career self-preservation, which meant that appeasing his departmental and political bosses was always foremost among his priorities. Add occasional twitches of irritation when he was overloaded with conflicting demands and a certain preset vindictiveness if his sensors detected a real or perceived threat to his sphere of authority, and you had the model bureaucrat.

When the sheriff's office was given oversight of the criminalistics bureau some months back, Ecklie had become its chief liaison with its supervisor, Catherine Willows. She wouldn't have said she particularly liked or disliked him; it seemed too strong to measure her reactions to Ecklie in those terms. Willows tended to gird herself for their meetings as she would getting ready to deal with bank loan officers or utility company service reps. Her wish was only that their encounters were brief and professionally courteous and passed with a bare minimum of trouble. The idea was to coexist with him and avoid pushing his buttons by any dignified, reasonable means.

Driving back to the lab from the library, Willows had gotten an e-mail on her cell requesting her immediate presence in Ecklie's office. The summons was copied to Nick Stokes, whose path she had crossed early that morning as he'd hoofed toward the autopsy room after returning from a four-nineteen on Koval Lane.

A shapely, long-legged, strawberry blonde who spun heads mostly without acknowledging the looks, Willows had reached headquarters first and gone hustling through the corridors to Ecklie's office. She owed her good genes to her mother, Lily Flynn, once a cocktail waitress and showgirl who had performed across the Western states. Jumping from school to school, Willows had become unsettled at her core, toughened on the exterior. Her ex-husband's bad habits acquired and mercifully kicked, she had danced like her mother to support their child and pay her own tuition at UNLV, earning her bachelor's in medical technology.

But Catherine had followed in Lily's footsteps only so far—and right now, she could not have been further from them, her own hurried steps having led her to the heart of Ecklie's domain, where she sat beside the second-to-arrive Stokes, both CSIs listening to the undersheriff give his bit from behind his desk.

"I've heard some discussion about the possibility of a link between the library killing and the Tattoo Man probe," he said. Lean, balding, the skin of his face taut over his cheekbones, he peered at them with the expression of a gliding raptor.

Catherine knew how quickly word spread through the grapevine. Still, she was puzzled. "What sort of discussion?" she said. "Greg and I haven't even filed our report."

"Sergeant Ayers radioed headquarters from the scene."

Ah-ha, Catherine thought. One of the uniforms she'd sent off to the reading room. It appeared he hadn't found any literary diversions.

"The victim was seriously into tattoos," she said. "She had a lot of work done on her."

"Her name was Laurel Whitsen, correct?"

Catherine nodded. "Our on-site examination of her body showed more than ink. She had scarification designs on her shoulder, strike branding on the chest—"

"What was that?"

"Strike branding," Catherine repeated. "The same process used on cattle."

"Scars and brands . . . wouldn't this be masochistic?"

"I suppose it depends whom you ask."

Ecklie formed a cradle with his hands and rested his chin on it. "Is it accurate that a tattoo was removed from her arm?"

"We think it was cut around the borders and then peeled away," Catherine said. "Greg unlocked Laurel's smart phone. There were pictures of her in short sleeves, so we know what it looked like."

"Can you describe it?"

"Yeah, the art's very distinctive," Catherine said. "A rabbit riding a deer . . . well, a buck, actually. The rabbit's waving a handsaw in the air and has antlers and a bandage around its head where they were transplanted. It looks happy." She paused. "The buck has stumps where the antlers used to be, and there's a teardrop coming from its eye like it's sad."

"Do you infer any special meaning there?"

Catherine ignored her better judgment. "If that buck had gotten hold of the saw first, the rabbit might not be smiling."

Ecklie frowned, unamused. "The tattoo might tell us about the victim's lifestyle. It isn't unreasonable to think there's some symbolism, or message, call it what you want, in the imagery." His eyes beaded in on Nick. "Captain Brass feels it's probably true of what was done to Quentin Dorset and the rest of Tattoo Man's victims."

"It's one theory." Nick shrugged. "But I don't see how that's got anything to do with the librarian."

"You think it's a coincidence that we had two similar crimes in a single night?"

"If similar's only about tats for you, sure. The judge turned up dead last night, but he was snatched weeks ago. The woman at the library's a consenting adult into body art and whatnot. I'm hearing from Catherine that her tattoo was *removed*, the opposite of what happened to Dorset."

"Nick's right," Catherine said. "There are different MOs and not a single piece of evidence tying Laurel Whitsen's murder to the Tattoo Man abductions."

Ecklie unmeshed his hands, set them flat on the desk, and leaned back. Catherine heard the springs of his chair creak in the silence. "We have to be concerned with perceptions," he said slowly. "I shouldn't have to explain."

She looked at him. "Maybe you'd better. Because I'm a little confused."

"Really, Catherine?" Ecklie's eyes met hers. "None of us in this room just fell off the turnip truck. The press hasn't gone too crazy starting an uproar over the Tattoo Man, maybe because there weren't any killings to this point. But that changed overnight. Once these stories circulate through the media, Sheriff Mobley's going to feel the heat."

"With all due respect to the sheriff, that isn't our problem—"

"Mobley already spoke to me this morning. He believes the cases might be somehow related. Or that a relationship is at least worth preliminary consideration."

"Somehow?" Nick said. He made no attempt to conceal his disdain for Ecklie. "You worked the field once upon a time. Let's hear what you think."

Ecklie tightened his lips. "When there's a buildup of pressure within a closed system, it does damage at the point of greatest vulnerability. Mobley is an elected official who recently suffered a very public embarrassment. He's eager for his office to rebuild its credibility."

Embarrassment, Catherine thought. As in her dear friend and teammate Warrick Brown getting murdered by Ecklie's corrupt predecessor. She felt her molars grit but kept her gaze leveled on the undersheriff, unwilling to let Nick into its periphery. He would be openly seething, and that wouldn't help her hang on to her own poise. "You're asking us to jump to a conclusion and work backward from it. Violate every sound investigative principle—"

"No," Ecklie said. "I only want you to satisfy Mobley that his . . . postulate, let's say, is being fully explored. There is a difference. But whether or not you agree with me, it's important that we understand each other."

Catherine inhaled, exhaled. "I think we're clear on things," she said. "Now, if you don't mind, we'd like to get back to work."

Ecklie studied the CSIs for a moment, his eyes

briefly holding on Nick. Nick didn't wait for him to complete his nod before pushing off his chair.

Catherine hurried after him in the corridor. "Nicky," she said. "Hang on."

He only stopped to turn around when he felt her grip his arm. "I can't stand that dude," he said, nodding back toward Ecklie's office. "It's tough enough making sense of things without worrying about politics. Grissom taught me to follow the evidence. That's all I know how to do."

Catherine leaned close to him, smiled a conspiratorial smile. "Then do what you do, and leave the politics to me," she said.

4

"YOU CAN PRETEND I'M NOT HERE," David Hodges said, approaching the conference room's rectangular table. "I'm just sitting in for the fun of it."

This was in response to Catherine asking why he'd arrived for her all-hands-on-deck meeting of the division's criminalists. Being a laboratory technician and not a CSI, he hadn't been required to attend her little Saturday morning confab about the macabre deaths of Quentin Dorset and Laurel Whitsen—cases that hadn't even begun to rise and take shape in their investigative oven but that Undersheriff Ecklie had suggested his politically shell-shocked boss leaned toward squeezing ass backward into a single bakery box.

In the glass-walled room were the CSIs directly involved in the probes—a tired-looking Nick Stokes, Sara Sidle, Greg Sanders, and Catherine herself. Rounding out the group was Raymond Langston, a criminal pathologist and published academic to boot, who was the section's senior member agewise but, as its most recent hire, remained a Level Two.

No one in the room knew whether Hodges's answer had been intended as a cheeky quip. His perpetual taciturn manner made him a tough read. Hodges could be bothersome that way. Among other ways too numerous to count. But the criminalists knew he was as sharp as Occam's metaphorical razor and had contributed to solving some of the most difficult forensic mysteries they'd tackled—once matter-of-factly uncovering a decisive piece of evidence while assisting the shorthanded criminalists in the field and seemingly staring into space as they were busily going about their work in earnest.

"Well, knock yourself out," Catherine said, nodding him toward the table.

"Long as you don't glom a custard doughnut," Nick said. He pointed to a cardboard assortment tray in the middle of the table. "That's where the fun ends."

Hodges gave Nick a flat look, strode past him, and took an empty chair between Sidle and Langston.

Catherine watched him get settled over the rim of her paper coffee cup. "Okay, let's compare notes," she said. "Nick, how about you get us started on Dorset?"

He nodded, got out his pocket computer, and opened his notes folder. "About three o'clock yesterday morning, some clubbers from Philadelphia discover his body in a trailer depot on Koval Lane. They'd been bounced from a taxi out toward the airport—"

Greg looked at him. "How do you get bounced from a *cab*?"

Nick produced one of those weary, sighing laughs. "Weekends in Vegas, dude," he said, and went on to sum up the rest. "Doc Robbins gave the body a preliminary exam when it came in, took some test samples. He's doing the full autopsy today."

"Any COD?" Catherine asked.

"Nothing positive," Nick said. "Looks like he was given an intravenous anesthetic. Same as with the prior abductions."

"Do we know what drug was used?"

"Could be Diprivan. Toxicology is working on it."

"So maybe we're looking at an overdose."

"Either as a primary cause of death or with other complications," Nick said. "Again, the tox results should help."

Catherine clucked her tongue. "I think we should be asking if there is anything to substantiate that the Tattoo Man abductions were committed by a single person."

"Or group of people," Sara said. "We can't rule out multiple perpetrators."

"Are you talking cult crime?"

"Gang, cult, whatever," she said. "I'm just saying it's possible more than a single person is involved."

Catherine was nodding. "In a way, that goes right back to my question," she said. "How are or aren't the attacks consistent?"

"I've boned up some on the other two cases just to make sure everything's current between us and the detectives," Nick said. He thumbed his keypad, consulting his notes. "Just to review everything we know, the first victim's a woman named Stacy Ebstein. Fortyish, worked as a special-events coordinator at the Starglow Hotel and Casino. Grabbed while getting out of her car late one night. Remembers seeing a nondescript white male on the street but doesn't even know for sure if he's the guilty party. One minute she's stepping into her driveway, the next she's dead to the world. And that's how she stays till she wakes up in Cave Lake State Park—with a scary-as-hell interlude that her mind blocks out till Brass persuades her to see a police psychologist."

"Namely?"

"At some point, she regained consciousness in a room or closet with mirrors all around her," Nick said. "She was tied or handcuffed to a chair and shown the tattoo work on her face. She described it as being like an unveiling. Also used the word *ritual*."

"And then?"

"From what we know, everything else is mostly a blank. She refused to cooperate after that first shrink session. Brass tells us it made her pretty hysterical. She does recall someone in the room with her, though. A man wearing a hood or mask. But not much else before the park."

Catherine felt a cold spot like an icy thumbprint in her stomach. She sipped her coffee to thaw it, hoping her shudder went unnoticed. "And the second case?"

"Mitchell Noble, twenty-seven, adult-novelty-store manager. He's pulling down the security gates after the place closes when somebody knocks him out from behind. Thinks he might've taken a blow to the head, but there's something else, too. Like needles or pins in the back of his neck. He's in limbo till he opens his eyes in a room full of mirrors. Gets a look at what's been done to him, passes out, comes to in a school yard a few days later."

Catherine sighed. "Stacy Ebstein's nightmare all over again."

"Yeah," Nick said. "Just with different scenery at the end."

"Do we have photos of the victims?"

"Before *and* after," Catherine said. She took several shots from a large brown envelope in front of her and passed them around the table. By the time they came back to Catherine, she knew she had company in having to suppress chills. "Is there anything to suggest that these people are somehow interconnected?" she asked. "Even without being aware of it?"

"Not that we know," Nick said. "There's no

apparent relevance to the time frame between the abductions . . . but I'll keep looking into that angle."

"Any chance that they're all customers of that sex shop?"

"They weren't, as far as the police reports go."

Nick's look said they could only wish things were that simple. She was reaching, and they both knew it. Brass's detectives would have picked up on those links—which wasn't to rule out the chance that there might be others. Catherine tapped Sara's photos. "How about their tattoos? The method, designs, dyes . . ."

"Nick and I plan to visit them and request that they submit to voluntary epithelials," Sara said. "Neither has had any taken yet. That would give us a solid basis for comparison."

Hodges cleared his throat. "Ah," he said. "I noticed something about the composition of *one* of the inks."

The CSIs gave him a moment to savor their combined attention.

"I haven't had a chance to analyze Dorset's facial excisions," he went on. "But Robbins also sent me eye swabs, and the pigments are mainly natural indigo and powdered lignite—or soft coal. There's a bit of logwood, too. The carrier's plant-derived glycerin and water."

"Is that significant?" Catherine asked.

Hodges shrugged. "It's a very low-irritant vegan formulation. In contrast to dyes that use animal and mineral products."

Catherine waited for the rest, but he was still basking. She wound her hand in the air. "Let's have it."

"It could be whoever tattooed the judge's eyes is a card-carrying member of PETA. But I think he was being very careful not to blind him with a harsher ink," he said. "It fits what his other victims said about him. That he wanted them to see what he'd done."

Hodges reclined in his chair, clearly pleased with himself. Catherine decided that he was entitled. But his ego would be fine without a massage. She glanced around the conference table. "Does he want to torment these people with his work, or is he looking for admiration?"

"Both," Langston said, breaking his attentive silence. "He takes them against their will. Exerts his power and control. These are classic sociopathies. But he isn't just mutilating his captives. He's transforming them into perverse, living works of art." He paused and folded his hands on the table. "What we don't know at this stage is how he selects them—whether they're random targets, have some relationship to him, or are typed by certain characteristics."

Catherine looked at Nick and Sara. "We'll see if you two turn up any new details when you talk to his earlier vics," she said. "Are we through with Dorset for now? Because I want to get to Laurel Whitsen."

No one offered anything. She nodded, gave them a rundown of the circumstances surrounding the discovery of the librarian's body, and nodded again, this time at Greg Sanders.

"Laurel was heavy into tats—the ink and branding we saw at the crime scene were just for openers," Greg said. "Phillips is autopsying her, and he photocopied me a rough chart based on his exterior exam." He opened a folder to review the diagram aloud. "She has nipple and genital piercings, plural in each case. Scarification tattoos on her breasts, including a Buddhist mandala. There's an elaborate skinning piece that covers most of her back from her waist to her shoulders. Flowers and branches. They could be apple blossoms, cherry blossoms, dogwood, I'm not sure. Also . . ."

"Hold on," Sara said. "*Skinning?*"

"Right," Greg said. "It's what it sounds like. The skin's removed to create scar patterns."

She shook her head. "Sounds painful."

"Just a little." Greg combed a hand through his hair. "Laurel had four tattoo parlors in her cell phone's address book. Two in Boston, another in San Francisco, one here in Vegas called Raven Lunar. Her friend listings had photos attached to them, and, surprise, they're mostly tattoo freaks."

Langston raised his hand. Catherine tried not to smile. Broad, bespectacled, his skin a light mocha color, the former college educator still occasionally fell back on lecture-hall protocols and tended to dress as if a sport jacket were a strict professorial must.

"Ray," she said.

"I believe we should make an effort to steer clear of preconceptions about the victim's way of life and the lifestyles of the people she knew," he said. "When I was growing up, my father liked to remind me that tattoos were for jailbirds and what he'd call 'gutter boys.' The grunge movement popularized them in the nineties, and later on, athletes and movie stars brought them closer to the mainstream, but it doesn't mean that the social stigma attached to body art has been removed. A lot of people still assume that lower-back tattoos on young women are signs of promiscuity—"

"Tramp stamps," Sara said. "I get your point, Ray. But don't you think voluntarily being skinned constitutes self-punishment?"

Catherine recalled the term Ecklie had used in his office: *masochistic.*

Langston adjusted his eyeglasses. "It might. Or not. Depending on the individual. Scarification is regarded by some as the purest form of body art, shaped from a person's own flesh and healing abilities, with nothing to mediate between the hand of the artist and the recipient. This creates an intimate bond between them. Very few cultures don't have some traditional form of it. Africans, Asians, Native Americans . . . it's an ancient practice around the world, with social and spiritual connotations."

"So you're saying you wouldn't consider it *peculiar*?"

He shrugged. "My understanding is that our job requires we keep open minds."

Sara frowned but gave no response.

Catherine had listened to them thoughtfully. "I think we can all agree that there's nothing spiritual about putting a bullet in a woman's head and then cutting half the flesh off her arm," she said, and checked her watch. "Okay, let's wrap this up. I'm going to drop in on Phillips, then head over to ballistics. It's a long shot, but maybe we can track the gun." She drained her coffee. "Greg, where do we stand with Laurel's next of kin?"

"Her mom's flying in from California—the head librarian kept her number on record as an emergency contact."

"Good. You should start getting in touch with the people in her address book, see what leads you can pick up about who might've done this. And that local tattoo parlor . . . Lunar something?"

"Raven Lunar."

"Why don't you pay it a visit?" Catherine said. She paused and glanced over at Langston. "In fact, Ray, I'd like you to join him."

He showed a wry smile. "For social and cultural perspective?"

"There's that," she said, and winked. "But I also thought you'd look great sporting some neck ink above your collar."

* * *

"If I was giving you a house edge," Phillips was explaining, "I would've said to put money on this woman dying from a bullet wound to the head."

"Right," Catherine said.

"So it seemed like the reasonable place to start."

"Right."

"My autopsy, that is."

"Right."

"Sometimes I have to follow the bouncing ball."

Catherine looked at him. "Okay, Dave," she said. "I get you."

Phillips stood beside the dissection table in his scrub suit, nodding as he displayed the top of Laurel Whitsen's skull in his gloved hands. He had seemed to loosen up before Catherine's eyes, reassured that she was genuinely *simpatico*. For the most part in criminal investigations, the dissection began with a Y incision from the shoulders and breastbone down to the pelvis, the purpose of which was to expose the rib cage, abdomen, and vital organs. But with the probable cause of Laurel's death fairly obvious, he'd followed his "bouncing ball"—the hole and cranial damage left by the nine-millimeter slug's entry—and sawed into the skull first, separating the top from the lower sections with a chisel.

Catherine supposed that Phillips's tendency to overexplain his procedures stemmed from playing second fiddle to Al Robbins for so long. While

Robbins did not seem at all the morgue-room autocrat, his presence loomed large over its post-mortem affairs.

Phillips held the inverted skull lid in one hand and motioned to three distinct marks with the other. Two were shallow nicks. The third, a wider fracture, had radial lines spreading from it like a concave glass surface hit by a stone. "You see the scoring in the bone? The projectile ricocheted inside this woman's head. Glancing off the skull here and then here." He touched the nicks and put his finger on the larger area of damage. "This is where it hit before deflecting downward and out behind her ear. It's a stellate fracture caused by blunt-force impact— imagine getting clubbed from *inside* the head."

Catherine mulled that over. "The gun was a nine, Dave," she said. "Wouldn't it be unusual for anything but a very small-caliber slug—say, a twenty-two—to start rattling around in there?"

"As a general rule, yeah," Phillips said. "Bigger bullets tend to go in and out. Smaller ones are sometimes retained and act like pinballs. But I ran a trajectory rod through the brain from the entrance wound. It went straight to the first point of deflection. There are also tiny bullet fragments and bone chips in the brain itself."

Catherine thought another moment, then nodded toward the body on the morgue table. "You think she could have stayed conscious for any length of time after she was shot?"

"Absolutely. Some people with a bullet in the brain don't lose their neurological functions all at once. They can stay alert or semialert for hours if the medulla or a major artery isn't struck." He stood thoughtfully regarding the damaged white roof of Laurel Whitsen's skull. "There's an Alabama woman who took a forty-five between the eyes in the middle of a traffic incident. She wasn't even aware of it till she pulled off the highway to report it to the police. Another lady in London was shot point-blank in the head by her husband, watched him commit suicide, and brewed herself a cup of tea before phoning for help."

"How proper." Catherine sighed. "Our vic seems to have found the strength and presence of mind to get up and place a call to nine-one-one. But when she reached the emergency operator, Laurel said something about having to return a book to the shelf and then went back to the next room to do it before she collapsed."

Phillips nodded and carefully placed the skull top on a tray. "I have her brain in the scale," he said. "Come take a look."

They moved to the hanging metal pan above the dissection table. Phillips lifted out the brain and showed it to Catherine, turning the soft, creased mass so she could see its rear portion.

"Notice anything about the parietal lobe?"

Catherine nodded. It would have been difficult *not* to notice the soft, swollen red lesion. "A hematoma," she said. "Does it align with the blunt-force damage to the skull?"

"Very closely," Phillips said. He pressed his thumb into the swelling, and red fluid welled up. "This section was basically turned to mush. But my CT scan revealed even more problems—give me a second, and I'll show you." He reached for a scalpel, held the brain over his sink, sliced it along the fissure separating the right and left hemispheres, and then split it cleanly in half with his hands. A juice of blood sloshed down between them into the basin.

Catherine shook her head. "Boy, she really hemorrhaged."

"There was no room for all that bleeding. It caused a pressure buildup in her skull and brain, even with some of it draining from her wounds." Phillips held one of the oval halves to display its interior. "The majority of burst cerebral capillaries are here in the left hemisphere."

The part of the brain responsible for linear, sequential thought and long- and short-term memory. Catherine's next question was meant to confirm what she'd already deduced. "How would that have affected Laurel's mental condition?"

"She'd have become increasingly confused," Phillips said. "Disoriented . . ."

"Maybe even gotten up to phone the police, then gone back to replace a book without knowing the state she was in?"

"One woman's tea is another's copy of Darwin." Phillips gave a thready smile. "In view of the evidence, it's a distinct likelihood that's what happened. It's even possible she was too zoned out at that stage to be aware of the wound on her arm." He shrugged. "Her loss of consciousness was progressive and gradual. As the pressure in her head reached a critical stage, she would have suffered an acute traumatic stroke. I'd guess that's the cause of death, though hypotension from general blood loss could have contributed."

Catherine let that settle in. "Assuming that Laurel blacked out when she was shot, do you think she could've come around again and *then* gotten up to make her call?"

Phillips slowly returned to his scale and redeposited the brain segments into the pan. "When she finally slipped into a coma, she stayed that way." He exhaled and went on without facing her. "In my opinion, Laurel Whitsen was still conscious when she was skinned alive. She would've known—and felt—everything the killer did to her. If that's what you're asking me, Catherine."

She stared at his back in silence. Pictured Laurel staring up at the killer while he crouched over her with his cutting tools.

As she left the room, Catherine started peeling off her surgical gloves and realized her hand had tightened into a fist. She had to wait a few moments before it would unclench.

*   *   *

Langston swung the Ford Taurus beater toward the parking lot in front of Raven Lunar, one of several tattoo shops lined in close proximity along South Valley View Boulevard, a tidy commercial strip on the west side of McCarran International Airport. The car knocked over the curb cut.

"Wow," Greg said from the passenger seat. "Shocks must be optional these days."

Langston smiled a little. Although he'd eyed a brand-new Mustang back at headquarters, it came as no surprise to him when the req officer on duty instead handed those keys to Nick and Sara. All things within the LVPD, including its criminalistics bureau, had a pecking order based on status and seniority. He had learned this with some embarrassment in his first days at the lab, when he'd found nowhere to put his crime-scene kit, boxes of case files, or even his sport jacket, forcing him to haul everything from room to room on a luggage cart, only to be repeatedly—and unceremoniously—told to run along.

He keyed off his ignition now, checking the dash clock as the Ford groaned to a halt. It was eleven forty-five, slightly more than three hours from the time Laurel Whitsen made her strange, disjointed 911 call from the library. Although it opened at noon according to Raven Lunar's website, Langston saw a silver Lexus hybrid had pulled up to its entrance, stylized versions of the studio's name and blue moon logo painted on the flanks, hood, and bumpers. Someone was already there.

"We're definitely in the wrong line of work," Greg said. He was looking out at the vehicle. "That's some chariot. Tattoos and all."

Langston smiled a little. "Have you ever considered one?"

"A tat?"

"Right."

Greg shook his head. "I keep changing how I get my hair cut," he said. "It's hard to see doing anything that permanent to my body."

Langston sat quietly a moment. "I have," he said. "Once or twice."

"You aren't serious." Greg looked at him and pulled a face. "You are serious, huh?"

Langston continued to smile. "Why do you sound so surprised?"

"I don't know." Greg hesitated. "I'm not sure I can picture you rolling up your sleeves to show off a fire-breathing dragon on a pile of demon skulls."

Langston was quiet again, his expression growing thoughtful. "I'd actually considered something hidden," he said. "Of very personal significance."

"Like . . . ?"

"I think that if I shared it with you, it would no longer be personal." Langston nodded toward the tattoo shop. "Come on. Let's see if anyone in there will speak with us about Laurel."

They found the place still closed. Langston cupped

a hand over his eyes, peered through the glass door, and saw a woman with short, choppy black hair sitting behind a computer at the front desk.

He was about to ring the bell when she glanced up from her screen, motioned for him to wait, then rose from her chair. The CSIs had their ID cards on lanyards around their necks, and she quickly scanned them through the door before unlocking it.

"Hi," she said. "I'm Raven."

Langston looked at her. "Lunar?"

"Right."

Langston paused. He supposed he hadn't expected her name to match the shop's. Why, though? Bringing presumptions into the field—large or small—left him vaguely disappointed with himself.

"May we speak to you?" he said. "I realize it's before business hours . . ."

"Are you here about Laurel?"

Langston could see now that her mascara was smudged. She'd been crying.

"Yes." He tilted his head sideways. "How did you know?"

"I listened to the radio driving in," she said. "They had a story on the news. I heard her name . . . she's one of my clients."

He nodded. "We have some questions," he said. "If you don't mind."

Raven Lunar stood there nervously ruffling her hair. She was pretty, full-figured, and in her early to mid-thirties, wearing black three-quarter tights and a low-cut violet tank top that showed a large rose tattoo on her arm and offered a deep view of silver-blue mermaids riding dolphins bareback across her generous cleavage. She had a row of small purple rings in her left eyebrow, a black stud in her right, what looked like spiral loops in the upper rim of one ear, and assorted metal tapers and hooks in the other.

"Come in," she said. "I'll tell you whatever I can."

The CSIs entered, Langston making introductions as she held the door for them. The studio was small but bright, with traditional green and blue Japanese fish kites on the wall beside the front desk and a black leather tattoo chair, wall mirror, and countertops toward the rear.

"*Koinbori*," Langston said. He was pointing up at the windsocks. "They're very nice. In Japan, they're hung each year on Children's Day—the fifth of May, I think. They symbolize courage and perseverance—"

"Because carp can swim against the strongest currents," she said, finishing the sentence. "I kind of understand how that feels. But I also like fish, the ocean, anything to do with mermaids."

Langston was slightly embarrassed to realize he'd noticed. He nodded toward the chair in back. "Is that where you apply your tattoos?"

"Yeah," she said. "Well, *mostly*. I've got a second studio upstairs if people want privacy. For certain areas on the body."

"And is the same true for scarifications?"

Raven shook her head. "I wouldn't attempt them."

"Oh," Langston said. "I thought you might. Laurel Whitsen had several."

"Yes," Raven said. "They're beautiful. But scarification and implant art are a specialty. You can count the real experts on your fingers."

"Do you know who did the work on her?"

"Sure," Raven said. "Mick's place is close by. Right down the street, actually . . ."

"One second, please." Langston reached into a trouser pocket for his digital voice recorder and thumbed it on. "Can you give me his full name?"

"Mick Aztec. He might be the best in the country. Everybody's trying to copy his techniques."

Langston nodded in silence. He'd heard of him, and recently, too. But at the moment, he couldn't recall where.

"The work Mick did for Laurel is . . . *was* . . . exceptional," Raven went on. Her voice caught. "We collaborated on a back piece together."

"The flowers and branches," Greg said.

"That's right." Raven turned to face him. "You've seen it?"

"She's been examined by the coroner," he said, his gaze meeting hers. "He took photos."

Raven's eyes lowered as that sank in. "Oh, right," she said in a sorrowful tone. "Mick and I were very proud of how it turned out. It's composed of features from different blossoming trees. Plus some imaginary ones."

"Ah," Greg said. "I was wondering."

"We used creative license. Laurel's two big things were flowers and fantasy stories. In fact, she was writing a novel. A modern mythology, she called it." Raven shook her head. "Laurel was one of the sweetest people you'd ever meet . . . it's hard to imagine anyone wanting to hurt her. I can't believe we're talking about her in the past tense."

"I'm sorry," Langston said, reclaiming her attention from Greg. He'd meant to ask something else about the scarification artist. "About Mick Aztec. Your working with him, that is. I thought you didn't . . . "

"Do skin mod, right. That part was totally Mick. I worked on original design sketches. And then did my tattooing over the scar tissue."

Langston quietly mulled how to ease into his next set of questions. But he'd learned since joining the crime lab that delicacy was often an impossible luxury. "Raven . . . can you tell us anything about the tattoo on Laurel's arm?"

"Yes. Well, she had a few of them. But I'm guessing you mean the one on her right . . ."

He raised an eyebrow. "Why would that be?"

"It was on *Flash Ink*," she said. "I figured you knew."

Langston shook his head. "No, I've never heard of—"

"*Flash Ink* is the name of an online tattoo magazine," Greg explained. "It's been spun off on cable TV . . . sort of a reality show. Pulls huge ratings."

Raven was nodding in agreement. "They follow a dozen body artists and their clients through the whole tattoo process and end with a big stage contest," she added. "The series moves to a different city every year. This season, it was Vegas. Before that, they went to Canada. Toronto, I think."

"The tattoo with the rabbit and deer was yours?"

"Well, I created and applied it. But it was on Laurel's skin, which in my mind makes it hers," Raven said. "We called it 'Transfornatural.' " She furrowed her brow. "Why do you want to know about her tattoo if you never heard of the contest?"

Langston decided to change the subject briefly. The details weren't pretty. But he also hadn't forgotten Hodges's eye swabs and still wanted to explore a possible link between that morning's two newly discovered murders.

"Raven, can you tell me anything about the ingredients of certain colors? And how they're mixed?"

She shook her head. "Not a whole lot beyond the really basic stuff. But I know a couple of people who make up my caps when I need a particular shade."

"Would you be able to steer us in their direction?"

"Sure. If it'll help. In fact, one of my color guys shares studio space with Mick."

Langston nodded. He would want to pay them a visit after finishing with Raven. "As far as the contest, am I correct in understanding that you're judged as teams?"

"Right. It comes down to two in the final round. The winning team splits ten thousand dollars. The runners-up get five. Laurel and I only reached the semifinals, though I think our piece might've been a little subtle for the panel. We got all kinds of positive viewer feedback. And my business doubled afterward."

"I'm curious . . . is there any symbolic meaning to the illustration?"

She shrugged. "I'd categorize it as neo-surrealist fairy tale. It's more narrative than symbolic."

Langston involuntarily widened his eyes.

"Blame that on my graduate degree in fine arts from Berkeley," she said with a thin smile. "The piece is really playful. But if you want to look for subtext, I suppose it tells how some of us feel about being modded and about what it takes to do it. The bunny's a sort of cartoon character. Small, mischievous. We thought it was kind of funny that he'd saw off the buck's antlers and then have the stones to ride him bareback."

"That pesky rabbit," Langston said.

"Basically," Raven said with a nod. "When I got my first tattoo, it was like winning the Revolutionary War. I was ecstatic."

"So the rabbit's celebrating its victory."

"Yeah," Raven said. "Even though it might've hurt. He needed courage to saw off the buck's antlers and then implant them in his own head. But it's all growing pains. Change doesn't come easy. He's won the freedom to change and express who he is."

"And the buck?" Langston looked at her. "Feel any sympathy for him?"

"Some. He's a big, hopeless lunk. Stuck on keeping his antlers because he thinks they make him powerful. If he only knew . . ."

"True empowerment is being able to let go of them," Langston said.

Raven smiled again and aimed her index finger at him. But her features were heavy with sadness. "There's your meaning, I guess. And why Laurel loved that piece. It isn't easy fighting your own hangups, and everything society says you should be, to get to who you are. She could've stayed out in Frisco, taken over her dad's investment firm, been set for life. Instead, she worked as a librarian and wrote fantasy novels that nobody published."

Langston heard the tremor in the young woman's voice and paused so she could gather herself. He truly wished he didn't have to tell her the rest. "Raven," he said, "the tattoo was removed from her arm."

She looked stunned. "No, it can't be. That would take months with a laser, and it was there when I saw her a couple of weeks ago. Besides, why would Laurel even want to—"

"I don't mean she intentionally had it taken off." Langston pressed his lips together. "Someone did it to her at the crime scene . . . in the library this morning."

Raven stared at him with dawning comprehension. "How . . ."

"We have reason to suspect the person used a surgical knife," Langston said. "It was expertly done."

"I can't believe it." Her face had gone a pasty white. "Why . . . my God . . . *who* would do anything that sick?"

"That's what we're trying to find out," Greg said. He thoughtfully scratched behind his ear. "Do you know if *Flash Ink* gave viewers any of Laurel's personal information?"

Raven was shaking her head. "Not the kind that would tell where she lived or worked. They were really careful about it."

"Didn't they show you giving her the tattoo?"

"Yeah, they had cameras on us the whole time," Raven said. "They would've mentioned that I'm in Las Vegas, but I don't think they gave my full address."

"It would be easy enough to look up," Greg said. "Let's say someone fixated on Laurel. The person could have watched for when she visited here, tailed her home or to work, and gotten familiar with her normal routines. Then waited for the right opportunity to attack her."

She shook her head again. "No, I can't believe it happened that way."

"Any reason?" Greg asked.

"You must have seen the other tattoo studios on the boulevard."

"Right, but yours is the only one called Raven Lunar. "

"You don't understand," she said. "We're all tight. We *look out* for each other. Somebody would have noticed if there was a stranger standing around outside, sitting in a parked car, or whatever."

"Many predators are good at being inconspicuous," Langston said. "I have some background in that area. They can be very clever at stalking their victims."

"I guess," Raven said. "But we get different types in this neighborhood. And we know the scaries. I still don't see—"

The CSIs looked at her. She'd abruptly cut herself short and snapped her head around toward the computer on the front desk.

"Is anything the matter?" Langston asked.

"I don't know." She turned to face him. "It just came to me about the website. Because of Laurel."

"I'm not sure I follow."

"*Flash Ink* has an online version of the magazine. But it's got other content for paid subscribers."

"Besides the e-zine," Greg prompted.

She nodded. "You need a user name and a password to access it. There are videos, heavy-mod photo galleries, an Internet store, that kind of thing. After I heard about Laurel on the radio, I logged on to check out some pictures of us from the contest. Don't ask why. Maybe just so I could see her alive. And then I read a post about what happened."

"Her murder, you mean?"

"It was on a message board," Raven said. "I wasn't surprised. Community forums, chat rooms—Laurel was on them a lot. Connecting to all kinds of different people."

"Are you saying . . . ?"

"I told you I never worry about scaries on the street," Raven said. "You can spot them in a minute. But you know . . ."

"Cyber-scaries are invisible," Greg said. "Ghosts in the machine."

She said nothing and stared grimly over at the computer, Greg and Langston joining in the silence. They were wondering exactly what kind of case they had on their hands.

Stacy Ebstein—the Tattoo Man's first victim—lived in an upper-middle-class Henderson subdivision a few miles southwest of Green Valley, her tract home's stucco walls, red tile roof, attached garage, and small rectangular lawn in neat conformity with the rest of the street's master-planned properties.

Nick rolled up to the house in his unmarked

black Mustang and noticed the blinds were drawn against the bright morning sunshine.

"Stacy's sister has been staying with her," he said. "She wasn't too keen on our visit."

"Stacy or the sister?" Sara said from the passenger seat.

"Stacy, sorry," he said. "She claimed over the phone that it was because it's the Jewish sabbath."

"Sounds like you think she might have a different reason."

Nick shrugged. "The sabbath ends after sundown. When I offered to drop by tonight instead of this morning, Stacy said she goes to bed early."

"Uh-huh." Sara looked out at the house with its lowered blinds. "So is that when you poured on the Texas charm?"

"Not this boy—though maybe I should've." He thumbed his chest. "Actually, I get a call back from the sister about fifteen minutes after Stacy hangs up. She tells me it's okay to come right over."

"Hope she bothered to inform Stacy."

Nick grinned. He swung into the driveway and pulled behind a lime Subaru wagon with New York plates. Sara unclipped her seat belt, then reached back for her evidence kit.

They went up to the house, buzzed, waited. It took only a few seconds for the front door to open.

The woman framed in the entry was thirtyish and very attractive. Cropped blond hair, blue eyes, slender figure. She had on olive capri cargo pants, a white tank top, and sandal wedges.

"Officer Stokes?" she asked, offering a hand. "I'm Ellen Lerner, Stacy's sister."

Nick was surprised by her youth. Her flat, worn-out tone over the telephone had led him to expect someone much older.

"I'm not an officer, ma'am," he said, and introduced Sara. "We're with the forensics lab."

"Oh." It was her turn to be surprised. "I must've misunderstood."

"Police get badges." Nick tapped the CSI patch on his Windbreaker and smiled. "We get these patches."

She returned his smile and moved aside to let them through the door.

The gloom within fell over them at once. Nick looked around the living room and realized its shades had blackout liners.

Ellen read his expression and grew uncomfortable. "You'll both have to excuse me," she said. "It's Stacy's wish that the lights stay low."

"Don't apologize," Sara said. "We appreciate being able to visit on short notice."

Ellen nodded. "My sister was always an active, upbeat woman—we called her the family extrovert. She used to say her job at the hotel was to make sure people left there with bigger smiles than they had when they arrived." She spread her hands as if to indicate the surrounding dimness. "Everything is different now."

"We won't take up much of Stacy's time," Nick said. "If we could speak with her . . ."

"Of course," Ellen said. "Come with me—she's in her room."

They followed her to a door at the end of a short hall. Their footsteps made no sound on the thick-napped carpeting.

Ellen knocked on the door.

"Yes?" softly from behind it.

"The gentleman who called earlier is here," Ellen said. "He's with his partner, Ms. Sidle."

Ellen waited a moment with her hand on the doorknob, then opened the door and motioned them in. Nick breathed and took the lead without betraying perceptible hesitation.

The room was on the small side and even darker than the other rooms. There was a bed against one wall, a dresser opposite, a corner bookshelf. That was it for the furniture, besides an armchair at the far end, facing the door.

Spectral in the dimness, Stacy Ebstein sat on the chair with her back to the blackout shades.

"Please stop right there," she said.

The CSIs stood just inside the door as it clicked shut behind them. Nick was thinking the air smelled of stale perfume. Then checked that. *No, not perfume. Makeup.*

"I should have had chairs ready," Stacy said. "You have nowhere to sit."

Nick couldn't make out her features. Bangs covered her forehead, the hair falling over either side of her face in long, straight sheets.

"That's okay," he said. "We don't mind standing."

"No, it's unacceptable," she said. "I used to organize parties for hundreds of VIPs. You know of my career at the Starglow?"

"Yes."

"I catered to A-list celebrities, top business executives," she said. "Hundreds and hundreds of them."

"Ms. Ebstein—"

"First names are fine . . . Nick, is it?"

"Right."

She turned her head slightly toward Sara. "And, again, you're . . . ?"

"Sara Sidle."

"Nick and Sara, I'll remember now," Stacy Ebstein said. "I was once quite good with names." She expelled a long sigh. "I wish I'd prepared chairs for the two of you."

Nick's eyes had begun adjusting to the weak light. He could see the heavy makeup on her chin. It had a thick, caked-on look.

"Stacy," he said, "we've come to talk about what happened to you."

"I've spoken to the detectives. At the hospital after I was found and then here at my home. They asked their questions, and I answered those I could."

"I understand," Nick said. "But there've been some new developments."

"So my sister insisted. She urged me to see you."

Nick said nothing.

"These developments," Stacy said. "Tell me about them, please."

He didn't hesitate now. "Do you know a man named Quentin Dorset?"

"No."

"He's a retired district judge," Nick said.

"I don't recognize the name."

"Is it possible he attended any of your events at the Starglow? Or even booked one?"

"I couldn't say. That's all in the past, Nick."

"But would there be guest lists? Records we could check?"

"I did keep them, yes. On my computer."

"Here or at the hotel?"

"The hotel. You'd need to find out if anyone held on to them. It's been months but seems so much longer ago. Why do you ask about the judge, Nick?"

"He was abducted and held against his will. Almost certainly by the same person who kidnapped you."

"Was he . . . *changed*?"

"Yes."

A momentary silence. "Oh," she said. "I see."

"Judge Dorset is dead, Stacy," Nick said. "We think he might have overdosed on a tranquilizer called Diprivan."

"The one the police say I was given."

"Yes."

Stacy Ebstein shifted in her chair. Nick noticed

that she stayed very straight, barely moving her head, careful not to let the hair move away from her face. "I wish you hadn't told me this news," she said. "I find it quite distressful."

"We didn't come here to upset you, Stacy."

"Well, you have. I don't know why Ellen was so adamant that we meet. Possibly that other man can help you."

"Mitchell Noble, you mean?"

"Yes. The shopkeeper. I don't recall our crossing paths, either."

"We plan to speak with him."

"Good. "

"But the more we know, the better," Nick said. "The tattoo inks that were used on you and the judge might have some unique qualities. If we can identify them, there's a chance it might lead us to the person responsible for these crimes."

"I wish you luck. Sincerely, Nick."

Nick paused. *Easy does it.* "There are comparisons we can make with our equipment," he said, his voice calm and level. "A skin sample from you would be very useful."

She stiffened. "The detectives also wanted samples. They asked to take them at your laboratory. Didn't you know?"

"I did, Stacy—"

"And are you aware I declined?"

"It's in their reports, yes. But the procedure's quick and painless . . ."

"So I'm expected to believe." She grew more

rigid in the chair, gripping its armrests. Nick saw a caddy of some kind on the right one but couldn't discern what was on it. "I'm afraid you'll have to leave now. My life is already difficult. Ellen shouldn't have told you to come."

Nick glanced at Sara. She nodded slightly, picking up the ball. "Stacy, you can trust us," she said. "We'd be very mindful of your privacy at the lab. But we could take the cultures right here if you prefer." She raised her kit. "I'd do it myself—just a few small scrapings of skin. Nick wouldn't even have to be in the room with us."

"Do you want to see my face?"

Sara seemed not to know how to take her question.

"I don't necessarily mean for your tests," Stacy said. "Say I refuse them. Would what I've become still matter?"

"Of course, Stacy."

"Because what I *am* is a freak. Or, in politer terms, a human oddity. One that some people can't resist gawking at out of curiosity and others force themselves not to turn away from out of pity. I haven't decided which looks are harder to bear." Her fingers were clawing into the armrest now. "What sort of person are you, I wonder? And Nick? But maybe it's best some questions aren't answered."

Sara had remained unruffled. "All we want is to find the person who's responsible, Stacy. That's why these epithelial samples are so important."

Stacy Ebstein stared at her across the room. After a long silence, she lifted a hand off the armrest and took what Nick thought might be a small round jar from the caddy. And something else . . . a ball?

"Sara, there's a dimmer knob on the wall to your right. Beside the door frame. Would you be so kind as to turn the light up, please?"

Sara nodded. Cool, deliberate. She brightened the ceiling lamp.

Nick could see the items she'd taken from the caddy now. The first object was, in fact, a jar. The second was not a ball but a natural sponge.

"This cold cream works well to remove my makeup." She screwed off the jar's lid. "It just needs a minute to sit."

Nick felt his heart skip a beat as she pushed the hair back from her face, spread on the white emollient with her fingertips, and slowly, almost primly, used the sponge to wipe it away. He'd known what to expect—but the pictures were one thing.

Reality was another.

Stacy Ebstein's face had been turned into a clock, or an eccentric *Alice in Wonderland* version of one, its black-ink numerals about where they belonged but somehow swimming toward the axis of the dial in varied sizes and styles. Almost, Nick thought, as if they'd been drawn freehand on a chalkboard. There was a thick, moonlike twelve on her forehead. A one and a two of different heights tilted together under her left eye. The balloon numbers three, four, and five tumbling down toward her jaw. On her chin was a rubbery six and then a normally proportioned seven under the right corner of her mouth. The top and bottom lines of the eight were missing so it resembled a cursive letter X on her lower right cheek. Above it, a dense number nine with bleeding edges bumped up against the elongated ten and eleven.

The position of the clock hands showed the time of a quarter past three. Nick had remembered that from the photos taken by the sheriff's deputies who'd found her roaming around Cave Lake in a daze. Remembered, too, that the hour and minute markings were accurately placed around the circumference of the dial.

The dial, he thought. *No, a woman's face.*

Nick watched her lean forward in her chair, the jar and sponge returned to the caddy now, her hands back on the armrests.

"I was raised an observant Jew," she said. Her voice choked. "It was always my belief that tattoos were forbidden. And that anyone who wears them could not be interred in a Jewish cemetery."

The CSIs listened in silence.

"My rabbi assured me the burial prohibition is a myth," she said. "I was relieved to learn my body will not be refused a proper place of rest."

Nick exhaled. "Stacy . . . we're trying to find a dangerous maniac. Help us before anyone else has to suffer."

She shook her head, her eyes wet. "The world embarrasses me, and I cannot dream that this watch exists and has no watchmaker," she said. "Sara, I would be appreciative if you'd dim the lights again."

Sara had kept her hand on the knob. She turned it.

"Thank you," Stacy said in the restored gloom. She'd draped her hair back over her face. "Now I'd ask to be left alone."

Nick considered asking her to reconsider, but Sara touched his arm. "Let's go," she said. "She's had enough."

Ellen Lerner was apologetic when she showed them out. It did nothing to remedy Nick's disappointment as he got into the Mustang and drove back toward the southbound interstate. He'd wanted that skin culture.

"I'm telling myself we should've pressed Stacy harder," he said, and turned to Sara. "I understand you feeling sympathetic—"

"I don't."

"Hold on." He stared at her across his seat. "I could've sworn it was you back there saying to leave her be."

"It was more like me wanting to make a graceful exit." Sara shrugged "What was the point of her whole performance? She definitely had no intention of helping anyone."

"I wasn't too specific over the phone with her sister. Stacy might've thought we'd have information for *her*."

"So? She finds out a man's been killed. You

don't think that should persuade her to donate some skin cells? Instead, she tries to get a reaction out of us."

Nick whistled. "Whoa," he said. "Those are some harsh words."

"I'd have knelt at Stacy Ebstein's feet and wrung my hands to get her to cooperate. She's had a terrible thing happen to her, but so have a lot of other people in this world . . . and what are we really asking of her?" Sara paused. "She's too full of self-pity to give a damn about anyone. I just didn't feel like wasting more time with the woman, her bad theater, and her Voltaire—Nick, you'd better watch where you're going."

Nick looked out his windshield, saw he was precariously close to running a stoplight, and braked. The Mustang halted with a sudden lurch.

He sat waiting for the light to turn green, then rolled silently on toward the intersection.

5

BOCKEM HAD SPOTTED the old coyote on his first day at the cabin. He was emptying groceries and supplies from his station wagon when it appeared down the ridge, its fur pale gray and natty, an observable stiffness in its gait as it moved closer to investigate his presence. This had been at high noon, with the bright, cold sun peaking in a crystalline blue sky, and Bockem had checked his watch on reflex to make sure he hadn't somehow lost track of the time. Coyotes were crepuscular in their normal prowling habits and would often drowse away the daylight hours.

As he'd carried his bags inside, the scrawny creature had been bold or desperate enough to come into open sight on the trail, although it had kept far enough away to make a safe retreat if he showed signs of hostility.

Bockem supposed it must have gotten used to foraging through the trash when hikers and sightseers arrived to rent the cabin during the tourist season. But that was still more than a month off, and the coyote would have relied on its skills as a predator and an opportunistic scavenger to survive the winter. Its rangy leanness and scruffy coat indicated it had not fared well. The slowness of age and instincts dulled by contact with humans had done little for its prospects.

After eating lunch, Bockem had left his table scraps in an open bag outside the kitchen window and watched as the coyote had loped up the mountain trail—pausing warily once or twice to sniff the wind with its triangular ears perked, then approaching the cabin to devour them. It had since lost much of its tentativeness, arriving early each morning on the same trail, hovering near the lodge for hours on end in eager anticipation of Bockem's throwaways. But he still made it wait, consistently putting out the discarded morsels at one o'clock in the afternoon, as he had the day he'd arrived.

Bockem held what the creature wanted, and his father had raised him to understand that nothing desired should ever be freely given. Patience only increased its value.

He finished washing his scraper, gently scrubbing its teeth clean with a brush under the open tap. With the hot water running, he could still hear the sounds from the sitting room—the skin flapping rhythmically against the sides of the rotating drum he'd set up there.

Putting his scraper aside to dry, Bockem sprayed

the basin to rinse away the blood drippings, turned from the kitchen sink, and glanced out the window into the swirling, windblown dust of yet another day—his fourth on the isolated valley rim. It had been three hours since he'd returned to the lodge, and with noon already approaching, the coyote would be eyeing its small front yard from the near distance. He meant to reward its latest visit with a taste of something different.

Bockem had wiped his hands on a dish towel and started toward the fleshing board and bucket when his cell phone vibrated against his leg. He reached into his pocket for it, read the name on the display, and frowned even while pressing the answer button.

"Mr. Chenard," he said. "What do you think you're doing?"

"My apologies for the disturbance, should I have caused one," Chenard said. "As you know, I browse certain galleries and keep an eye on current events. There was a breaking news story in the Las Vegas area—"

"Keep it to yourself," Bockem snapped. He flared with anger over Chenard's carelessness. "You shouldn't be calling now."

"I realize this is irregular. However, the piece is truly fabulous, its artist an unacknowledged master. And I would like to extend an offer."

"There's a proper time for that," Bockem said. "This isn't it."

"Possibly I wasn't clear enough. My hope is to make a preemptive bid."

"So I assumed," Bockem said. "But I'd expected you would understand my reasons for establishing certain procedures."

"Would sixty thousand dollars relax them?"

"No."

"Seventy-five, then."

"Mr. Chenard, you verge on disrespect."

A pause. Then Chenard resumed in a less stubborn tone. "Nothing could be further from my intent. In fact—"

"Your intentions are of no concern to me. I'm not some street-market vendor who haggles over prices," Bockem said. He was thinking Chenard had to be put in his place despite being a highly valued client. Men of his wealth and position were used to setting the rules, not abiding by them. "I would ask that you don't participate if you're unwilling or unable to follow my terms."

"I have no difficulty with them," Chenard said. "Please consider this matter resolved. I'll be waiting for your usual notification."

Bockem was thinking Chenard had been sufficiently admonished; a conciliatory gesture would do no harm. "Thank you, Mister Chenard. I appreciate your understanding my position and believe you'll find that patience has its definite rewards. If my plans hold, there will be more than a single additional offering."

"Of the same quality—if I may ask?"

Bockem had heard the hitch of barely suppressed excitement in his voice. "I expect them to be among my best to date," he said.

Bockem clicked the cell phone's disconnect button. *Waiting.* Of that he had no doubt.

A smile scratched across his lips as he thought of the coyote sniffing the wind. He put down the phone, turned toward his fleshing board, picked up the bucket alongside it on the sink counter, and went out to dispose of his scrapings.

Ray Langston was driving over to Mick Aztec's studio in the Ford when he realized why that name had sounded so familiar.

"The Tattoo Man case reports!" he said, slapping his forehead.

"What about 'em?" Greg asked

"Brass's men interviewed Aztec after the second abduction."

"The sex-toy salesman, right?"

"Noble, yes."

Greg looked at him. "The name doesn't *quite* fit the line of work."

Langston smiled a little and swung into the parking area. "My point is that Raven told us Aztec is recognized for his scarification and implants."

"Which were used on Noble," Greg said. "You don't figure . . .?"

"The detectives seemed to feel he's clean," Langston said. "We'll see what *we* think."

Getting out of the car, Langston noticed a tall,

thirtyish man with a shaved head having a smoke in front of the studio. He watched the CSIs closely as they approached. "I've kind of been expecting you." He offered his hand, speaking softly, his cigarette poking from his lips. "I'm Mike Aztec. I assume you're the two from the crime lab. Raven phoned to give me a heads-up that you might be coming here."

Langston nodded and got their introductions out of the way. "Is it okay if we talk inside?"

Wearing black Dockers, black high-top sneakers, and a dark blue ribbed sweater, Aztec studied him through a puff of tobacco smoke. Then he flicked his cigarette stub to the ground and crushed it out with his sneaker bottom. "I've got fifteen, twenty minutes until my one-thirty appointment. Sound like enough time for you?"

"If it has to be," Langston said, and followed him to his door.

The shop was about the same size as Raven Lunar's, with a padded black leather waiting bench to the right of the door, a flight of stairs descending to the left, and a glass display case filled with piercing jewelry toward the back. There was a natural sandstone veneer on the walls, a gallery of tattoo design sheets covering the light brown tiles on one side. Langston studied their complicated interlocking patterns and lines for a moment, then turned toward the stairway.

"The workshop's down there," Aztec said, noting

his curiosity. "That's where I do my thing. Cody's area is divided off from it."

"Cody?"

"Cody Vaega. He's a tattooer."

"The one who prepares colors for Raven."

"Sometimes," Aztec said. "He does it as a favor for different artists in our community."

"Is he in now?"

Aztec shook his head. "Cody's a road dog . . . travels around and hits the convention scene. He's out of town this weekend giving a seminar at one in Dallas. Also does a lot of ink-and-stays, you know?"

Langston gave him a look that said he didn't.

"They're hotel packages. Guests book weekend getaways and get tattoo vouchers with their accommodations."

Langston grunted. "Creative," he said.

"In these tough times, they'd better be if they want to fill their rooms," Aztec said. "Some places have in-house artists. They mostly use local tattooers. But someone like Cody can pull in more business through his rep."

Greg had been looking around as they talked. "Is the flash yours or his?"

"Cody did the majority of it. He's Polynesian . . . you can see the tribal influence. I'm just a dabbler."

"Stick to skin mod otherwise?"

"It's what I love doing," Aztec said with a nod.

Langston decided to get to the point. "I assume you've heard about Laurel Whitsen."

"Raven broke it to me over the phone." Aztec's face expressed regret. "It really hasn't sunk in. Laurel was my client. But we were also friends. She was one of the gentlest people I've ever met."

Langston recalled Raven Lunar describing her in approximately the same terms. He made a low, thoughtful sound in his throat. "How long had she been coming here?"

"I'd say a year. Maybe a little more," Aztec said. "Laurel was still living in California the first time. She flew in to get specked on her arm."

"Specked?"

"It's a stippling technique I developed. We did a fancy leaf pattern."

"How had she heard about you?"

"I think it was through an e-magazine."

"*Flash Ink*?"

"This was a while back, so I can't swear to it. But I have a running ad that links to my Web page and networking sites."

Langston regarded Aztec closely through his spectacles. "Is that how you get all of your out-of-town contacts?"

"Some. More than eighty percent is still word-of-mouth," Aztec said. His dark eyes returned Langston's interest. "Raven told me a stalker killed Laurel."

"It's among the possibilities."

"She said it might have been someone who saw her on television and then looked her up on the Internet. "

"Again, we don't know," Langston said. He paused. "Did Raven mention what happened to the tattoo on Laurel's arm?"

" 'Transfornatural'?"

"Yes."

A moment passed. They looked at each other in the pendant silence. "I'm sick about it," Aztec said finally. He hesitated. "I suppose I should ask if I'm a suspect."

"Should you be?"

Aztec was quiet another moment. "The detectives already paid me a visit about the Tattoo Man kidnappings. And I was expecting them."

Langston was thinking they would have only spoken to him about Mitchell Noble and Stacy Ebstein. The specifics about Dorset hadn't yet been released for public consumption. "What made you certain they would come?" he asked.

Aztec meshed his hands at his chest, bowed his head, and studied them as if in deliberation, remaining very still for a while. Then his eyes lifted. "Local cops, feds . . . I'm on all kinds of hot lists. They'd deny I've been typed, but there aren't a lot of people with my skills and rep. They know who I am."

Another silence. Langston waited for him to continue.

"What I do is about love and sharing," Aztec said. His voice remained very soft. "There's a bond between an artist and a client. You wouldn't understand."

"Now you're typing me," Langston said. "Making assumptions that might not be true."

Aztec shook his head a little, looking skeptical. "If you don't think I did anything wrong, why are you here?"

"We need help finding a killer," Langston said. "It's that simple."

Aztec gave him a long, assaying glance. Langston waited patiently again, saw a slight shift in his doubtful expression. But he wasn't sure how much could be read into it.

"Come on," Aztec said at last, motioning toward the stairs. "Let's talk down in my workshop. I can show you some things."

Langston could tell from his tone that he was the only one who'd been invited. He shot a look at Greg, who gave a shrug indicating he wouldn't object to staying put. Then he returned his eyes to Aztec. "Lead the way," he said.

Nick and Sara's second stop of the day was on the east side of town off Boulder Highway, a fifteen-minute drive from Stacy Ebstein's home.

" 'Intimate Sexy Adult Fantasies.' " Nick read the lettering on the store's plate-glass window as he slid the Mustang against the curb. "Now, that's a name."

"At least you know what you're getting," Sara said, and exited the car.

They walked into the shop, and as the door shut

behind them with a jingle of overhead chimes, it suddenly occurred to Nick that Sara was wrong, dead wrong. Whatever you were getting here was anything *but* what was touted up front. The walls and counters were full of battery-powered stimulators and massagers and enhancers and pumps and probes, pornographic movies in Blu-ray and DVD and mark-down videocassette formats, assorted sprays and gels and lotions and powders with names like *Make Me Groan* and *Heat Seeker* and *Coochy Lube* and *Orgasmix*, bondage costumes and masks and chastity belts and stand-up cages, cuffs and whips and cat-o'-nine-tails—everything in sight collectively geared toward fantasies Nick did not find at all intimate or sexy but instead just considered dreary and tiresome.

"No lingerie department?" Sara asked.

Nick motioned to a flesh-colored female body form in a leather strap harness. "I think that's it right there."

A smile tweaked her lips. "I prefer everyday comfort."

They had spent a minute looking around when they heard movement elsewhere in the shop. The sales counter was at the rear, a doorless entry behind it presumably leading to a stockroom. Someone had emerged from it, a man with a red-and-white-checked Saudi *ghoutra* wound around his head do-rag style. Its long tails spilled over his shoulder.

"Can I help you two?" he said from behind the counter. Then he noticed their Windbreakers. "Oh, sorry. This is an official visit . . . I didn't see the patches. You're investigators?"

"Las Vegas Crime Lab," Nick said, and gave his name. "My partner's Sara Sidle."

The man nodded. "Mitchell Noble," he said.

Nick watched him come around into the aisle. Brass's case files described Noble as Caucasian. The tattoo needle had left his face black, with a faint enamel gloss to the pigment. His visible implants were metallic. Those covered by the headscarf bulged under its tightly wrapped fabric.

Later on, Nick would think it lucky he'd reviewed the snapshots at headquarters—still, photos weren't always adequate preparation. The tug of simultaneously wanting to stare and look away made him acutely self-conscious—perhaps because he knew what Stacy Ebstein would have said.

Noble seemed to pick up on it. He stopped in the aisle and ran his open hands down over his cheeks. "It's a camera, an antique box camera," he said, and then touched the large round knob on his temple with a finger. "You recognize this right here?"

Nick shook his head. He wished he'd been better at hiding his reaction.

"That's supposed to be a dial for winding the film. You can see the finger grips if you look closer. The stud underneath is for a lanyard—*wheeee*, don't hang me from it!" Noble swallowed his chuckle. "A little joke there. Don't mind me. I try to have a sense of humor. It helps settle people down when they get a load of me."

Nick took a rasping breath. The spit had drained from his mouth.

"There's a shutter switch on the other side." Noble turned his head slightly away from Nick and Sara to show them. "It's kind of wide, but that's how they were on these cameras. The fucker worked to scale." He faced the CSIs again. "An Ensign Ful-Vue, that's the model. Big in England in the late thirties. *Clever* choice. It's shaped like a helmet, and guess what? A helmet fits on a head! I wrapped the scarf around the photo and viewfinder lenses on mine. They're titanium rings under the skin—you can probably make out the outlines. Goggle, goggle."

Nick breathed dryly again. He felt spiders scrabbling over the back of his neck.

"He really messed me up at first," Noble said. "My life, my business, everything. How'm I gonna make the overhead when even the kinkers are creeped out by my looks? But then I tell myself, 'Mike, give yourself a hug and think about mail order.' "

Sara interrupted. "Mr. Noble—"

"I know. You're busy. It's a busy world. But I tried telling the detectives what I remember. It's just that I don't remember much. I'm outside rolling down the store gates when the fucker comes up behind me, and *bam*."

"Mr. Noble, listen to me," she said. "There was

another abduction. The man was a former chief judge."

"Boy, oh, boy. What'd he get turned into? A flying gavel?"

"He died, Mr. Noble. His body was found last night."

"Does he have a name?"

"Quentin Dorset."

"Eighth Judicial District Court," Noble said. "Clark County Criminal Division. Department Four, wasn't it?"

"Tell me how you know."

"I was a spot-news photographer back in the day. Freelance. Wasn't that in the detective reports?"

"Yes."

"Good. I thought I'd talked about it with them. You're a *whole* lot hotter than they were, incidentally."

Sidle ignored that. "What sort of stories did you cover?"

"Hit-and-runs, wildfires, strangled hookers, mob killings, you name it." He touched the button-shaped implant on his temple. "Here and there I'd do weddings and bar mitzvahs to pay the rent. Say cheese, snap-snap."

"Let's stick to your news photography. I think it's obvious your kidnapper knew you once did it for a living. We have reason to believe he also knew Dorset was a judge. Could you have worked any trials he oversaw?"

"Lots, I'm sure. Dorset was around for twenty years." Noble glanced over at Nick. "What's wrong? Not joining in on the conversation?"

"I'm the one talking to you now, Mr. Noble, so pay attention," Sara said, her eyes flatly on his. "Back to Dorset. Do any of his cases stand out in your mind?"

"What mind? I've got a stale roll of film inside my head." He made another chortling sound. "Just kidding, beautiful. Your question was?"

"Don't insult me, Mr. Noble. I've been nothing but respectful."

He looked at her and kept looking. "I didn't mean to—"

"Forget it. But we have to stay on track."

Nick regarded Sara in the brief silence that followed. It had only been a short while since her return to the CSI team after a long personal hiatus, which had included marrying Gil Grissom and going off on a research trip to Costa Rica. But watching her take hold of the ball, he was reminded of the purposeful intensity and focus that had always impressed him about her.

"I need to know if you remember Dorset's trials," she said, her eyes on Noble. "Or were involved with any in particular."

"Involved?"

"Say one of your photos was used as evidence? Swung a verdict or sentencing decision? Something like that . . . I'm just guessing."

He absently raised a hand to the *ghoutra* and ran a finger around the larger of the two circles pushing out its fabric. "The district had thirty-seven judges. You want me to run off their names in alphabetical order? Be easy. I'd start every day of the week checking their dockets. Did it for five solid years. You realize how many cases that comes to?"

"I'd gather quite a few."

"Dozens times thirty-seven," Noble said. "I sold my pictures to the local newspapers, national papers, and magazines. They pay late and print credits that wouldn't show up under a microscope. But I never hit the big piñata. The hero fireman after a bombing. A high school massacre. A Vietnam vet holding a convent full of nuns hostage. Some little girl rescued from a well—ooh, lawdy, that's Pulitzer material!" He kept tracing the forehead implants with his finger. "Shutterbugs don't rate. Ain't no money in it, honey. You better believe I'd know if I got mileage from anything that had to do with Dorset."

"And what about Stacy Jacobson?"

"The tick-tock lady?"

Sara remained expressionless. "Mr. Noble, it's important that you cooperate here. I'm wondering if your paths could have crossed at some point."

Noble shook his head with a mock grin. "You know, I wondered the same thing when I first got my new look," he said. "But far as I can tell, all we have in common is a psycho kidnapper."

Nick decided to take his crack at him. A thought was fluttering around the edges of his brain, but he'd been unable to grab hold of it—and for him, questions always spun the net that caught the moth. "You said you freelanced for five years. When did you give it up?"

"Well, look who's talking to me again."

"Come on, Noble," Nick said. "When?"

"I did it for Y2K. Photojournalism's spotty. I ran into a guy who was selling this shithole of earthly delights on the cheap and figured, sex merch, *there's* a reliable income."

"Did you hang on to your pictures?"

"Listen, I'm a pro, dig? No matter how I choose to pursue the American dream."

"So the answer's yes."

Noble produced a long sigh. "They're all catalogued and cross-indexed on disc," he said. "My photo library's in the stockroom. Next shelf over from some great dual-action toys."

"We might want to have a look, even burn some copies," Nick said. "That okay?"

"Oh, sure, be my guests." Noble flashed his simulated grin. "Depending on your tastes, I can also recommend an excellent selection of videos."

Sara gave Nick a communicative glance. He nodded almost imperceptibly. "There's something else we'd rather have from you," she said, taking the lead.

"And what would that be?"

"Skin specimens," she said.

"Epithelials?"

She gave him a questioning look.

"The detectives wanted them, too," he said.

"And?"

"Their attitude put me off. Much too cagey, no give and take."

Sara considered that. "Mr. Noble, you told me you followed dozens of trials, is that right?"

"Dozens and dozens."

"So you know we can run lab comparisons with Dorset's tissues," she said. "The dyes that were used might tell us something, provide us with valuable leads."

Noble was staring at her. "*I've* been told there'd be minimal facial scarring if I hired the right doctor to remove the implants, really not much that can be seen. I've even got health insurance to cover the surgeries, yet I haven't looked into it," he said. "Can you guess the reason?"

"Give us the samples, and I promise I'll get back to you."

Noble regarded her for a full thirty seconds. "I like how you work," he said finally.

"I appreciate that."

"I'm serious."

"So am I."

Noble smiled, his eyes still on her face. "You can take whatever samples you want," he said. "Why not? They're only skin deep."

Watching him, Nick decided that this time, the smile was authentic. Although until further notice, he wasn't at all certain he preferred it to the outright fakes.

He had known of the place for a long time. It was down below a saddle in the canyon wall and across a wash where the Joshua trees stood in rooted assembly, a dozen or more of them, tall and grizzled, their shadows dark, dusty, and as tattered as the robes of ancient clerics. There beyond the trailheads frequented by hikers, in a deep notch cut into the canyon's bare bedrock, he had once found an outcropping that rose from the ground in the shape of an altar.

Like the slopes around it, the projection was composed of red sandstone. It came almost up to his knees, its top flattened and smoothed by erosion to a platform that was five feet long and easily two feet wide. There were no other formations of any appreciable size around it, no large boulders, nothing of a similar shape, only the windblown bed of powdery gray sand and loose, scattered stones and pebbles spreading from its base, the coarser deposits as red as the altar and the overarching cliffs.

Early that afternoon, he'd driven out to an overlook spurring off the loop road, pulled his car in, and descended from the saddle on foot, taking a natural pass that wound to the bottom in slow bends and curves. Although he had known another, more direct route, this was far less strenuous. He'd realized his bloodstream was still flooded with endorphins and would not be fooled into thinking he was fully recovered from his suspension. In a sense, though, the peptides in his brain had helped him make the trip out there, dulling the pain of the cancer growing inside him.

The sunlight was angling into the notch when he reached it, warming the air pocketed inside, brightening its high stone walls so that they seemed almost luminescent. He stood for a while and took in the brilliant crimsons, the pink, purple, and vermillion striations. Yes, he thought. Once consecrated, it would make an ideal chapel.

At the altar, he crouched, shrugged off the shoulder pack he'd carried with him, removed his kit, and set it on the ground. Then he opened its lid and uncapped the inks he had prepared. He was confident the porous surfaces below the altar's platform would let them take as if they were colored paints.

On his knees now, he shut his eyes tightly and recalled the picture that had come to him the night before, appearing even as the sight and scent of sagebrush left him. It was as if a wave had overtaken his mind's interior and then withdrawn to leave behind the second image . . . or possibly to expose one that had already existed there, hidden away in his subconscious.

A child with the face of a lamb lying with his hands and legs bound together, a yellow circle of light around his head, his eyes closed almost as if in peaceful repose. A white resurrection banner emblazoned with a red crucifix waving from a sword or a knife above him, the edge of its blade low across the boy's throat.

The image was as vivid as a stencil illustration, and he closely examined it, his consciousness turned upon itself. The moment he felt ready, he reopened his eyes and took a fine-tipped artist's paintbrush from his kit. Gripped by an exalted feeling that was something greater than mere inspiration, he would reproduce the image exactly as it had been revealed to him.

Concentrating to his fullest, he dipped the brush into an ink bottle and applied his first stroke to the rock.

"I can't help you with what happened to Laurel," Mick Aztec was saying to Langston. "I would if I had any information for you. Anything. Do you know what that means?"

"I believe it speaks to how you felt about her," Langston replied. He was sitting near the bottom of the stairs that descended to the workshop, his hands meshed on his lap. "But why don't you tell me?"

Aztec stood in front of him below the flight of steps. "Body artists, we're a tight group," he said, and crossed his fingers together for emphasis. "I don't like talking to you."

"Because I'm with the police?"

"And an outsider," Aztec said. "It isn't personal."

Langston nodded his understanding. "I appreciate your frankness—"

"Laurel was special," Aztec said abruptly. "It's like I told you upstairs. We loved each other."

Langston was recalling that Aztec had actually told him the *work* he'd done on her was a loving act, which was not quite the same thing. "Were you in a relationship with her?"

"It wasn't sexual," Aztec said. "Laurel heard about me about two, three years ago through word-of-mouth. Then she saw my online portfolio and flew here from San Francisco to get a scarification."

"Her first?"

"She never went to anyone else afterward," Aztec said. "I understood what she wanted."

"Aesthetically?"

"And based on how her body would respond. As an artist, I do my best to envision how scar patterns will look on a client. Flesh is my medium, and I have a feel for its qualities."

"Your techniques . . . I imagine they would vary from person to person."

"Yes. Everyone heals differently. I can't say why, but it was easy with Laurel."

"Knowing how she would heal, you mean."

Aztec looked at him. "We had an immediate harmony."

"So after you did your initial work on her . . ."

"She came back here every few months. She was breaking ties with Frisco anyway—her family was giving her grief about the mod—but I think she moved to Vegas partly to cut down on her travel expenses."

Langston nodded, his eyes moving around the room. Small, unadorned, and immaculate, it had soft overhead lighting, with a tattoo chair like the one upstairs in front of the counter, a massage table, a couple of storage cabinets, and a trolley with several rows of pullout bins and trays. There was an adjustable standing lamp near the table, another near the chair, both switched off. He noticed an autoclave of the type used to sterilize medical instruments on a salon counter, the counter itself under a mirror covering the upper half of an entire wall.

"You brought me down here for a reason," he said finally. "I still have no idea what it is."

Aztec started to reply, seemed to think twice. "Cody's had this place for five years," he said after a moment. "We're certified in blood-borne pathogen and infectious disease control, CPR, and first aid. Compliant with Clark County health regs for tattoo practitioners. But there are people who don't like some of what we do here."

"*We*," Langston said. "Or you?"

"It's all the same if they want to shut us down." Aztec shrugged. "Cody's strictly into permanent cosmetics and body piercing. He's clear with the law."

"But you aren't."

"It depends," Aztec said. "My art is defined as extreme body modification. Somebody objects to it morally or whatever, they can interpret the regs so we're slapped with all kinds of misdemeanors. Use them as excuses to call us public nuisances."

"The potential spread of hepatitis B and C and HIV isn't an excuse," Langston said. "I'd say the same for viral, fungal, or bacterial infections."

Aztec looked at him sharply. "I keep a clean room."

"And you'll vouch for everyone else in your profession?" Langston caught another look. He sat forward, his fingers still meshed, his elbows resting on his knees. "I didn't come here to run you out of town on health-code violations," he said. "Anything you tell me stays off the record."

"That sounds fine right now," Aztec said. "How do I know it stays that way?"

"It's possible I'm flattering myself," Langston said, "but I think you only brought me down here because you sense it will."

They kept their eyes steady on each other for a long moment. Then Langston saw Aztec straighten up as if in decision. He finally turned, went over to one of the trolleys, reached into a bin, and came back holding a large assortment of stainless-steel instruments in his hand.

"This is my basic tool set," he said. "The ones I use for scarifications and implants."

Langston studied them. Most were surgical scalpels, scissors, and forceps. But there were some he didn't entirely recognize—long-handled instruments with blunt, flatly circular tips of different sizes. "These tools," he said, pointing to them. "They almost resemble root elevators, the kind that would be used in dental procedures."

Aztec looked surprised. "You know your stuff," he said.

"I'm a medical doctor," Langston said. "A nonpracticing forensic pathologist."

Aztec's eyes widened on him. "You're serious."

"Yes."

" 'Nonpracticing,' " Aztec said. "Is that anything like a lapsed Catholic?"

Langston gave a thin smile and saw Aztec do the same. "A little," he said. "Tell me about the instruments."

"They're dermal elevators." Aztec slid one out from the rest to exhibit it in his free hand. "The dental tools you mentioned separate the gum from the root of a tooth. Mine do the same with layers of skin. Whenever you implant something, you make an incision and insert it between the layers. But if you go down as far as you need to all at once . . ."

"There would be swelling and bruising," Langston said. "A significant amount, I imagine."

Aztec nodded. "I take my time with the elevators to enlarge the space in graduated stages. It causes less trauma and speeds up the healing process.

Anything that helps the tissues rejuvenate quicker gives me better results."

Langston took a moment to digest that. "You're talking about the Tattoo Man as well as yourself."

"The pictures of the people he grabbed were all over the newspapers and the Net," Aztec said. "He's a genius . . . anybody could see it just from looking at them. But they tell *me* he's got some years on him."

"By that you mean . . . ?"

"He's thirty-five, forty, at least."

Langston suddenly felt very ancient. "How can you be sure?"

"Guys don't share their techniques till they do some hanging out with you, loosen up, show off their work. Then they *might* swap some tricks of the trade . . . usually after you've had a few drinks together. I can tell he's learned a lot from the old-school pros."

"Just from looking at those photos?"

Aztec nodded. "His colors aren't typical. Some of them have to be his own formulations."

"You're certain of this as well?"

"I know what I see. Cody can give you the detailed ins and outs," he said. "Another thing . . . if the news stories are right, he held the people he kidnapped for about a week. But there's no peeling where he did his tattoos. No swelling, no discoloration. Same goes for the skin around his implants. Not a mark. When you're experienced with ink or mod, you plan around the normal healing cycle. He has a light touch. Knows his anatomy, too."

"And you?"

"Hmm?"

"Human anatomy," Langston said. "I'm guessing you've also studied it."

"Of course," Aztec said. "Since I was about twelve." A shrug. "Just not in school, you know."

Langston, guilty over his sudden smile, could tell it simply puzzled Aztec. Then he remembered his question to Raven Lunar about symbolism and decided to do more fishing. "Is there anything else you see?" he said. "Some special meaning in what he did to his victims?"

"I couldn't say unless I knew him. Or them. And even then, your guess might be as good as mine." Aztec looked thoughtful. "Hang on, I'll show you something."

He went over to the trolley and put away his instruments. Then he returned, pushed up the sleeve of his sweater, and revealed a multitude of skulls covering most of his forearm. The distorted, socketed bone faces were rendered in black and gray washes.

"Aztec isn't my birth name," he said, which for Langston was hardly a shock. "I lived in Mexico for a while and got interested in their culture. These are a few of their gods." He pointed to one, another, a third. "This is Mictlantecuhtli, the king of the underworld. This here has sacrificial stone blades coming from the eyes and is based on a museum piece. And this, my favorite, has mystical carvings from the priesthood. But as far as their meaning . . . the history's fun, but it's really that the artwork was done by a friend."

Langston waited. Aztec turned his arm over, showing the face of a spike-haired blonde on the soft flesh below the elbow.

"She's Nina Tyford," he said. "A singer-songwriter. Remember 'Angel Heart' from a couple years back?"

Langston shook his head in the negative.

"It was her big hit. Then she committed suicide. I wear the portrait because I was a fan. Nothing profound."

Langston nodded and found himself looking at the small tattoo on Aztec's neck. The doughnut hooked to a pair of dangling chains.

"And the one over there?" he said, touching his own neck. "Out of curiosity . . . I noticed it before."

Aztec shrugged. "I like doughnuts," he said. "And I like hanging from hooks."

Langston opened his mouth, closed it, his question aborted. Aztec had rolled down his sleeve and was looking past him up the stairs, a signal that was easy enough to read. And he hadn't forgotten that Greg was waiting for him.

He rose from the step on which he'd perched and smoothed the front of his trousers. "You've been a great help," he said, putting out his hand.

Aztec nodded and took it. "You'll still want to talk to Cody," he said.

To Cody, and maybe to Aztec again, Langston thought. But he'd learned when to push and when not to.

Aztec motioned him upstairs with a polite wave, pausing to turn off the lights in his workshop before Langston heard him following closely behind.

6

Scheduled to have Saturday night free—his first partial weekend in a month—Nick had told Greg Sanders in passing that he might head out to catch an R&B band at a local club that served the best authentic Tex-Mex food in Vegas. Greg had given him a dubious glance and said he hoped he had a great time. Later, Nick mentioned to one of the techs that he might just choose to stay home, take a crack at clearing away the mess that had accumulated over the last month or so of missed off nights, pick up the novel he'd been trying to finish forever, and hit the sack a little early. The tech hadn't sounded convinced while saying she hoped he got some rest.

A short while afterward, he'd shared a combined and amended version of those plans with Sara, saying he'd decided to stop at the supermarket on the way home, restock his fridge, fix himself a hearty dinner that included burritos and nachos with guacamole, then relax to a country-and-western

CD or watch one of the blockbuster action flicks he had missed last summer—or had it been among the crop he'd failed to see the previous year?— on DVD. Her only response had been to roll her eyes.

Refusing to let their skepticism bother him, he'd gone about getting the box of photo discs obtained from Mitchell Noble catalogued as evidence, asking David Hodges—whose lab was just down the hall from the evidence room and who was familiar with the necessary paperwork—to assist him because the clerk was nowhere in sight. Hodges hadn't looked pleased and was even less thrilled when Nick asked if he could help him get a jump on things by taking care of it pronto, but he'd taken the box from his hands nonetheless.

Now the midnight hour had come and gone, Sunday having crept up on Nick to find him still hanging around his office, his eyes grainy from staring at the computer screen. Hodges had managed to process and return the discs to him within a couple of hours, and he'd decided to give them a quick look before signing out. Although that had been around six P.M., Nick was still optimistic that he'd be able to knock off before too much longer, then maybe swing by the late-night taco joint on South Durango and grab some takeout. When it came to a CSI's personal life, expectations were on a sliding scale, and they generally trended toward the downside.

The thing was that he'd gotten on a roll and

hated to quit. Noble, as it turned out, had not been exaggerating when he'd claimed to be a thorough archivist. The photos for each of the criminal cases he'd followed as a freelance shutterbug were kept in separate folders searchable by docket numbers, the court's ruling dates, and the names of their respective plaintiffs, defendants, and presiding judges. The majority also cross-linked to scanned-in court documents obtained from the county clerk's office. Browsing the contents of the index disc on his computer, Nick had found there were photographs relating to thirty-seven cases that had fallen into Judge Quentin Dorset's lap, dating back to 1998, when Noble began his photography career.

Recalling his conversation with Stacy Ebstein, Nick had looked up the Starglow's general information number and punched it into his phone. This was at half past seven. Ten minutes of navigating the automated menu had finally put him through to a human being, whom he'd asked to connect him with the person in charge of special events. The request had led to a series of inexplicable misroutings, including one to the resort's box office, where he'd gotten another automated list of showtimes for the comedy-magic act currently running in its theater and then been disconnected. Cursing under his breath, he dialed general info again, this time introduced himself as an investigator with the LVPD, and again asked to be put on with somebody in special events, curtly emphasizing that he was calling in an official police capacity. That seemed to break through the operator's wall of confusion, and Nick had finally reached the banquet manager's line twenty minutes after he'd first called the resort.

Unfortunately, he'd gotten a recorded message: "Hello, this is Karen Esco. You can reach me during business hours Monday through Friday and on Sundays between noon and five P.M. For questions about banquets or conferences currently taking place at the resort, you may phone the concierge's desk. The number is . . . "

Nick had hung up without bothering to note it, deciding he would wait till midday on Sunday and then try Karen Esco again.

After that, he went back to Noble's photo collection, carefully perusing the Dorset cases one at a time—the pictures, the associated documents, everything. They ran the familiar gamut of murders, rapes, robberies, assaults, weapon and/or drug busts, mob racketeering prosecutions, and a smidgen of political corruption and fraud indictments thrown in for good measure. In no instance was there an apparent link to Stacy Ebstein. She wasn't shown in any photos or named in the court papers. And Nick had similarly found nothing that mentioned tattoos or a tattooer.

It was three in the morning when Nick realized he was down to the last nine or ten cases with Dorset's name attached to them. With so few left, his energy waning, and his body slumping in his chair, it seemed the right time to call it quits. The taco stand he'd considered swinging by would be closed at this later-than-late hour, but he knew an open 7-Eleven where he could pick up some cold cuts or canned tuna for sandwich fixings. Either that, or he could stop at a diner for something. Or, talk about downward trends, he could forget about eating for now. Just head home, hit the sack, sleep in, and maybe grab a bite when he woke up—

Nick's thoughts abruptly broke off, and he sat up straight. He'd been idly clicking his mouse, scrolling down the list of photo-archive folders, when one near the bottom caught his eye and he'd half-consciously opened it. The title read, "Child abd./hom. (Dumas)—8th District Court v. Clarkson (Hon. Dorset)—Vegas Globe News—7-14-2000.

The dozen or so photos in the folder captured the same scene from different positions and angles. A man in a T-shirt and blue jeans, on his knees in a large area of blooming sagebrush, cradling a young boy in his arms. Nick didn't need to zoom in on any of the pictures to see that the child was dead. There were distinctive signs of small wildlife predation and bruising on his neck. And his body had the unmistakable stiffness of early rigor.

As in the other folders associated with Dorset, the judge's name appeared not only in the folder's title but also as a highlighted embedded link beneath the images.

Nick told himself that this could wait till tomorrow. It was a child murder, yes, so it naturally jumped out. Child murders always did to him. Bottom line, though, it was still just one of thirty-odd cases. It could wait. He'd be at it the rest of the night unless he closed the folder, turned off the damned computer, and went home. Might as well sign on for pulling his third consecutive extra shift in the last three weeks if he didn't do himself a favor and quit while he was ahead . . .

Sighing, he clicked on Dorset's name, and a short list of document files appeared onscreen. There was the court docket sheet with relevant filings and motions, an official summary of the judge's ruling on dismissal without prejudice, and then what looked like headers from several news-paper articles.

Nick skipped the docket sheet and opened the ruling summary. It began:

"In the case at bar, based on the circumstances sur-rounding Kyle Dumas's death, the court is satisfied that some type of criminal agency caused his de-mise. The testimony also satisfies the court that the defendant, Ronald Clarkson, might have been the last person to see him alive. He might have had a prior allegation of sexual misconduct, but charges were dropped by the complainant, a female adult who could later admit the events were consensual. He might have had a means and opportunity of ab-duction, but there is no physical or circumstantial evidence that he did so. There is no circumstantial

*evidence that he committed violence against Kyle
Dumas, no murder weapon, and, most important,
no direct evidence presented before the court that it
finds to be uncontaminated and admissible, including DNA, fingerprints, and bloodstains . . ."*

His eyes narrowed, Nick read the rest of the
summary and moved on to the newspaper articles
about Kyle Dumas's murder, resigned that Saturday night was lost and Sunday had found him right
where he should have figured it would all along.

Blue-spectrum radiance always suffused the criminalistics bureau at police headquarters, emanat-
ing from the confined spaces where lab rats and
investigators would peer into microscopes, hunch
over dusting stations, and stand at forensic exam
tables in their gloves, goggles, and smocks, studying latents and biologicals under a range of light
sources.

Visitors and new employees commonly insisted
that the blueness darkened from pale aqua to cobalt
as the hour grew late—noticing, too, a sound that
seemed almost imperceptible by day. Throughout the
building, one could discern the subaudible pulse of
compressors, water chillers, laser-deposition chambers, gas chromatographs, fume-exhaust systems,
recirculated-air pumps, and all manner of other specialized electrical apparatus.

Catherine Willows no longer consciously registered any of this as she walked the halls. For her, the deep blue glow was as ordinary as the film noir posters lining her daughter's bedroom walls, the throb of equipment as normal as the music from Lindsey's mp3 docking station. She had been with the unit a very long time, and it was in these surroundings that she was Catherine raised to her highest power—confident, efficient, in control

Now she strode from her office into the outer corridor, passing lab cubicle after glass-walled lab cubicle as her graveyard shift went about its quiet, systematic work. It was almost five o'clock in the gray hours bridging Saturday midnight and Sunday morning, and she was past due for a caffeine recharge to boost her tso the far side.

Catherine figured she'd drop in on Nick once she slugged back her coffee. Although she'd penciled him in to take half the weekend off starting Saturday night, he hadn't swung by her door to offer his customary wave before departing, and she had a suspicion she might find him reviewing the items he obtained from the shutterbug sex-toy hawker who'd been Tattoo Man's earliest number.

She turned a corner toward the break room, and lo and behold, Hodges was meandering toward her in his white smock, his face saturnine even by his glum standard.

"Catherine," he said, moving up the hall. "I was just on my way to see you."

"Oh?"

He nodded. "I've decided things need changing around here," he said.

"What things?"

A deep breath. "Things," he said, "that lead to distractions for me."

She wondered if he was referring to Wendy Simms, the DNA tech. Everybody at headquarters and their long-lost fourth cousins in outer Belgrade knew he was infatuated with her.

"What sort of distractions?" she said.

"The sort that negatively impact my job performance," he said, "and divert my concentration from where it should be."

Catherine looked at him. She was convinced that had been an oblique reference to Wendy. "Oh," she said. "I see."

Hodges straightened, inhaled again, and tipped his chin up toward the ceiling as he visibly inflated his confidence. "It can't go on. We need to make some changes."

Yes, Catherine thought, *here it comes*. And LVPD regulations would, of course, require one or the other to change shifts if they got openly involved. In *that* respect, the techs becoming an item would be worse than having them live with their unrequited affections, since Catherine was not eager to lose either to days. Nor, as supervisor, could she explicitly encourage a don't ask, don't tell policy. Suggesting that they keep their amorous intentions to themselves would be a breach of her professional obligations. At the same time, however, it would place her in a bind if Hodges actually came out with his dilemma, since that would mean she'd have to enforce the regs, remind him that workplace hanky-panky was forbidden, and discourage it between him and his lovely Wendy. Either that, or put one of them down for a mandatory transfer.

Catherine frowned. It was enough for her to get involved with her daughter's romantic problems. Two intelligent and supposedly mature adults ought to be able to figure out the dating game for themselves. "Hodges, you might want to think about this before we talk," she said.

"I've thought enough about it, Catherine," he said. "It's big and hard. But it belongs firmly in your hands."

She bit her tongue. "Look, I was just about to get some coffee. If this can wait awhile—"

"It can't," Hodges said. "You need to set our evidence clerk straight about staying on post."

Catherine looked at him. "The evidence clerk."

"He's constantly derelict."

"Oh."

"Absent without leave."

"Uh-huh."

"Nowhere to be found," Hodges said. "Leaving me to pick up his slack because my lab is down the hall from the evidence room."

She tucked a loose wisp of hair behind her ear. "I'll straighten the situation out with him," she said.

"Remedy it, I hope."

"I think that's what I said."

"I just want to be sure I'm understood," Hodges said. "This has been an ongoing problem, Catherine. And thanks to his latest unannounced departure, I've been logging in items all night."

Catherine was thinking she desperately needed to chug down some coffee. "What items?"

"Nick's computer discs," he said. "And Sara's epithelials. Which I not only checked in but delivered to the appropriate lab for analysis."

"If I'm not mistaken, wouldn't that be *your* lab?"

"That's beside the point," Hodges said. "Or on second thought, perhaps it is the point. I should have gotten started on those skin samples by now. But the discs had to be tagged and coded, and Nick didn't know the correct procedure. So naturally, the task fell to me."

"Nick's still here?"

"Yes," he said. "While some might stray from their posts, other soldiers of the night boldly hold the line."

Catherine gave a vague nod. She'd blearily set aside her thoughts on whatever he'd been complaining about, remembering that she'd meant to drop in on Nick, not yet having gotten a chance to find out exactly what he meant to do with the boxload of CDs he had brought back from the sex shop. "Later, Hodges," she said, abruptly brushing past him.

Catherine ducked into the break room a moment later, figuring she'd pick up an extra cup of java and carry it over to Nick's office so they could drink while they powwowed.

She was hardly stunned to find Langston hovering over the machine. When she filled out her monthly supply forms, coffee ranked a consistent third behind only dusting powder and petri dishes.

"Hey there, soldier," she said.

He looked up at her. "Catherine," he said, sounding a bit out of sorts. "Sorry, what was it you said?"

"Nothing." She shook her head. "Anything left in the pot?"

"I'm about finished brewing up a fresh one," he said. "Excuse my vacant stare . . . I didn't hear you come in."

Catherine, wearing a trim sharkskin pantsuit, glanced down at the high-heeled boots under her slacks. "Are these things really that quiet?"

"The truth is, I'm really that preoccupied," Langston said. He reached for the coffeepot, poured two cups, handed one to Catherine. They stood silently and drank, Catherine recalling a brief account he and Greg had given her of what they'd picked up at the tattoo parlors back when Saturday was still young.

"Making progress?" she asked.

"I think so," Langston said. "I've been at my computer most of the night. But I placed several calls to the Toronto police earlier."

Catherine nodded. "Toronto's where that *Flash Ink* tattoo competition was taped last season."

"Before the show came to Vegas, yes," he said. "I wanted to find out if there were any homicides in Canada with characteristics at all similar to the Laurel Whitsen killing. Or the Tattoo Man crimes."

"You think Ecklie might be right lumping them together?"

"It seemed logical to cover all bases," Langston said with a small shrug. "But I agree with you that there's no real evidence pointing to it."

Catherine looked at him over her steaming cup. "Any luck with our colleagues up north?"

"After a bit of doing, yes," Langston said. "The Toronto Police Service is divided into two divisional commands. One covers the downtown part of the city, the other the outlying areas. Theoretically, central field and area field—that's what they're called—operate in tight sync."

"Which means that, in fact, they're all fouled up."

"It could have been worse. The people I reached at first were cagey—I think they would have rather spoken to a fellow officer. But I was finally able to reach a deputy chief, Davis Reynolds, who directs operations between the commands. He was fairly accommodating . . . and informative."

She waited out a brief silence, her cup steaming in her hand.

"There were three murders in Canada between

nine and twelve months ago that draw strong comparisons to Laurel Whitsen's," Langston said. "Two fell within jurisdiction of the TPS. The third was up in Alberta and went to the Mounties."

"By comparisons, you mean . . ."

"The victims were partially skinned," Langston said. "The Toronto cops guessed that tattoos had been removed from their bodies and theorized the motive was to delay their identification, hide street-gang affiliations, or both."

"I can see why they'd consider it," Catherine said. "There's enough precedent in criminal-case files."

Langston was nodding. "Toronto has two major street gangs in addition to their offshoots and smaller posse-style crews. And the triads have been embedded in its Chinatown area for decades—the Big Circle Boys and the Ghost Shadows are the most notorious. Since one of the DBs was an Asian male, it raised some antennas."

"But we've got a very different situation here," Catherine said.

"Yes. Laurel Whitsen was killed where she worked and had her personal belongings with her. Nobody cared about hiding who she was."

"And I doubt many gangbangers study the Dewey decimal system," Catherine said with a grim smile. She drank some coffee, pulled a face. "Do you *like* how this tastes?"

"I suppose it turned out a little weak."

"Maybe just a little, Ray." She paused. "I take it the Canadians didn't associate the killings with the TV contest?"

"Not that they told me," Langston said. "My sense, though, was that the DC wasn't aware of the show or the Internet magazine."

A grim smile. "Where's Dudley Do-Right when you need him?"

Langston smiled back at her and sipped quietly from his cup.

"Did you get the vics' IDs?" Catherine asked.

"Yes, Reynolds was especially cooperative in that respect," Langston said. "He e-mailed names and photos to me as we spoke."

"And were you able to find out if the Canadian vics were contestants?"

Langston nodded. "I established an account with the e-zine that gave me access to its social-networking features. There are archived galleries for every season's episodes, and I found photos of all three."

"So we've established that someone's picking his targets from the board."

"For a fact."

"Notice any common threads besides?"

"Not yet," Langston said. "The body art they display is exceptional, but that's a basic prerequisite for getting past the cattle-call auditions. The themes, motifs, and styles are all very different."

"And as far as which level of the contest they reached . . . ?"

"Two were semifinalists, the other an early-round elimination."

"Could they have been clients of the same tattooer? Maybe even friends?" Catherine asked. "What I'm wondering is if they had any kind of ties, before, during, or after the contest."

"The same questions occurred to me," Langston said. "Well, aside from the first."

Catherine gave him an interested look.

"Tattoo artists and recipients win or lose as teams, and the rule is that each artist pair up with a single client," he said. "Remember, the contest is only *Flash Ink*'s season finale—its last episode or two. The rest is like any reality show. It follows the tattoo process from conception onward, follows the recipient at home with the family, captures the artist-client bond. It would be impractical to film that if a particular artist had several clients. And I'd imagine their one-on-one rapport generates viewer involvement with the characters."

"They win or lose together, and we root for them," Catherine said. "Modern drama."

"Or sport." Langston nodded again. "About their possible relationships, I won't have an idea until I've thoroughly explored the networking area. And even then, there's no assurance I'll find conclusive answers. It's reasonable to surmise they connected on the site if they mixed outside it—but by no means definite."

Catherine produced a sigh. "We'll have to wait

and see," she said. "Keep me posted if anything turns up."

"Will do," Langston said. "I've also left cell-phone messages for Cody Vaega, the expert on ink formulations."

"He's off somewhere or other giving a lecture, right?"

"Holding a class on tribal body art," Langston said.

"Got it," Catherine said. She took a halfhearted sip of the watery coffee. Better than a cupful of nothing, she figured. "Okay, I'm gonna drop by Nick's office—"

"Knock, knock."

Catherine and Langston both turned toward the sound of the voice and saw Sara Sidle leaning into the room from the corridor.

"Sorry to interrupt," she said. "I was trying to find Hodges—either of you see him?"

"Yeah," Catherine said. "Around ten minutes ago."

"In his lab?"

"Down the hall toward my office," Catherine said. "I thought he might've been on his way back to the lab."

"I just came from there," Sara said. "He wasn't around."

"Did you check the evidence room?"

"No," Sara said. "Should I?"

Catherine nodded. "He's been busy logging stuff."

"Log—" Sara cut herself off and frowned. "What about my epithelials?"

"I don't think he's gotten around to them."

Sara looked surprised. "He told me he'd rush the analysis."

"The evidence clerk's nowhere to be found." Catherine shrugged. "Hodges bitched about having to do his job tagging and coding Nick's photo discs." She paused a beat. "Has he told you what he's hoping will turn up on them, by the way?"

"Photos that might link Noble to Judge Dorset," Sara said. "I'm not sure if there's more to it . . . you know how he is sometimes."

Catherine thought the word was *quiet*—for the most part when he was chasing a hunch. And generally, the quieter he got, the stronger the hunch.

She drank as much of what was left in her coffee cup as she could bear and tossed the rest. "I'm heading over to see Nick. If I bump into Hodges again, I'll tell him—"

The cell phone rang in Catherine's waist pouch, her eyes automatically flicking to the wall clock as she reached for it. Five A.M. on Sunday, still well before daybreak—nothing good ever came of the phone ringing at this hour. She thought of Lindsey at home alone—God, she *hoped* Lindsey was home; the kid had gotten into trouble more than once being someplace besides where she was supposed to be—but then she saw Brass's name flashing on the caller display.

"Jim," she said, "what's up?" And was silent as he told her and signed off.

Catherine lowered the phone from her ear. Nothing good, no. But her heartbeat had slowed in her chest. The bad news wasn't about Lindsey. In this world, where lightning struck with such random mercilessness, there was no guilt in feeling relieved that you'd dodged a bolt.

"It's a double homicide at Floyd Lamb Park," she told Langston. He was now her only audience, Sara having already ducked back into the hall. "We'd better hurry."

"There's more," he said, reading her face.

Catherine nodded. "Let's go," she said. "I'll give it to you on the way."

Heading out the door to the car lot, Catherine realized she had never gotten around to dropping in on Nick. Not that she wouldn't have her chance. For a CSI, all things usually lead back to the lab— and when it came to urgent interruptions from Jim Brass, you could pretty well count on it.

7

As Catherine would have discovered had she not gotten repeatedly and variously sidetracked, Nick wasn't in his office but had left it to bring one of Noble's photo discs over to Archie Johnson in the audiovisual tech's minuscule lab cubicle, which happened to be three or four steps down the hall from where she was standing when her cell phone rang.

The two men turned to look out its glass partition into the corridor, watching as she and Langston swept past them.

"Somebody's in a big hurry to get somewhere," Archie said.

"Always, around here," Nick said with a yawn, looking tired and distracted.

Archie shrugged and brought his attention back to the disc in Nick's hand. "Now, what was it you were asking me again?"

"About a map," Nick said. "Whether you can put one together. I'd want a three-dimensional, panoramic, street-level view."

Archie thought a second. "Of . . . "

"That's the thing," Nick said. "Could be Fremont. Or the Strip. Probably both. And maybe some other areas. I'm not sure. But I should know soon."

Archie regarded Nick with open puzzlement. "Great that you're being unequivocal," he said under his breath.

"Huh?"

"Forget it," Archie said. "If you don't mind, I have a question of my own."

Nick nodded, stifling another yawn.

"What's wrong with the navigable street maps you can find on the Internet? The kind that use pictures taken by guys riding vans and tricycles with funny-looking cameras on top?"

"They wouldn't do any good," Nick said. "Way too current."

"So you want an *outdated* street-level view?"

"You got it," Nick said. "Well, not to split hairs, a view of a particular date and time that happens to go back a ways."

Archie frowned. "Exactly how far back are we talking?"

"Ten years." Nick wobbled the disc between them. "Think you can put one together for me?"

Archie mulled that over. "Are the photo captures I'd need on your disc?"

"Some."

"Meaning . . . ?"

"A dozen, maybe two."

Archie looked at him. "Do you know how many images are compiled and integrated for mapping a single street? I think the ratio's something like one for every three feet."

"Right," Nick said. "That's why I told you I've only got *some* of 'em on disc."

Archie took a deep breath. For him, a major distinction between criminalists and humble techs like himself was that the former's thought processes lacked specificity. Were all over the map, pun intended. Of course, one could make allowances because the nature of their work required taking a broad perspective, whereas he was all about bringing things into full focus. Which in this case was literally the problem.

"Just so I'm not in a complete state of confusion," he said after a moment, "where would we get the several thousand odd images that *aren't* coming off the disc?"

"I was figuring security cameras. They've got installations over the entrances to every hotel and casino in town."

"Nick, that's all very well in theory. But you're talking Y2K. That's a long time ago."

"And . . . ?"

"And you have to think about how much CCTV systems have changed since then," Archie said. "I'd guess most places still had videotape surveillance. Digital recording was an option, but system upgrades are expensive, and it takes a while for users to catch up with the available technology. Even assuming a given casino or resort was ahead of the curve and had switched from an analog to a digital network, the images probably would have been kept on disc. I doubt any of them were stored in the virtual archives everyone uses nowadays. High-capacity databases weren't common—"

"Archie, now I'm the one who's missing something," Nick interrupted. "What's wrong with us using old videotapes and discs?"

"Nothing. Again, theoretically. The issue is what we can get our hands on. We're talking about three conversions in *less than* a decade. Analog to digital media to mass virtual storage. Do you have any idea how many places transferred their recordings from one to the other or how far back they would have gone with it chronologically?"

Nick shook his head.

"Me, neither," Archie said. "But when you consider the cost, it's a safe assumption not all of the recordings were saved."

Nick gave him a wearily impatient look. "Listen, man, I always say you don't have to know every star in a constellation to draw in the lines."

"And I wouldn't argue it," Archie said. "My point, though, is you usually need to see more than a couple of dozen."

Nick started to reply, hesitated, rubbed the back of his neck. "This could be important, Arch."

Archie was thinking he hadn't needed to be

reminded. Everything was important when you dealt with crimes like murder. He didn't take the remark personally—the dark circles under Nick's eyes were pretty good indicators that he'd been doing a double shift. But the lab was understaffed and overtaxed, and that went for the techs as well as the criminalists. When one of them walked out after making a request, you could start ticking off the minutes until another walked in.

Archie produced a long sigh. "I'll have a better sense of what we can do once I know the area that has to be mapped out. Then we can start checking in to who saved what and going back to when."

Nick looked at him. "Meaning you're down with me on this."

"Yeah." Archie nodded slowly. "I'm down."

Nick grunted and slapped his shoulder. "You're my man," he said, and rotated toward the entrance.

Archie watched him step out into the hall, then sat at his computer screen and got to work, the lab rat's familiar countdown starting in the back of his mind, hoping to make some progress on the job he was doing before the next one came blowing through his door.

Catherine and Langston arrived at the park to find Brass grunting orders at the uniforms busily securing the crime scene. They ducked under the yellow tape and went straight over to him for the lowdown.

The detective gave it in a hurry, starting with what he knew about the man who'd called the police. "His name's Linus Tyrone. Comes here to do bird watching, brings his dog sometimes," he said. "He was out for a stroll with the dog when it found the DBs."

Catherine glanced in Tyrone's direction. Wearing jeans, a heavy knit sweater, and running shoes, with a binocular camera hanging from his neck, he stood within earshot behind the line of tape, where a uni had moved him and the dog. A black Labrador retriever, it was heeled obediently at his side, its leash wrapped around his hand.

"He's on his way to the pond over on the north side of the park when Edgar—his dog—takes off in that direction," Brass said, nodding toward a thick growth of cottonwoods and shrubs over to his right. "It isn't on a leash, obviously, so he chases after it and then sees what got its attention."

"I wish I'd walked him in my yard and brought him back upstairs," Tyrone said, overhearing him. "Especially this morning."

Catherine turned to him. "Why?" she asked, thinking he was probably referring to its having led him to the bodies.

"What do you mean?"

"You said you *especially* wished you'd come without your dog," Catherine said.

"Yes."

"And I was wondering why that would be. As opposed to other days."

"Oh, I see," Tyrone said, looking flustered. "It's

because of the rusty blackbird. They're quite rare in Nevada. Excuse me for being scatterbrained."

"Is the blackbird what you meant to photograph over by the pond?"

"Actually, no," Tyrone said, shaking his head. "I was heading there for the waterfowl. We have a great many species in the winter. But then I heard a red-breasted nuthatch in the trees . . . they're native songbirds with a very distinctive warble. Common but a pretty sight when they're all fluffed out. So I thought I would take a picture."

Catherine looked at him, bunching the collar of her jacket against the morning chill. She wasn't eager to waste another minute here. Not with Langston already having gone over to snap pictures of the dead man and woman on the ground several yards away. But she realized she had to go easier on Tyrone. Besides being scatterbrained, he was clearly shaken up.

"Mr. Tyrone, can you describe exactly how your dog found the bodies? If you can recall. And try keeping it brief, please."

He nodded. "I spotted the rusty while scanning for the nuthatch through my binoculars. It was a thrill—my club only has three verified sightings this year. But before I could snap a picture, Edgar launched at the trees and startled it away. I hope you won't summons me for taking off the leash, by the way. He's normally very obedient and stays right at my side."

"I'm not an animal control officer, Mr. Tyrone."

"I just want to avoid problems, being that I'm trying to cooperate," he said. "Anyway, it was really unusual."

"What was?"

"Edgar getting so excited. He was whimpering, running in circles . . . I've never seen him so agitated. And no wonder, given the condition of those two people." Tyrone paused, fanned his face with his hand. "I'm sweating, can you believe it? In this cold weather. It must be my nerves. My God, that poor man and woman. I feel flushed—"

Brass cleared his throat. "Mr. Tyrone went chasing after Edgar and then saw the ladder and the bodies," he broke in. "Retrievers are sight hounds. I figure it must've scoped the vics on the ground and gotten curious."

Catherine was looking at Tyrone. "You didn't notice them at all before that? Or see anyone else in the park? A person loitering around, a conspicuous vehicle?"

Tyrone shook his head. "Eyes up," he said.

She gave him a questioning look.

"That's our club's motto. Mine were on the tree-tops."

"Lucky for us Edgar's weren't," Catherine said with a sideways glance at Brass. Then she hurried to join Langston, who was taking pictures of the victims under the bare, sprawling limbs of a nearby cottonwood.

"Anything interesting out of him?" He nodded

back at Tyrone without lowering the camera lens from his eye.

"Not much besides what we already know." Catherine stood over the bodies, getting her first good look at them, bunching the collar of her jacket in her fist as a gust of wind rattled the branches above. She had seen Laurel Whitsen's remains in the library less than twenty-four hours ago. And while making hasty assumptions was a cardinal sin for forensic examiners, this morning's double homicide undeniably resembled the work of her killer. "I'm getting a bad sense of déjà vu, Ray."

Langston nodded again and snapped more photos. The dead man was a black-haired, dark-complected Asian of about thirty-five. He lay with one cheek to the ground, his head turned sideways. A fair-skinned blonde, the woman, also in her mid-thirties, was facedown beside him in the dewy winter grass. Both of them had been shot in the head and then clearly moved to where they were now under the cottonwood, shoulder to shoulder, their arms at their sides. Both were nude from the waist up—there were no jackets, no shirt or blouse, no bra on the woman. They had on jeans, shoes, and nothing else, although the male vic still wore a pair of work gloves.

Finally, both of them had the skin peeled away from their bare backs and shoulders to expose the layers of muscle, adipose tissue, and white bone underneath.

Catherine noticed an electric pole saw on the ground beside the three-legged stepladder, then another smaller curved blade in a strap harness around the man's calf. She got onto her haunches to examine the second tool.

"A pruning saw," she said, slipping the latex over her fingers.

"They say late winter's a good time for it," Langston said.

She looked at him, her eyes distant with concentration.

"Cutting back the branches," he said.

"Oh, right." Catherine returned her gaze to the bodies. "We have IDs on these two?"

"A name, address, and DOB for the male," Brass said. He'd come up behind her. "You're looking at Diachi Sato, thirty-one. Or what's left of him. He parked his vehicle in a little turnaround back of these trees . . . a Volvo wagon."

She looked around at him. He held a wallet in his own white-gloved hand.

"I took it from his pocket," he explained, nodding down at the body. "It's got a driver's license, credit cards, employment identification. Sato was an arborist with the Nevada Division of State Parks."

"Explains the ladder and the cutting tools," she said. "Nothing for his lady friend?"

"Not yet."

Catherine nodded. She saw that the leg of the

woman's jeans was hitched up above her right ankle and carefully raised it a little more, baring the flesh above her athletic sock. Her calf was discolored—the purplish stain of developing livor mortis as blood settled to the lower limbs.

She applied gentle pressure to the area with her thumb, and the bruisiness dissipated, the skin turning milky white. The pale splotch remained there after she'd removed her finger.

"Her blood isn't fixed," she said. "This woman's been dead a couple of hours, max."

Brass seemed about to comment when his cell phone jingled in his sport jacket. He answered it and drifted away from the CSIs, the phone to his ear.

Crouched over Sato, meanwhile, Langston was manipulating his jaw and eyelids. "I would guess his TOD is the same as the woman's—his body is still prerigor," he told Catherine. Then he got out his voice recorder and opened a file for his verbal observations. "Decedent shows slight lividity consistent with prone position. Musculature appears relaxed." Raising the dead man's head slightly off the ground, he examined the gunshot's entry wound and then looked over his face, inserting his pointer and index fingers into the mouth. Loose, broken teeth slipped around their knuckles and tips. "There's no external scorching, no visible grease or metallic residue. The victim appears to have been shot from a distance of a yard or beyond. It appears the bullet penetrated his right temporal bone, leaving extensive collateral damage to the upper jaw . . ."

A few feet away, Catherine had carefully plucked the matted, bloody hair away from the woman's gunshot wound. Her eyes narrowed. "Ray?"

He touched the pause button, looked at her.

"There's a distinct contusion ring on the back of her head," she said. "And I see burnt skin around the wound cavity."

"She was killed at close range."

"Maybe even point-blank." *Like Laurel Whitsen,* Catherine thought but did not bother adding aloud. Langston would grasp the implication.

He rose and went over to the ladder under the cottonwood. Cut twigs and branches littered the ground around it. He brought up his gaze and saw where the tree's crown had been trimmed. Then he dropped his eyes to the trunk.

"We know Sato came here to do some work," he said. "I think we also can be fairly sure of something else. But give me a moment with this evidence."

Catherine nodded. She watched him drop some markers around the pole saw, photograph it from several angles to document its position on their arrival at the crime scene, then get his fingerprint kit out of his carrying case and dust the handle for latents. A few partial fingerprints came up, probably Sato's, deposited before he'd put on the work gloves. There wasn't much chance they would be useful. Again, though, you assumed at risk of inviting someone with horns and a pitchfork to the dance.

Langston lifted the prints with tape, transferred them to a backing card, and carefully put the card into an evidence envelope. When he had sealed and put it away, he recovered the saw from the grass and climbed several rungs up the ladder.

Catherine noted that he'd processed the scene in less than five minutes. It wasn't too long ago when he would have needed twenty to get through the whole thing. Clumsily.

"Okay . . . Sato's my approximate height," he said, gripping the handle and extending it over his head so its blade reached the pruned section of the cottonwood. The bark at eye level was spattered with a tarry amalgam of blood and tissue. "He would have been standing on this rung or the next highest when he was shot."

Catherine strode over to the ladder. She looked down at where the pole saw had lain relative to it and raised her eyes to the bloodied tree trunk. *Sato's going up to trim the branches and asks his friend to be his spotter. She waits here, right here, holds the ladder for him in case it gets a little shaky or he loses his balance. And then . . .*

She peered over her shoulder at a dense tangle of trees and coyote brush about five yards from where she stood. "The shooter could've been hiding over there," she said, gesturing at the thicket. "The electric saw's buzzing away, and neither of them hears him coming close over the racket. Sato doesn't see him because he has to pay attention to what he's doing. And the woman doesn't see him because *she's* paying attention to Sato."

"So he slips up behind her and fires a shot into her head," Langston said. "Before Sato can react or possibly even realizes what's happening . . . "

Catherine formed a gun with her thumb and forefinger and aimed it at him. "Bang. The killer does him, too," she said. "That saw has a safety switch, right?"

Langston squeezed the bar on its handle. It throbbed noisily to life, its blade vibrating in his hand. After a moment, he released the bar, and it went silent.

"Sato gets shot, lets go of the saw, and it drops right where we found it," Catherine said. "He lands in almost the same place, but the killer drags him and his lady friend a few feet away and lays them out alongside each other."

"And then he partially skins them," Langston said, climbing down from the ladder.

He lowered his eyes to the woman. "It would help to know who she was. Odd she didn't leave a purse in the car."

"You need to get out more often." Catherine's lips hinted at a smile. "Women take their purses everywhere. They carry around too many personal items to leave them behind. She would have brought it with her."

"Even out here trimming trees?"

"Everywhere."

"Which would mean the shooter either took it with him or disposed of it," Langston said. "But why didn't he bother with Sato's wallet?"

Catherine shrugged. "He'd have had to fish it out of his pocket. If she had a bag, it would have been easier pickings. He might've even heard the dog coming and rushed off before he finished." A second shrug. "I don't think he was too worried about their being identified. He'd have known they had to bring their pruning equipment in some sort of vehicle. And that once we found it, we'd trace the owner from the plates and go from there. Snatching their personal ID wouldn't stall things long."

Langston stood there looking thoughtful.

"What do you bet they had tattoos on their backs?" Catherine said, then saw that he'd reached into his jacket for his palmtop. She watched him rapidly thumb-type something on its touchpad. "You bringing up that e-zine? What was it called?"

"*Flash Ink*. I opened a user account last night," Langston said with an affirmative nod. "I'm browsing the photo gallery of participants in the latest television competition."

"The same one Laurel Whitsen was in."

"Yes, right." Langston scrolled and clicked for

a while. Then he glanced up at her over his spectacles. "Catherine, come take a look."

She walked over and found herself examining a screen image of the victims. Labeled "Daichi and Lynda," it had been taken from behind and showed them nude from their waists up, turned away from the camera to display the tattoos that had covered their bare backs. They stood side-by-side, holding hands, their hips touching.

Catherine suddenly felt tired. *In life as in death—almost.* The object of theft here had not been a purse.

"The art looks Japanese," she said, raising an eyebrow as she studied the fine lines and subtle color gradations. "Like ancient woodcuts."

"Or panel art." Langston framed the woman, zoomed in. "The figure on her back is Benzaiten, the folk goddess of love and music. She's usually depicted as she is here. Near a river playing a *biwa* . . . that's the four-stringed instrument in her arms."

Catherine watched as he zoomed in on Sato's back piece.

"This is Bishamon, one of the protector gods," he said. "A bringer of good fortune and guardian against evil."

She motioned at the bodies on the ground. "Somebody must've caught him napping on the job."

Langston took a breath and slowly let the air out. "*Flash Ink* is owned by a limited-liability corporation in San Diego," he said. "The contact pages list several e-mail addresses, and I wrote to inform them we have to talk. I also obtained a phone number and left a voice message. But it's the weekend, and I did all that after midnight."

Catherine was nodding her commiseration. At the LVPD forensics lab, where everyone from investigators to techs put in endless hours of unpaid overtime probing, dissecting, and analyzing evidence gathered from crime scenes and corpses, the night shift was a term of convenience, a theoretical construct, a general if highly malleable guideline you followed so you knew if your kids were supposed to be home or at school, or eating breakfast or dinner, or if your husband or wife had gone into absentia due to spousal neglect. It maybe even gave you some vague sense of when to let the cat in—or, more likely, ask a friend to do it. But insofar as the work itself was concerned, the practical drawback of being on a reverse clock from the rest of the world was that you were always ready to make calls when nobody was there to answer and go knocking on doors when the lights were out in the offices behind them.

Almost a full minute passed as Catherine assembled her thoughts. "That tattoo artist you and Greg went to see, didn't she say a log-on's needed to access the magazine's content?" she said at last.

Langston nodded. "It has some free public areas, the contestant gallery among them," he said. "But the short answer is yes. The chat rooms, community boards, and other areas are reserved for paid password accounts. And there are different membership tiers."

"Based on?"

"Subscription length, special interests, whether someone wants to view or download videos, essentially what you might expect."

She looked at him. "Ray, you know where I'm heading. The magazine would have a user database. With e-mail addresses and credit-card information."

"Only to an extent. I opened an account last night using my credit card. Unfortunately, *Flash Ink* also accepts money orders as a payment option."

"That's unusual for an online service, isn't it?"

"Somewhat. But I've come to see why individuals at the extremes of body-modification culture might want their information private for personal and legal reasons."

Catherine was curious. "Come to see *how*?"

"Through a source," he said vaguely, seeming a bit uncomfortable with the question. "The law's spotty for body-modification salons and their customers. People who object to the lifestyle can pressure local governments to hit them with health-code violations I'd consider very much up for interpretation. What's pertinent is that anyone can buy and send a money order without giving a name or a valid return address."

Catherine frowned. His caginess did not exactly delight her, but that issue was for another time and place. "Okay. Let's see if Archie can come up with any ideas."

Langston nodded his agreement. Archie Johnson being their unit's resident technophile, the CSIs were used to leaning on his computer savvy.

The wind intensified now, bending and swaying the long, interwoven shadows of the cottonwood's leafless branches. Catherine saw it rustle Lynda's hair where it wasn't glued down with drying blood, shivered, and turned to gaze past the knot of officers around the crime scene. The evidence-collection van and the coroner's wagon were arriving on an access road. When Dave Phillips was on shift, he would usually beat the CSIs to the scene—though he'd never admit it, it was as if he was in some kind of race with them. Could be he thought his promotion to assistant ME a couple of years back was a prize for it. Who knew?

But Super Dave was off this morning. And once she gave the techs her instructions, Catherine would be, too, spending what was left of the weekend at home with her daughter. Lindsey had probably grown a couple of inches since they'd last spent a quiet Sunday together. She would also probably want to spend this one with friends rather than an exhausted mom carrying around the image of two dead lovers who had taken gunshot wounds to their heads and had matching tattoos stripped from their backs along with every ounce of meat.

She huddled into her collar and was still watching the two vehicles wind closer when Brass returned from wherever he'd gone to talk on his cell phone.

"How's it going?" he said, putting away the phone.

Catherine shrugged. "Somebody makes a mess, we sift through it," she said.

He studied her wearily. "That was Ecklie who called."

"Uh-oh."

"He asked what we found here."

"And when you told him?"

"He said the mayor and the sheriff's office will be holding a joint press conference about the Tattoo Man crimes this afternoon."

"On a Sunday? Doesn't he know the media hates paying camera crews double time?"

"They're trying to get a jump on the Monday morning news cycle," Brass said. "And want to send out a message that they're on the ball twenty-four-seven."

"All it does for me is signal panic."

"Characterize it however you want," Brass said. "Ecklie plans to reassure people that the city of Las Vegas is committed to restoring their safety. That residents and tourists should know there'll be additional manpower watching out for them. And that efforts to apprehend the culprit will be escalated."

"*Culprit.* Singular."

"That's what he said."

"And what do you say?"

"Doesn't make a difference right now. And it'll make less after tomorrow."

Catherine frowned. "These crimes shouldn't be bundled together, Jim. You know it. I know it. And my gut feeling's that Ecklie knows it, too."

"I notice you didn't mention the mayor."

"Because the pressure has to be coming from the top. Ecklie's too smart for this dog and pony show on his own. It can only confuse things."

Brass looked at her and rubbed his hands together. "Cold outside," he said. "Feels like Ash Wednesday was ages ago. Where the hell's the Easter Bunny hiding his ass?"

"Does that mean you intend to ignore me?"

"Not possible," he said.

"Then tell me what we're supposed to do, Jim."

Brass gave her a blunt look, shoving his hands into his pockets. "Unconfuse things fast," he said.

As he pulled to a halt at his lodge, Bockem noticed the coyote waiting nearby out of the bushes. Squatted on its rear haunches, it had not been at all alarmed by the sound of his approaching station wagon, making no attempt to retreat.

He stared at the creature through his windshield and reflected in silence, a slight metallic taste rising into his mouth. When he was still very young, four or five at most, his father had begun to school him in life's hard realities. He recalled the first of his frequent lessons quite clearly. It had been at their

Manhattan brownstone when his uncle Gunter came to visit from Europe.

All fair-haired innocence, Bockem was a contented, sociable child. His mother had lavished him with attention, and her friends, charmed by his outgoing nature, had often traded small gifts and candies for hugs, holding him to their warm bosoms.

One night before dinner, Bockem had offered to show Uncle Gunter how well he could run across the parlor. That was after Gunter had playfully surprised him after bouncing him in his lap to a children's rhyme.

In his mind's eye, Bockem could picture his uncle as a hefty, smiling man with wisps of thin white hair combed sideways over his mostly bald head. The skin at its crown was pink with spots of brown, and without even knowing he was born eight years before his father, Bockem had somehow recognized those blotches as signs of greater age. Uncle Gunter had spoken in a thickly accented English that the boy found difficult to understand, the half-smoked cigar that was constantly between his lips making it an even greater task. In fact, Bockem had found it easier to decipher his German, since his parents sometimes spoke it when they were alone at home. And an agreeable warmth had come through despite the language barrier.

He remembered giggling wildly when Uncle

Gunter bumped him up and down on his knee while reciting the German rhyme:

> *Hoppe hoppe Reiter,*
> *Wenn er fällt, dann schreit er,*
> *Fällt er in de Hecken,*
> *Tut er sich erschrecken.*

> *Hoppe hoppe Reiter,*
> *Wenn er fällt, dann schreit er,*
> *Fällt er auf die Steine,*
> *Tun ihm weh die Beine.*

> *Hoppe hoppe Reiter,*
> *Wenn er fällt, dann schreit er,*
> *Fällt er in den Graben,*
> *Fressen ihn die Raben.*

> *Hoppe hoppe Reiter,*
> *Wenn er fällt, dann schreit er,*
> *Fällt er in den Sumpf,*
> *Dann macht der Reiter . . . plumps!*

At the rhyme's conclusion—*plumps!*—Gunter had abruptly swung Bockem off his lap and across his body with both of his wide, strong hands, the boy's legs flying horizontally through the air before he was set down standing on the carpet.

Bockem had let out high squeals of laughter when his uncle tricked him like that. He recalled

hearing his mother laughing as well from the hallway, where she'd stood watching. Father, though,
had looked just faintly amused, if even that, smiling quietly from his favorite chair against the wall
opposite the sofa. He had never been demonstra-
tive with his affection.

It was after the nursery rhyme ended that
Bockem had wanted to show off his running ability.
Gunter had asked his father if it would be all right in
English, then repeated the question in German as if
to make sure it would not be misinterpreted—"*Wäre
ei in Ordnung?*"

Father had looked steadily at the boy as he gave
his conditional approval, saying he could run back
and forth between his armchair and the sofa only
once—and reminding him to be careful.

His hands out behind him, Bockem had pushed
off from the sofa beside his uncle and darted over
to his father, tagging up with his knees, then turning to sprint back across the room.

He did not immediately realize what had happened when he fell. He only knew that one moment he was running toward his uncle, and the
next his feet had flipped up underneath him, and
he'd felt a hard shove between his shoulder blades.
Then he was sprawled on the parlor floor, his nose
and mouth mashed into the carpet.

Red-faced with embarrassment, Bockem had
stood up, gathered himself, then registered his
uncle's dismayed expression and turned to see
what he'd stumbled over.

Still watching Bockem with dispassionate eyes, Father had sat there with his leg stuck straight out, patting it above the ankle to show where he'd tripped him.

"You should trust no one, *Junge*," he said. "And beware of life's random cruelties."

Bockem had not forgotten that lesson. And if ever he'd done so, Father's many subsequent reminders would have drilled it into him.

Now he pulled his eyes from the coyote, got out of his vehicle, went around back to open the hatch, and folded back the blanket he'd thrown over the large plastic storage bin in which he'd transported his raw skins from the park. He had laid them out flat in the opaque blue bin, separating them with multiple sheets of waxed paper, then carefully placing another layer of waxed paper on the top skin before the cooling packs went in. Colder than ice, the packs could burn a skin if pressed directly against it, marring its artwork.

Bockem felt the skins slide a little inside their container as he pulled it from the rear compartment—their juices would have been seeping to the bottom. Momentarily setting it down on the ground, he slammed the hatch shut and locked the car with his keychain remote. Then he bent to lift the bin and carry it into the cabin.

A sound, soft but recognizable, snared his attention before it was back in his hands.

He straightened and saw the coyote skulking

toward him, its head hung in abject submission. It moved another half foot and stopped, and he smiled. How quickly it had grown dependent on him.

"Pathetic, needful thing," he said quietly. "I think you will miss me when I leave."

The coyote stared at him with its insipid brown eyes, keeping its head lowered below the bony shoulders of its forelegs.

"Come to me," Bockem said, gesturing for it to come closer with a wag of his fingers. "Do not be afraid—you know better, do you not?"

Its natural suspicion diminished, the creature inched closer. *Needful, cringing, weak.* Bockem all at once felt wiry inside, his mouth full of metal.

"*Hoppe hoppe Reiter, wenn er fällt, dann schreit er, fällt er in de Hecken, tut er sich erschrecken,*" he sang in a gentle voice, reaching under his jacket for his holstered pistol. The coyote looked at him timidly as he raised the Glock in both hands and slid his right index finger out along its barrel, first aiming at its head, then changing his mind and shifting the bore of the gun toward its hindquarters.

"*Hoppe hoppe Reite, wenn er fällt, dann schreit er, fällt er auf die Steine, tun ihm weh die Beine.*"

The animal watched him, sloe-eyed and docile, expecting fresh morsels for its belly. Bockem held the gun steady, his extended arms slightly bent, hands wrapped around the grip, their thumbs married against it.

"Hoppe hoppe Reiter, wenn er fällt, dann schreit er, fällt er in den Graben, fressen ihn die Raben."

The creature watched. Bockem's index finger dropped from the barrel and curled around the trigger.

"Fällt er in den Sumpf, dann macht der Reiter . . . plumps!" he sang in his utter loathing.

And then his heart beat faster, and he fired his pistol, the weapon's recoil bouncing his arms upward as the coyote howled out in pain. Bockem had hit the creature in its right rear leg, the bullet shattering its thigh bones with an explosive spray of blood, instantly laming it. His eyes followed it now, watched it break away from the clearing in shock and panic, seeking cover in the chamise scrub along the mountain trail it had come from days ago. It scrambled for the brush with its leg dragging behind its body, bent at a loose, crooked angle, bleeding out a trail of bright, venous red.

Bockem let the gun sink in his hands until its snout was pointing straight down at the hard, dry earth, stood listening to the coyote crash through the bushes along the trail. Its wild, shrill cries reminded him of the screams of a tortured woman or child.

"Trust no one," he said into the high desert silence. "And beware."

He returned the pistol to its holster and brought his container inside to the kitchen sink.

Now and then throughout the day, Bockem paused in his work to hear the coyote's fading yelps and whimpers. It was not till quite late that he realized he would need to find a new way to dispose of his scrapings.

8

"CATHERINE," SAID Dave Phillips, sounding as though his head was stuffed with cotton. "Got a second?"

Catherine paused in the corridor outside her office. It was a little after eight o'clock in the morning, and she'd just returned from Floyd Lamb Park to type out her crime-scene reports and supervise the processing of evidence. She'd already phoned Lindsey to apologize and cancel their planned Sunday crêpe brunch at the new neighborhood trattoria, saying she'd try to make up for it with dinner reservations. Lindsey hadn't sounded convinced, and Catherine didn't blame her. She hadn't bought it, either.

She turned to face the assistant coroner. His eyes swollen and red, his nostrils chafed, he'd reached the park twenty minutes after she and Langston arrived and returned with the bodies in the meat wagon well before the CSIs wrapped up there.

"Dave, you look awful," she said, thinking she'd been too busy to mention it earlier. "Have you got a cold or something?"

"No," he said. "Cats. A pair. They're kittens. Cute white ones. From the shelter."

"But aren't you allergic to cats?"

"Yes," he said. "My wife isn't, though."

"Did you ever bother *telling* her you're allergic?"

He nodded. "Before we were married."

"And she brought them home anyway?"

"Actually, I did it. For her birthday."

Catherine raised an eyebrow. "Let me get this straight," she said. "Kitties make you gag and sneeze, but you go out and adopt not one but two at the same time."

"For my wife who loves cats and who celebrated a special birthday yesterday," Phillips said, dabbing his runny left eye with a tissue. "It *is* possible to develop an immunological tolerance to allergens through prolonged exposure."

"And what? You figured a double dose of fur would do it twice as fast?"

Phillips shrugged. "Snowflake and Sugar are litter mates," he said. "I didn't have the heart to separate them."

Catherine looked at him. "Dave," she said, grinning.

"Yes?"

"Your wife is one lucky woman."

Phillips stood there a moment, his cheeks turning the same shade of red as the tip of his nose. "Uh," he said, "did I mention why I came to see you?"

"Nope."

"Something occurred to me while I was zipping that man and woman in the park into body bags," he said. "A professor who taught a basic forensics course—this was in my second year of college—he took us to the National Museum of Health and Medicine. It's run by AFIP, the Armed Forces Institute of Pathology, in D.C."

"On the Walter Reed campus," Catherine said, nodding. "If you've paid the price of admission, you're probably a forensics expert researching an obscure subject or a weirdo looking for the two-headed grail."

"Since when is there a difference?" Phillips said with a morbid grin. "Anyway, the museum's got hundreds of specimens. The bullet that killed Lincoln, the leg of an amputated Civil War soldier, preserved organs and skeletons taken from people who had rare diseases, genetic conditions, anatomical deviations—it's an amazing collection."

It had abruptly struck Catherine that if Gil Grissom were God, that museum would be the afterworld he chose to create. "So what made you think of it while you were packing up the DBs?" she asked.

"The skinnings," Phillips said. His tone had sobered. "Most of the exhibits at the museum were open to the public. But there was a roomful of stuff, environmentally controlled and with restricted access. Our class never would've been granted permission to get in, but our professor had written a book or article and talked our way into a walkthrough. Not that I'm sure we were grateful afterward."

Catherine was silent. Phillips was not easily overcome. But there was a look in his eyes, a recalled horror and disgust, that bore no resemblance to anything she'd ever glimpsed in them. "What is it, Dave?"

"We saw five tattooed human skins taken from the bodies of Holocaust victims," he said. "The cabinets in that room were numbered, and they were in cabinet twenty-four. I can picture them. They were in acrylic frames. I remember the curator explaining that they were seized from Buchenwald's pathology section when American GIs liberated the concentration camps back in World War II. The Germans claimed to be using them for research. One scientist even wrote a dissertation on the sociology of tattooing."

"Scientist, huh?"

"Scientist, sadist, for the Nazis, those terms could be interchangeable," Phillips said. "The fact is that they took the skins as keepsakes or artwork to exhibit on their walls."

As she had the day before, Catherine felt an icy finger in her belly. She was becoming far too well acquainted with its touch. "Wasn't there a conviction for that at Nuremberg?"

"Ilse Koch," Phillips said. "The Witch of Buchenwald. She didn't bother with scholarly pretenses. Inmates testified that she kept a whole collection of skins. Some were tanned and sewn into lampshades. Billy Wilder, the Hollywood director, documented the liberation on film for the U.S. Army. He took footage of a whole table full of Ilse's souvenirs. There were preserved human organs, two shrunken heads, and fourteen tattooed skins. And a lamp with one of the shades."

"But didn't you say there were only five at the museum?"

"Right," Phillips said. "And just one skin was entered into evidence at the trial, a woman with butterfly wings." He paused. "Ilse got a life sentence before an Army review board commuted it to four years."

"They let her walk?"

"And the story gets worse before it gets better," Phillips said. "A couple of years later, the military governor of the American zone in Germany pardoned her."

"Why?"

"Good question." Phillips shrugged, shaking his head. "Luckily, it caused such an international commotion that the Germans rearrested her to save face and gave her a new life sentence. She served fifteen, sixteen years before she hung herself in her cell."

"Let's just hope she dangled awhile before she died." Catherine regarded Phillips for a long moment, those cold fingers leaving their prints everywhere inside her now. "Dave . . . what happened to the other tattooed skins in the film?"

"Another good question," Phillips said. "We know the tattoo of the woman with wings is in the National Archives."

"And the rest?"

"They disappeared."

"What about the lampshade?"

"Gone, too," he said. "So are the shrunken heads and preserved organs . . . for reasons unknown."

"Anybody ever try figuring out those reasons? Or where everything that's missing went?"

"I talked about it with somebody around here once," Phillips said. And then he gave her a look that told her exactly who that somebody had been.

"Grissom?" she said.

Phillips nodded. "It was a while ago," he said. "I think he mentioned that he was also in the non-public room at the museum once. I wish I could remember how the subject came up. Wish even more that he wasn't off in Europe somewhere so you could ask him yourself. But I was thinking . . ."

"Sara's back with us." Catherine looked at him. "She ought to be able to help with it."

"Exactly."

Catherine looked at him another second, smiling a little. "Dave," she said, "if anyone ever wants to know why we call you 'super' around here, just send that person straight to me."

*   *   *

Vern and Reginald Miriam founded the town that would take on their family name in 1858, the same year that arid Comstock territory revealed its silver lode to the brothers and six years before it became part of the newly recognized state of Nevada. In 1866, Our Lady of Guidance Church had its cornerstone set at the north end of Miriam, the construction financed by Catholic miners who were grateful for their inestimable success, eager to ensure heaven's continued generosity with the earth's precious resources, and keen on a good, strong dose of Sunday worship to mitigate the sins of their weeklong excesses in local saloons and brothels.

In their religious dedication, and possibly to one-up the competitive miners building their own church over in Carson City, the Miriams and other wealthy local mining families spared no expense giving the towering structure every ornamental and architectural adornment to fall within the era's bounds of tastefulness. Slender minarets lined up around its soaring bell tower. The sun entering its stained-glass windows spilled onto elaborate painted wall mosaics, delicately sculpted saints and archangels, and sacramental vessels of fine gold and silver. During services, tapering candelabras flickered in a choir loft supported by massive wooden pillars, its cedar rail carved with winged, prayerful cherubs.

Although still several months shy of his tenth

birthday, Jake Clarkson knew a great deal about Miriam's olden days. Father Molanez, who relished telling stories about them—along with occasional corny bathroom jokes ("What did the toilet say to the other toilet? You look flushed!")—had never spoken a word to him about Sugar Alley, but he was an intelligent, inquisitive boy and had picked up a tale or two on his own. It wasn't hard. Lying midway between Carson City and Reno, with Lake Tahoe only forty miles east across the state border, Miriam was itself a minor tourist stop, and many of the brochures in its little visitors' center made mention of the Sunday morning in 1874 when Judith Abigail, "Hatchet Judy," led her Women's Christian Temperance League on a furious rampage that left the district's saloons and brothels in splintered ruins. His omission of that episode aside, Father Molanez *did* regale the altar boy with stories of the Trappist order known to villagers as the Crazy Monks, who purchased the church from the parish in the 1930s after the silver ore dried up and three-quarters of the congregation went away with it, leaving Miriam's population more than halved. In their avowed silence and austerity, the Trappists were quick to strip away the building's classically beautiful features. The terraces around the minarets were dismantled, the art torn from the walls, the precious vessels and appointments sold or traded off for mules, hoes, and sacks of alfalfa seed for planting in the field. But for some reason, the choir loft was overlooked.

Then one day, as Father Molanez often told it with a mischievous lilt in his voice, the abbott sternly gathered his brothers in the nave, looked toward the back of the church, and turned his deep-set eyes up to the loft, lacing his hands over the middle of his apron.

"This abbott had kept a strict silence for ten years," Father Molanez would say. "The sign meant he'd been deep in thought."

Jake always humored him with a nod, as if he'd never heard it before. "Then, slowly, the abbott—did I ever tell you he had long white hair and a wild, shaggy beard to match?"

"That's how I picture him!" Jake would say to avoid admitting he'd heard that a hundred times, too, or having to lie that he hadn't. The father had silver hair himself and tended to be forgetful.

"Well, *very* slowly, the abbott did this." Father Molanez touched a fingertip to his lips and drew it away, little by little to build suspense. "It signaled he was about to speak, the rarest of things for any Trappist monk, and we know all about that fellow, Jakey. So naturally, the brothers thought their leader was about to share an important nugget of wisdom or reveal some glorious truth that came upon him in his silent meditations."

Jake would give a dutiful nod, waiting for the climactic line.

"Next, he thrusts his arm toward the choir loft like so." Father Molanez would spear the air with his finger to dramatize the moment. "And with his wild hair and beard flying this way and that, he shouts, 'A mouse up there just peed on my head! Now get rid of it before I pee on yours!'"

In the small room off the vestry used by the altar boys and choirboys, Jake reached into a large wooden chest for his neatly folded cassock and surplice, shrugged into them, then carefully snapped, buttoned, and straightened them over the dress shirt and slacks his dad had laid out for him that morning. Soon after he'd arrived at church to prepare for Sunday mass, Father Molanez was once again moved to tell his tale of the Crazy Monks and the choir loft, and Jake had forced a laugh, although its humor had long since grown stale. The story's timing wasn't at all unusual. Sunday communion—or, really, the part of the service that followed the sharing of the host—was when Jake got to take his brief turn with the choir, leaving the sanctuary for a hurried trip down the aisle that always drew glances and smiles from the congregation.

Although Jake found the attention a little embarrassing, he also secretly enjoyed it. He liked to sing, liked attending practices with the ensemble's regulars, and liked how he felt when Father Molanez and the instructors told him his voice was a special gift. He also liked how he felt inside when he sang the hymns at church—warm and settled, as if he was wrapped in a soft down blanket. Dad, who'd been saying a novena for his safety since the first time he stepped aboard a school bus, had told him it meant Jesus had placed a caring, protective hand on his shoulder as a reward for his devotion. When he'd mentioned the feeling to Father Molanez, the good-humored priest had joked that God was showing that he was grateful the choir had one member who could manage to stay on key. For his part, Jake only knew it was a very different kind of satisfaction from what he got out of anything else.

Now he went through the vestry door into the sacristy, still grinning over Father Molanez's favorite story. While his version of the abbott's decree was beyond goofy, Jake knew those monks had, in fact, torn down the loft way back when. As it turned out, though, they'd been experts at growing high-quality hay to sell to local horse ranchers but weren't too slick when it came to knowing how things were built . . . or *stayed* built.

The same tourist booklets that contained tales of Judith Abigail's Temperance League storming through Sugar Alley had sections about the history of the church, which was given official landmark status right around the year Jake was born and underwent a major restoration about three years later. According to what he'd read, the original pillars that held up the choir loft had also partly supported the roof above the entrance lobby—or the narthex, as Father Molanez always called it. A thin wall between the narthex and the main area of the church had hidden those huge structural beams, but when the Crazy Monks decided the loft had to go, they'd smashed through the wall so they could saw the pillars into scrap wood, then rebuilt the wall without the pillars, leaving nothing to help keep the roof of the narthex from falling in.

By the 1950s, the Trappists and their mules had quit the scene—Jake had no idea why or where they went—and Our Lady of Guidance had been returned to general usage by the town's Catholics. But over the decades, the roof over the narthex had begun to sag dangerously. When architects sketched out their plans for the church's refurbishment, they reviewed its early blueprints and agreed that the best way to prop up the roof was to replace the long-gone pillars with new ones that pretty much had identical dimensions. With that decided, one of the church's wealthier sponsors suggested that they might as well take things a step further and build a new choir loft right where the original had overhung the pews.

Coincidentally, Jake's father moved to town the very year Our Lady reopened to parishioners. Jake was barely out of diapers back then, and it would be several years before Ronald Clarkson enrolled him in Catholic school and only after his ninth birthday the previous July that he'd been eligible to become one of Father Molanez's servers. Of the four altar boys, he was the youngest, with the most senior being Pablo Rodriguez, who was almost thirteen. But the father had been quick to notice Jake's voice the first time he'd sung the Kyrie and the Gloria during services.

"Was there an angel on your shoulder, Jakey?" he'd said after the mass. "Because if that was you I heard, and not one that took flight while my back was turned, I think you might want to join the choir."

Although Jake had appreciated the compliment and had already realized he enjoyed singing, he'd wanted to continue as an altar boy. He liked being around Father Molanez and the other boys and had to admit, at least to himself, that he also liked getting out of class for eight o'clock weekday mass. When he'd gotten his first tip serving at a wedding last September, it had sealed things for him. He was adamant to the father about his preference, but the priest was equally insistent that his voice, which the choral teacher later described as a high alto verging on soprano, was "too good to waste while you make me look fit for my job."

After visiting with Jake and his dad at home to discuss the subject, Father Molanez had proposed a happy compromise. He would be proud and delighted to have Jake remain an acolyte, but if the boy so chose, he could attend choir rehearsals, train with its members, and discreetly ascend to the choir loft at certain times during the service to participate in the hymns and praises.

The father's solution had seemed just right, and Jake had readily embraced his unique dual roles, although his attempts at being inconspicuous hadn't prevented his dashes for the loft from becoming highlights to which the congregation looked forward with eagerness.

Of the servers at the church, Pablo was the crew head. He'd been an altar boy back in Mexico, where he and his family had come from not too long ago, and Father Molanez had entrusted him with the biggest responsibilities. He had the key to the tall maple cabinet in the sacristy where the vessels and linens were stored, and Jake would occasionally assist him in setting up the chancel. Although Pablo spoke very little English, he was always in a cheerful mood and managed to kid around a lot with Jake despite the language barrier. But he was very serious about his duties and about checking to see that the other boys on his crew were no less diligent.

Jake's regular job before mass was to make sure the water and wine cruets were filled and properly aligned on the credence. If Pablo arrived early enough, he would have everything ready for him on a small table in the hall, so Jake would only have to carry them out on a tray. And since Jake had spilled wine from the flagon more than once, he always appreciated it. But this morning, Pablo had showed up around the same time as Jake and hurried off to take care of his own tasks.

Well, not altogether—Jake noticed that the older boy *had* put the empty cruets on the hallway table. He turned toward the unlocked cabinet, where the wine and water pitcher sat in a cubby down near the floor, below the shelf that held the sacred vessels. His first order of business would be to bring the pitcher over to the sink at the far end of the sacristy.

He was crouching in front of the cabinet when someone came up from behind and grabbed him under the arms.

"*Grrrraoooooaoww!*"

Startled, Jake felt his spine bolt up straight at the sound of that roar. But he was already recovering as he snapped his head around to see Pablo there behind him, laughing hard.

"Definitely unfunny," he said, and wished he could have kept from grinning himself.

"*Sí* . . . funny, *poquito*!" Pablo removed his hands from Jake's sides to hook them into claws. "I am wine monster."

"Unfunny *and* lame," Jake said.

Pablo gave a furtive wink. "Wine monster, he catch you drinking wine."

Jake's smile faded. A couple of the boys claimed they'd been swigging from the flagon during wedding and funeral ceremonies. But it had never happened when he was with them. Besides, he couldn't stand how the stuff tasted and wouldn't have risked getting into trouble over something like that. "I was not—"

Pablo laughed again, his brown face crinkled

with amusement, his fingers still clawing at the air. Jake realized he'd been doubly zinged.

"You stink," he said, then pinched his nostrils shut to ensure that he hadn't been misunderstood. "You are stinko. Catch me?"

The boys were both cracking up now. After a moment, Pablo took a playful swat at Jake's hair. "Come." He gestured toward the cruets. "Señor Stinko help you."

Jake watched as Pablo came around him, bent, and reached into the cabinet for the wine flagon. "I guess you don't *totally* reek," he said, letting go of his nose with a magnanimous smile.

He had left Las Vegas before midnight Saturday for the now-familiar trip to Miriam, driving smoothly through the darkness on the long, empty band of northbound interstate. Although his body still felt some soreness from his suspension, he'd made a quick recovery afterward, taking in fluids and eating small high-protein meals throughout the day Saturday. With his contoured foam seat cushions reducing pressure on his back and shoulders, whatever discomfort he felt was acceptable.

Reaching the outskirts of town at eight-thirty, he parked his car at the tourist rail depot where black steam locomotives had once clanked in from the mines with their piles of raw silver ore. A log-cabin trading post stood beside the motel opposite the station, banners for hunting supplies in the window, a sign in the door indicating that it would open at noon.

He studied the signs a moment and bought his usual coffee at the motel diner. Then he went on foot toward the church spearing up between the hilltops, its tower bells clanging out their invitation to Sunday morning services.

Mass was at ten o'clock, and he felt no need to rush as he followed the steep, winding two-lane mountain road from the railway station into town. He experienced little pain for most of the walk there, and the one time he felt tightness in his chest, he was able to manage it with patterned breathing.

Across the street from the church, he paused to watch its congregants streaming through the tall paneled doors under the entrance arch. It was the third week of Lent, and the flock was thick. He had worn tinted lenses, but the sunlight was directly in his eyes as he looked eastward, and for a brief glare-shot moment, he imagined the people coming to worship were disembodied souls passing from the world's corruption and viciousness into golden transparency.

Blinking rapidly, he crossed to the church and went inside, removing his sunglasses as he passed through the inner set of doors to the nave.

The boy's father was seated toward the front of the church. He spotted him there while filing in with the congregants, and something inside him wound tight. As the torrent of memories, grief, and rage swept over him, he momentarily broke stride. It took all his will to force his legs to move and then slide himself into a rear pew off the aisle.

Minutes later, he thought he saw the father take a chance look back in his direction. But he was confident he wouldn't be recognized. His head was shaved, and he no longer wore a beard. He had lost weight, more than fifty pounds. And although the cancer had begun feeding on his muscle and sinews, his physical type was a far cry from what it had been eight years ago. He had changed in so many different ways.

He watched the processional from his spot at the end of the pew, the servers appearing with the crucifix and candles, the boy carrying the incense as the priest emerged from the sacristy to the harmonious singing of the choir. The ritual gave him powerful feelings. It was as if he had his own singular role to play as he answered the introductory prayers and allowed himself to be sprinkled with holy water. *Blessed be God the Father of our Lord Jesus Christ . . . may almighty God cleanse us of our sins . . . amen, amen, amen.*

His sense of immersion in the mass grew stronger as it continued, mingling with a kind of excitement. Eyes on the boy, he was stirred by the psalms and antiphons, the ringing of the altar bells. In partial kinship with the men and women around him, he joined in the Kyrie, shared the plea of all humanity while regretting that it wasn't nearly enough: *Kyrie eleison*, Lord have mercy on us, *Christe eleison*, Christ have mercy on us . . .

And when God's mercy fails, the visitor added silently at the hymn's conclusion, *I will give you something to replace it.*

He had anticipated the gray-haired priest's seasonal homily would relate to the coming of Easter, but it stunned him with its connection to his vision in the Mirror Chamber and the affirmation of the plan it had inspired. The priest spoke first of God commanding Abraham to kill his only son as a test of his love and faith in him. Incredibly, as if communicating to the visitor in words meant directly for his ears, he spoke of Abraham building an altar, laying out the wood for his burnt offering, then binding Isaac with rope and holding the knife over his throat. Of God staying his hand at the last moment, delivering a lamb for him to slaughter in his son's place, a ritual atonement that future generations of Hebrews would perform at Passover. The priest told how the story of Abraham and Isaac foreshadowed God's designs for his own son many centuries later—how for love of humanity, a love greater than he held for himself, he would make the very sacrifice he had not demanded of Abraham. Finally, the priest told of Jesus as the Lamb of God, redeeming mankind from sin by his death, and in his closing words reminded the congregants that through the Eucharistic blessings the sacra-

ments were converted into Christ's real and sub-
stantial presence, transformed into his very body
and blood, citing his words to the apostles at the
Last Supper: "Take, eat, this is my body. Drink ye
all of it, for this is my blood."

In accepting the consecrated bread and wine,
the faithful shared in the Lamb's sacrifice, pledged
to carry out his divine work, and dedicated themselves to making amends for the serious sins and
crimes of the world.

As he listened, thrills running up and down his
limbs, long-cold embers of emotion igniting as gal-
axies within him, the visitor was convinced beyond
a shred of doubt that the priest had been a mes-
senger, imparting God's approval to him through
his sermon.

He left a generous donation when the collection
basket was passed into his hands.

There were more prayers, and then a man beside
the visitor offered him his hand, and a woman in
front of him turned to do the same. The gestures
bothered him even as he returned them. It had
been an eternity since he'd had that sort of contact
with people, and it occurred to him that this might
have been the reason. But he also didn't want his
attention sidetracked from the boy.

Up at the altar, the priest was getting ready for
communion. The smiles and handshakes over with,
the choir singing, the visitor watched the boy assist
the other celebrants with their preparations.

And then, as the priest busied himself breaking

the wafer, the boy suddenly turned and left the altar area.

The visitor was careful not to betray the extent of his curiosity. This was unexpected. His white robe swishing around his knees, the boy raced down the aisle to smiles and rippling murmurs from the pews, sweeping past the visitor before he pushed out through the double doors into the narthex. Heads turned as they swung shut behind him, then tilted back toward the choir loft.

"Father Molanez's angel," someone said to him. It was the man who'd shaken his hand. "He has a beautiful voice . . . you've heard it before, yes?"

The visitor ignored him, his eyes fixed on the loft as the choir began the Agnus Dei, Lamb of God, the boy's voice sweetening its melodic and solemn strains, its imploring gentleness:

> *Agnus Dei, qui tollis peccata mundi, miserere nobis.*
> *Agnus Dei, qui tollis peccata mundi, miserere nobis.*
> *Agnus Dei, qui tollis peccata mundi, dona nobis pacem.*

The flutelike delicacy of the boy's petition, rising above the duskier voices, almost broke the visitor's heart. He could barely stave off tears. He smelled the sagebrush again or perhaps saw it rolling beneath an endless blue sky—he could not tell. It was as if the voices had evoked a merging of his senses.

Yellow perfumed sparks of sagebrush were in his eyes, in his nose, at the back of his tongue. And among them on a hill, the Lamb lying on a pyre of branches, crowned with a nimbus of golden light.

The communicants had risen from their seats to move toward the rail. Joining them in the aisle, the visitor looked back up at the boy in the loft more than once as he approached the front of the line. He felt doubled somehow, inside and outside his body, at once a participant and an observer.

When his turn came to receive the host and wine, he expressed his gratitude to the priest for his sermon, adding truthfully that it had overwhelmed him with emotion. The priest looked pleased and joked that he was just trying to stay gainfully employed.

As the service neared its conclusion, the visitor slipped from the nave before the others and took a minute or two to gather his composure in the narthex. He made note of a plain polished oak door to his right. Then he glanced over his opposite shoulder and saw a second door ornamented with elaborate metalwork seraphs and frosted glass. The embellishments were a likely indication that it opened on a baptismal area—in a church of this vintage, the fountain would be in a separate chapel. Which would mean that the door on the right led to the stairs running up to the choir loft.

He would have liked a chance to test both doors to be positive. But within moments, the congregation would be pushing into the vestibule. As an unfamiliar face in town, he didn't want to attract attention. It would have to wait until his return.

He put his sunglasses back on and strode down the stairs of the church to the street, turning back to the railway depot where he'd left his car. He could still see the image of the Lamb on the hill, lying near a pyre of branches in its heartbreaking innocence.

And he could still smell sagebrush.

"Archie, how're you doing?" Ray Langston asked.

The tech looked guardedly around from his bank of computer display panels, where he'd been mulling Nick's idea of putting together a ten-year-old street-view map from ancient security video footage. Criminalists didn't care how lab rats were doing. Ever. When one asked, it usually prefaced a request that would lead to hours of work on top of work.

"I'm a little busy with something right now, Dr. Ray," he said. "Otherwise, I'm all ri—"

"I wonder if you could help me out," Langston said. "Advise me on something."

Archie was thinking his retort of choice would be to suggest that he drop a handful of quarters into the meter and wait in line. "With regard to . . . ?"

"Getting information about an Internet subscriber account," Langston said.

"From a service provider?"

"No," Langston said. "A website."

Archie semirelaxed, thinking that this did not look like an issue that would require any cyberwizardry from him.

"Sometimes you just have to request it from the site," he said. "Practically all of them have you agree to terms of usage when you sign up. If people actually bothered reading the fine print, they'd know some state outright that they'll share info with law-enforcement and other agencies on request."

"This site won't comply voluntarily," Langston said. "I'm talking about *Flash Ink*."

"The tat-freak 'zine?"

"I'm not sure I'd characterize it that way . . . but yes," Langston said. "Its policies emphasize user privacy."

"Then you'll need a subpoena," Archie said. "I'm probably not the most qualified person around here to give you the skinny on how that works. You might want to ask one of the detectives next door. One thing I'd recommend is that you don't wait on the request to contact the magazine. Depending on what type of info you need, sites will only keep it for finite periods."

"For instance . . ."

"F'rinstance, log-on and log-off times might be stored for half a year. Since it eats up memory, mail could be wiped after thirty days. And IM—instant messaging—log data in two or three days. It all varies according to system capacities."

"Do you know how we'd find out about *Flash Ink*'s system?"

"You'll want to speak with the site's custodian of records," Archie said. "Word to the wise, expect those types to be protective."

"Even if we stipulate the information's wanted for a criminal investigation?"

"Sometimes *especially* if that's the situation," Archie said with a nod. "It gets to be a civil-liberties issue."

Langston looked thoughtful. "Greg's been trying to contact somebody at the website, but Sunday isn't the best time to pick," he said. "Let's assume there's an objection to providing us with the records. Would you think they'd retain them once they know we'll be applying for warrants?"

"Yeah, since it doesn't necessarily mean they'll have to share everything with you . . . and since they will want to avoid trouble with the courts," Archie said. "I think you'd need to give them a user name and stipulate the information you need. Screen aliases, profiles, friend lists, message-board postings—"

"We don't have anything like that."

"Oh," Archie said. "Well, then, I'm assuming you've got an IP address associated with somebody's computer. In that case, you'd request whatever info you'd want for a particular date and time, or range of dates, that the person was at the computer and logged on to the site. It gets sticky when users use proxy servers—middlemen between their computers and the Web. You can trace backward to the user from the proxy's IP address, but that's another reason you have to move fast. Websites don't store proxies too long—"

"I don't want to investigate a single IP address," Langston interrupted.

Archie shrugged. "Still shouldn't be too complicated. If you're looking at multiple users, my guess is you'd just list each of them on your request. Or maybe you'd need separate requests. And separate subpoenas. I don't know the legal formalities. Again, you might want to run next door—"

"*Flash Ink* has thousands of registered members," Langston broke in again. "I think the actual number it gives is ten thousand."

"Yeah, so?"

"I don't know how many need to be checked out," Langston said. "It could be a dozen, twenty, five hundred . . . at this stage, the pool includes all of them."

"*All?*"

"For now, yes."

Archie blinked. "Let me get this straight," he said. "You've got no names to check out."

"Correct."

"No IP addresses."

"Also correct."

"Absolutely none?"

"None."

"Then where are you going to *start*?"

Langston looked at him and smiled. "Right here with you, Archie," he said.

"Starglow banquets," the woman answered her phone. "This is Karen Esco."

Nick sat up behind his desk. It was a little past nine A.M. on Sunday, and his back felt tight and achy, a price he'd paid for having dozed off for several hours behind his desk. His stomach, meanwhile, wasn't in much better shape and had been making strange burbling noises thanks to the greasy sausage omelet he'd ordered from the breakfast joint around the corner. But by the time Nick had decided to stop pulling up reports and other info about the Dumas case late Saturday night—or early that same morning, however you chose to slice it calendarwise—he hadn't seen the point in going home just to crash for a while, jump out of bed, shower, and make a quick turnaround for the lab. Instead, he'd decided to save on time and gas and stay put in his office.

"Ms. Esco, I'm Nick Stokes, a criminalist with the LVPD," he said.

"A what?"

"Criminalist, ma'am."

"Isn't that kind of like a police scientist?"

"We have scientific backgrounds, yes."

"I saw a drama about it on television, and it seems fascinating. Though I wouldn't know if it's the same in reality."

"There's never a dull moment," Nick said. "Anyway, Ms. Esco—"

"Karen, please."

"Karen . . ."

"Oh, my dear!" she exclaimed with sudden concern.

"Something wrong?" Nick asked.

"That's what I just wondered," she said. "We haven't had an incident of some sort at the Starglow, have we?"

"Not that I know of."

"So nothing's gone on here overnight?"

"Not in terms of a crime," Nick said, thinking that if walls could talk, they'd have plenty to tell her about what went on at every hotel in Sin City after dark.

"Well, I'm certainly relieved," she said. "I walked in maybe fifteen minutes ago, then listened to my voicemail while having my coffee. When I heard you were with the LVPD, I figured I'd better get in touch right away . . . though, if I may ask, why would a criminalist be calling unless it *was* about a crime?"

"I was just getting to that," Nick said. "Karen, are you acquainted with Stacy Ebstein?"

"Of course, I know Stacy. I was her assistant before, you know, the incident. Reported directly to her. And then . . . oh, I'm sorry. I'm rambling. I must seem dizzy to you. But I generally come in to find messages from people wanting to throw catered affairs. Weddings, engagement parties, convention dinners, things of that variety. It's anything but a typical morning when I hear from someone investigating a *crime*. And now that I know this is about poor Stacy . . . is she all right?"

"I spoke with her a couple of days ago," Nick said, aware that wasn't really an answer. He didn't think Stacy Ebstein would ever be all right again. Not by any definition. "She indicated that she'd held her job at the Starglow for quite a few years."

"Over a decade, I believe," Karen said. "As I told you, she preceded me as banquet manager and was already a senior employee when I was hired. So brilliant—and she couldn't have been more generous as a mentor. We used to call the position 'special events coordinator' back when she held it, incidentally. Then new ownership came in when we renovated and changed things around. Basically just for the sake of change, you know how that goes."

"Uh-huh," Nick said. "Karen, are there still calendar listings on file for the affairs Stacy booked? She thought there might be."

"There are for the recent ones," Karen said. "We get many repeat clients, especially on the corporate side. So it makes sense to have a record of their preferences and so forth. Also, we occasionally mail solicitations to parties who've booked events with us before."

"What about listings of older events?"

"By older, you mean . . ."

"Going back about ten years."

"Ten?"

"Would you have them?"

"I'd have to check," Karen said. "If I may ask, does this have anything to do with finding out who kidnapped her?"

"It might," Nick said. "I won't know till I see those listings."

"Are there specific dates you require?"

"Yes and no," Nick said. "I'll give you a range. But I'd also want to know whether Karen ever booked any parties for someone named Quentin Dorset. Or if he happened to be a guest at a party she booked, if that information's available."

"Did you say Dorset?"

"Right, the spelling's D-o-r—"

"Isn't he the judge that was found murdered the other night?"

"That's right."

"My God, talk about dizzy, how big a numbskull must I seem?" Karen said. "I saw the news reports about his body being found in that truck lot. There was a mention that he'd been, you know, disfigured in the same manner as Stacy. Is the same person responsible? The one they're calling Tattoo Man?"

"I can't comment on the case, Karen," Nick told her, reminded that Ecklie and the mayor would be saying whatever they wanted about it at their press conference in a few hours. "Back to my question . . . do you think you can dig up the information?"

"I'm not sure," she said. "Stacy was meticulous. She kept everything in our computers. I'll do what I can—it's slow today, and I may have a chance to follow up. I'll need to check the files, then get permission from my superiors at the hotel to release them. I don't think that will be a problem . . . but with the changeover in ownership, I can't tell you what was retained."

"Try your best," Nick said. "Will you do that for me, Karen?"

A pause. His phone to his ear, Nick waited out the silence. "Yes, naturally," she said then. "And for Stacy."

The clock in Willows's office showed it to be ten-thirty in the morning in Las Vegas, which Sara Sidle had just wistfully pointed out was early evening five thousand miles away in Paris, where her husband, Gil Grissom, was trying to get the Sorbonne's board of trustees to shake loose some funds for a research project.

"You must miss him," Catherine said from behind her desk.

"I do," Sara said, sitting opposite her. "The separations are rough. But the one thing I realized being away from Vegas, from my work here, was how much a part of me it had become. I think distancing myself from it for a while left me . . . I'm not sure I can give you the right word for it."

"Refreshed?"

Sara smiled. "It shows, huh?" she said. "Score one for a half year of studying primate behavior in the Costa Rican rain forest—not that capuchin monkeys don't scheme, steal, go into jealous rages, fight turf wars, and exhibit occasional psychotic tendencies."

"Our closest living relatives?"

"You got it," Sara said with a chuckle. "When our research grants tapped out, it was off to Paris and the Sorbonne to try to refill the coffers. Gris is good at meeting with trustees in stuffy boardrooms, but I felt kind of superfluous and was itching to get back here to do something constructive."

Catherine was nodding. "Gris was such a rock. I never understood how much of a load he shouldered dealing with higher-ups. What it took to buffer us from outside pressures so we wouldn't be distracted."

"I think he always trusted us more than we trusted ourselves," Sara said. "It was his recommendation that you head the team after he left, Cath. My advice would be to remember that when things get tough."

Catherine smiled a little, then turned to her reason for calling Sara into the office. "Has Gris gotten a chance to read my e-mail about the . . . ?" Hesitating, she sought a suitable term for what Phillips had seen at the museum.

"He did," Sara said. "I spoke with him about an hour ago. Most of his files are in storage with the rest of our stuff."

"Here in Vegas?"

Sara nodded. "Right before he left for Costa Rica, Gris was actually working on a kind of minivid about the work he'd done on those artifacts."

Catherine was silent. *Artifacts.* Sara always had been a contradiction. The most clinical and dispassionate of investigators, she'd never shown how deeply she was affected by the nightmares every crime scene represented. But there had seemed to be an old wound inside her, and the horrors had penetrated it, darkness drawn to darkness, until something unbearable came seeping up. She'd left the job to purge it and mend her spirit, and Grissom had soon followed, adding his love to her healing.

"Okay," Catherine said. "What's our next step?"

"I'll head over to the storage warehouse. Gris archived all his research, including the video material, on flash drives. Once I get hold of them, I can shoot the files over to him via e-mail. It shouldn't take him long to pull everything together."

Catherine nodded.

"A request from Gris," Sara said. "He considers this one of his personal projects—an unfinished piece of historical detective work. He knows for sure he's on to something but hasn't been able to take it too far. If it'll help find our killer, we can run with it. Otherwise, he'd prefer we keep his research to ourselves—he doesn't want innocent people's reputations hurt."

"Sounds like a plan," Catherine said.

Sara rose from her chair. "I'd better get moving. I need to go see Hodges about my epithelials before shooting over to the storage place. If I have any problems finding the material—or uploading it—I'll give you a call."

Catherine nodded. "When you're sending Gris that e-mail, tell him I said thanks. I owe him, Sara. Seriously."

Sara gave her a smile. "Off to the races . . . *laissez les bons temps rouler*," she said, and left the office.

"Okay, what have you got for me?" Sara said.

Hodges turned to see her standing in his entryway. He'd been glancing back and forth between his high-powered microscope's binocular eyepiece and the large flat-panel display of the computer to which he'd output his comparative specimen images, calibrating their color and focus so Sara could see with her own two eyes what he was about to explain about his findings . . . not that she sounded significantly appreciative.

"Thank you, Hodges," he muttered under his breath. "I appreciate you busting it. On short notice. While subbing for an AWOL evidence clerk and acting as Nick's office gofer."

"Excuse me?"

"Oh, sorry," he said. "I was just contemplating the invariables of forensic lab work."

She pulled a face. "C'mon, Hodges," she said. "I've been waiting for these results."

Hodges decided not to reply that he heard that familiar refrain a dozen times a night on *average* shifts and that it had only grown in frequency and volume over the past few days, what with most of the CSIs on short strings, working nonstop to resolve two different cases Mayor Stancroft had been determined to blend into one.

"Just a second." He leaned over the ocular tubes, further sharpening the split-screen image. "I'll show you what intrigues me."

She took another couple of steps into the lab and waited, arms folded across her chest. Hodges made a final adjustment or two and decided he was satisfied.

"Notice anything about the images?" he said, nodding to indicate the screen. The image on its right side, tagged with a capital *D*, showed a wide granular patch of crimson with faint grayish vertical lines. The one on the left, tagged with an *N*, was exactly the same, red with those darker rodlike stains.

"They look identical," she said. "Are those the epithelials?"

"They're mineral traces I obtained from them," Hodges said. "Or, more precisely, that I extracted from their tattoo inks."

"Does the *D* stand for Dorset?"

He nodded. "The sample's from one of the lips on his backside."

"But if *N* is for Noble, where did the red pigment come from? The samples from his face were black."

"Some only appear to be," Hodges said. "The

base pigment is powdered jet and an iron oxide called wustite, which are used in some black tattoo inks. But if you carefully examine the photos, you'll see that his face has subtle accents. Mix red, blue, and green in equal proportions, and you'll have solid black. Vary the proportions, and you'll get the washes Tattoo Man used for his accents."

"In other words, the red pigment in those washes is exactly the same as the pigment in the butt kisses."

"Yes." Hodges was nodding. "It's an extremely fine-grained sandstone composed of quartz, feldspar, and metallic silicates, including hematite, a red iron oxide. I'd estimate it accounts for three percent of the material in the grains, which doesn't seem proportionately significant. But since the quartz, its primary constituent, is translucent and colorless, a thin layer of hematite is enough to give it a striking red color."

"Does any of this tell us where the pigment came from?"

"Generally, it's a type of red sandstone that dates back two hundred fifty years to the late Permian era—when the dinosaurs started dying off. Before that, the American Southwest was covered under an inland sea that left similar formations from the Colorado Rockies to California."

Sara frowned. "Half the country, in other words."

"True, unless we look at other features of the

sandstone," Hodges said. "The most conspicuous are those gray stripes. They don't show up to the naked eye in the pigment because only an infinitesimal portion of the sample material in the epithelials contains them. But when the grains *do* have these stains, they're the result of a type of lichen that forms encrustations on natural rock walls. That narrows our range to Utah, Nevada, and a slice of southeastern California. And I think I can bring us even closer to the source . . . much closer." He paused. "Do you know what tuff is? That's t-u-f-f."

She shrugged. "A word I see on shirts with reggae slogans."

"Very good—except we're discussing mineralogical science, not Jamaican patois," Hodges said. "There's another meaning. People sometimes call it tufa, like those stones you see in fish tanks. It's volcanic ejecta. Ash and other materials that blow from the caldera during an eruption."

"And?"

"And, you see, tuff from any given region has very distinct characteristics. You can tell one tuff from another by its makeup. Caetano tuff, for example. It comes from Mount Caetano up north in Lander County and is loaded with smoky quartz and a mineral called sanidine. Thirty-three million years ago, that mountain was a supervolcano, one of the biggest in the history of the earth. Its caldera was twelve miles wide and blew its guts hundreds of miles into the air. The ash was carried around by the wind, then deposited all over northern Nevada. Take a hike in the desert outside Vegas, I can virtually guarantee you're going to get Caetano tuff on the soles of your boots."

Sara looked at him. "Is this stuff—"

"Tuff."

"Is it in the pigment you took from the epithelials?" she said, no amusement whatsoever in her voice.

"It's loaded with geochemical traces, Sara," he said. "My educated guess is that Tattoo Man blends his own inks and that we can reasonably pinpoint the location of his source for red pigment."

Her eyes tightened. "Where?"

"Walk out my door, hang a left in the hallway, and keep walking for about twenty miles."

"And then?"

"Then you'll be at Red Rock Canyon," he said. "And you can stop."

"Got some bad news, man," Nick said, coming up behind Archie.

Archie frowned with his hands on the computer keyboard, thinking his neck was sore from cranking it around to face what seemed like a different CSI every fifteen seconds.

"No security video?" he said.

"Not so far." Nick looked dejected. "I've phoned a couple dozen places in the past hour. Hotels, casinos, shops, and so on. Same story from all of 'em. You were right, none stored anything for close to the length of time we need. And most never migrated older video from one format to the next—too expensive. It's basically routine to discard stuff after a while unless it's got image captures of known criminals, cheating rings, repeat scammers . . . people they want to stay on the lookout for."

Archie was thinking he ought to be relieved to get the job of making a retro photomap off his plate, considering he'd have his hands full tackling one problem at a time, among them sifting through mountains of electronic log-in data for Doc Ray's inside-out *Flash Ink* user-tracking quest.

Ah, well, sorry, wish you'd had better luck, he considered replying.

"Let's not quit on the idea," he instead heard himself say to his own consternation. "There might be sources that haven't occurred to us."

Nick rubbed his eyes with his knuckles.

"You're starting to remind me of Sleepy the dwarf," Archie said.

"I'm just a little dog-eared," Nick said. "Look, I need to track down Sara and Hodges—they've been working on some skin samples together. Then I'm supposed to head over to city hall with Catherine." He shrugged. "I guess Ecklie and the mayor want us to be stage props while they do their song and dance."

"Glad I don't have tickets to that show," Archie said.

"With luck, I'll stall out in heavy traffic on the way," Nick said. "In the meantime, I'm gonna keep racking my brain for places that might—"

Archie snapped his fingers and poked a finger through the air at him. *"Wham!"*

"Wham?"

"Wham, pow, you hit it right on the head," Archie said.

Nick looked at him. "Think you can explain what this is about?"

Archie spun around toward his displays and began typing away at his keyboard. "Traffic," he said. "It's about Las Vegas traffic."

Nick slapped his brow as Archie briefly explained what had started him blurting out cheesy comic-book sound effects. "Hoss, you're the best," he said. "Can't believe I never thought of it."

"Goes to show why you need techs around here," Archie said.

"Definitely. I—" Nick was interrupted by his cell phone's call-forwarding ringtone. He got it out of his pocket, glanced at the caller ID display, and his eyes grew large. "Hello?" he said.

"Hi, this is Karen Esco. The banquet manager from the Starglow."

"Yes, ma' . . . uh, Karen."

"I hope I'm not reaching you at an inconvenient moment."

"No, no, this is fine," Nick said.

"Could you possibly come over here? To the hotel? I can free up about half an hour around eleven-thirty, a quarter to twelve."

Which, Nick thought, was right when he and Catherine were supposed to show up at city hall together. Although, judging from her excited tone, he knew he wouldn't have said no even if he hadn't wanted an excuse to skip out on Ecklie's press conference

"Did you find something?"

He waited, hearing her lower the phone from her mouth and speak to someone at her end. "Sorry, we're getting the floral arrangements ready for a party, and it's a little hectic," she said after a moment. "What was it you asked?"

"I just wondered if you'd found something."

"Oh, yes," she said. "And not only that, but got the blessing of corporate counsel to show it to you. That's why I called right away, Mr. Stokes. I think it might be exactly what you need."

Catherine heard her office phone ring and grabbed the receiver. "Crime lab," she said. "Catherine Willows."

"Cath, it's Sara. I'm at the storage warehouse. And I've got some good news."

Catherine sat up straight. "I'm listening."

"The Ilse Koch material was right where I thought it would be. Luckily, I'm the one who did that packing and filing, or it might've been buried forever."

"I won't tell Gris you said that."

"Appreciated," Sara said. "Anyway, I'm uploading the information to his computer with my palmtop. His notes, images, everything. He's back from his dinner with the museum honchos, so hang tight at the office while he sets things up for a videoconference. It shouldn't be too long—Gris did a lot of work on the minivid for his own reference."

Catherine held on to the phone, nodding. "I'll be here," she said.

"Okay, Catherine, I should be watching the same images you are, so let me know if there are any syncing problems at your end," said Grissom's digitally transmitted voice over the Internet telephone connection. "Right now, you should be looking at Frederick Bachmann in nineteen forty-three. Approximate age twenty-seven. The photo was taken outside his home in the Wannsee suburb of Berlin . . . the same lovely town where German officials met to plot out their blueprint for the Final Solution about eighteen months earlier. Perhaps coincidentally, perhaps not."

About an hour after Sara had called from the storeroom, Catherine sat at her desk looking at the grainy black-and-white photo on her computer monitor. Posing with a small dachshund snuggled between his arm and his side, Bachmann was a tall, thin man in a double-breasted suit, his dark hair slicked back from his forehead in a sharp widow's peak.

"The picture came up fine, Gris," she said.

"Excellent." A pause. "Frederick—or Fritz, as he preferred to be called—was a third-generation dealer of fine art," Grissom explained. "When the Nazis began looting the homes of prominent Jewish families, he cut deals that allowed him to acquire confiscated paintings, sculptures, and antiquities and ship them off to family-owned warehouses in Switzerland or vaults in Swiss banks where they were favored account holders. In some instances, he was a commissioned middleman. In others, he bought the pieces outright from the Germans. Fritz sold works by Picasso, Cezanne, and Monet and hundreds of masterpieces by Rembrandt, relics from ancient Egypt, Greece, and Rome . . . I could go on and on. Some of them even wound up in American museums. What's interesting is that these upright institutions weren't concerned with the provenance of the works—their history of ownership running back to the creators. The only time that isn't a normal part of the authentication process is when you'd rather not know."

"Selective blinders," Catherine muttered. "Gotcha."

The still photo faded out, and another black-and-white image—or a series of movie images—faded in. The jerky film clip's upper margin was stamped with a serial number that read, "OMGUS Headquarters, Administrative Meeting, Frankfurt, ca Sept. 1945."

Catherine saw a group of American and German military representatives around a large conference table, engaging one another with the brittle cordiality typical of such official occasions. Then the moving picture froze.

"Bear with me, Catherine. I'm going to use my digital equivalent of a Telustrator, and you'll recall I'm not very adept with electronic contraptions," Grissom said as a circle appeared around a pair of men seated at one end of the table—one a German, the other in an American uniform. "It took me months to pry the snippet of film you're seeing out of our National Archives using the Freedom of Information Act. The American officer is Colonel Jonas Whitney Stevens. The German is Oberst Gunter Bachmann."

She crooked an eyebrow. "Bachmann?" she said.

"Right, there's that name again. Gunter was Fritz's older brother. Presumably, he hadn't been keen on the family art trade and decided to attend the German Army's Offizierschule in Dresden. Immediately after the war, he was appointed an official liaison to the Office of Military Government, United States—"

"OMGUS," Catherine said.

"—and struck up a chummy relationship with

Colonel Stevens that lasted for decades, as I'll show you in a bit," Grissom said. "A few years ago, I had a genealogist do up the Bachmann genealogical tree and discovered that Gunter Bachmann was married to a Hetta Köhler, who happened to be a close cousin of Ilse Köhler, who married Karl Otto Koch, a *Standartenführer* in the SS, who became—"

"The commander of Buchenwald," Catherine said. "That means our ghoulish Frau Koch—"

"—née Köhler was tied to the Bachmann clan through marriage," he was explaining over her speakers. "If you've followed me this far, Catherine—and you have, of course—then you probably see where this is headed. You should know that Gunter's buddy Colonel Stevens was a major figure with OMGUS. Which is to say that besides being one of the top brass in the U.S. constabulary that policed occupied Germany, he was influential with the panel that let Ilse Koch skate on some of her most heinous offenses. Another thing—the Bachmann family business thrived for decades after the war, with Gunter eventually retiring from the German army to rejoin the fold. In the nineteen-fifties, they went transcontinental. Gunter continued to run the galleries in Europe, while Fritz Bachmann moved to America with his wife, legally changed his name to Bockem, became a proud father, and opened an exclusive auction house in New York's Upper East Side with branches in London and

Berlin. He was a mainstay of Park Avenue society there until his passing in the mid-nineties . . . and if there's a good time to have your ticket punched, Fritz couldn't have done better. Because only a couple of years later, an investigative article in the *New York Times* revealed that he'd hung on to half a billion dollars' worth of artwork plundered from the Jews and continued quietly dealing it off to collectors."

Catherine inhaled through her front teeth. Fade out, fade in, and the freeze-framed image of the OMGUS conference was replaced by a color photograph of three elderly men eating at an outdoor café or restaurant. The man at the right of the screen, his hair turned silver but still dipping down the middle of his high brow in a kind of point, was instantly recognizable.

"This heartwarming reunion occurred at a swank resort in Hilton Head, South Carolina, about six months before Fritz passed away. The image isn't widely known to exist. I don't have it in my possession and therefore can't be showing it to you right now," Grissom said. "If we *could* somehow get a look at it, however, it would be courtesy of someone I know with Israel's Institute for Intelligence and Special Tasks."

"The Mossad," Catherine whispered as a large cursor arrow appeared onscreen. The arrow moved to the silver-haired figure.

"I probably don't have to point out Fritz to you,

so let's move on," Grissom said. An instant later, the arrow went to a heavy, bearded man on Bachmann's right, caught eating with his fork midway between his plate and his mouth. "This old fellow enjoying what appears to be pasta primavera is a little harder to recognize. But strip away the beard, about seventy pounds, and a half-century's worth of wear and tear on the skin from heavy drinking, and you'll see another familiar character. He, incidentally, is also now among the departed. Liver cancer."

Catherine read the name in the box and nodded her head. "Colonel Jonas W. Stevens," she said. "So, Gris, who's the other guy? Brother Gunter?" She was thinking that if he *was* Gunter Bachmann, he resembled his old self even less than Stevens did.

"The third man's a latecomer to the story . . . as I'm telling it," Grissom said. "His neighbors in Elm Creek, Illinois, knew him for forty years as Wallace Tindler, the owner of a moderately successful small-town contracting outfit before his retirement four or five years ago. But once upon a time, he was Oberstleutnant Kurt Deil, an SS guard in Block Two at Buchenwald, otherwise known as the Section of Human Pathology. Deil reported directly to Ilse Koch—he was her main henchman, in fact. No atrocity was committed without his approval. But like many lower-ranking men in the chain of command, he slipped off the radar and was able to live comfortably for more than sixty years. Then, last year, a criminal-justice grad student at Northwestern recognized him and reported him to authorities. He'd been working on a dissertation on former Nazis hiding in plain sight. After his arrest, Deil was extradited to his native Austria and convicted of war crimes that included the killing and torture of thousands of inmates."

But the Mossad knew about him more than a decade ago, Catherine thought. *Why not bring him in then?*

"I know what you must be wondering, Catherine. Bet you're rubbing your chin right now."

She lowered her hand. Son of a bitch.

"The Israelis didn't want Deil nabbed or deported," Grissom said. "They were casting a wider net. Holocaust deniers insist that Ilse Koch was a maligned, innocent victim of Zionist propaganda. That her human-skin lampshades and album bindings were mythical. And that Billy Wilder faked the documentary footage Phillips told you about. They say the tattooed skins in U.S. possession are also phonies. Instead of Jews, they claim they belong to German prisoners of war who were killed and mutilated to further the deception and point to the Jewish prohibition on marking the flesh as proof of the sham—ignoring documentation that hundreds of thousands of inmate Jews who'd culturally assimilated to one degree or another had decorative tattoos."

Catherine was nodding her head. "Israel was

after the missing items from Frau Ilse's collection," she said. "They figure Deil must have delivered them to Fritz Bachmann before the U.S. liberation force could get its hands on them . . ."

Or possibly afterward. It was obvious that the Bachmanns had gotten to Stevens during the occupation. Could be they'd blackmailed him somehow, could be he'd been war profiteering in the most monstrous way imaginable—it made no difference. One way or another, he'd assisted them. And sustained a relationship with them and Deil for half a century.

But Fritz Bachmann—Bockem—was dead now. Stevens, too. And Catherine was sure it would have made international headlines if Deil had confessed his role in seeing that crucial evidence from Ilse's chamber of horrors vanished before her trial. Catherine frowned. Vanished? Or was sold off?

"Gris, where are we going with this?"

"Fritz Bockem's auction house closed a year or two after he died. His wife, Hetta, survived him and returned to Germany, where she might or might not be alive to this day. I mentioned they had a son after coming to this country, though. William Bockem. My records indicate he's in his middle to late fifties. He went to Columbia University in New York, helped his father run the company. But once Fritz died, he dropped out of sight."

Silence. Catherine stopped herself from asking Grissom what he'd done to track him down, figuring it obviously involved sources he couldn't disclose.

"I'm not sure how much any of this has to do with your case," Grissom said. "It could easily turn out to be nothing. You might be dealing with a lone wolf. A serial killer-collector with a very unusual fetish. But I think it's worth a follow-up."

Catherine looked at the computer display and nodded. "Thank you, Gris," she said. "Needless to say, we all miss you. Things haven't been the same around here since you left."

"My regards to everyone, Catherine," Grissom said. "Man's yesterday may ne'er be like his morrow, naught may endure but mutability."

Catherine imagined Grissom at his computer in Paris, picturing him as he looked in the recent photos Sara had shown her. There was more gray in his hair nowadays than there used to be, and he'd grown a full beard, also flecked with white. But nothing had changed about those blue eyes that saw so much.

"Do I get to find out the source of that quote?" she asked.

"You know I'd never make things that easy on you," he said. She could hear the smile in his voice. "Good luck, Catherine. I'll be in touch."

And with that, her screen went blank.

9

Nick had no sooner left Archie's boxy little lab than he saw Catherine quickly approaching him from down the corridor. She had on her overcoat and gloves.

"Nicky," she said. "I've been looking for you high and low."

He poked a thumb over his shoulder at the lab entrance. "Me 'n' Arch been trying to get a handle on some things," he said. "We saw you zip past us a few hours ago. I need to fill you in."

"Let's swap progress reports heading over to city hall," she said, tilting her head toward the parking exit. "We'd better get rolling—"

"I was just on my way out," Nick said. "But I can't go with you."

"You have to," Catherine said. "Ecklie wants a couple of token CSIs as a show of interdepartmental commitment."

"Cath, we already know the press conference is a clown show."

"Doesn't matter. I gave my word we'd be there," Catherine said, glancing at her watch. "What's the problem, anyway?"

"I need to see someone at the Starglow," Nick said. "An employee who's helping me dig up old records. They might connect Stacy Ebstein to Dorset. And maybe the Tattoo Man."

She looked at him. "And exactly *why* didn't you give me a heads-up?"

"I would've if I'd known ahead of time. But I just heard from the woman at the hotel," Nick said. "I'm smelling a real break, Cath."

A brief silence, then Catherine sighed. "All right," she said. "It'll take you, what, two minutes to get to city hall from the hotel?"

"In slow traffic."

"Meet me there if you get through soon enough. The press conference is in that windy little plaza between the front wing and the tower. In the meantime, Jim will be there keeping me company while I freeze my butt off."

"Should be some media hounds, too."

Catherine frowned. "Appreciate the reminder," she said.

The Starglow, one of the original hotel-casinos in what used to be called Glitter Gulch, had undergone three extensive renovations since its grand opening in the late 1940s, a year after the Golden Nugget's famous pillowtop began slinging neon lights over the shiny limos met by curbside valets a little farther up Fremont Street, their tuxedoed and mink-stoled passengers dropped off with the ushers at its red-carpet entrance.

Now you couldn't drive your car along Fremont because of the big high-tech light-show canopy over the mall there, and the closest equivalents to ushers or valets were the slot-room hawkers with their discount coupons and the beautiful smiling showgirls out front of the strip club that Mom complained about on every budget trip to Vegas, while Dad tried not to sprain his neck turning to get a look, and the kids kept tugging both toward the video arcades.

Doing his best to avoid the usual clog of tourists, Nick had taken Carson Avenue down to South Third, left his car in the lot across the street from the county courthouse, then walked a block, turned left, and went through the Starglow's comparatively new entrance on South Fourth, adjacent to the mall.

The resort's corporate suites were on the eighteenth floor. Nick took the elevator up, found the one Karen Esco had given him over the phone, asked for her with the receptionist while displaying his ID, and was promptly shown back down a carpeted aisle to her office.

"Hi, Mr. Stokes." She smiled pleasantly, rose from behind her desk, and took his hand. "Let me bring you something to drink."

"That's all right, Karen."

"Are you sure? We have soda, juice, coffee . . ."

"I'm fine, really," Nick said. "If you don't mind, I'd like to get right to what you dug out of your files."

Karen nodded, motioned him into a chair in front of her desk, then went back around to her side and sat down. She was a good-looking blonde, maybe in her thirties, wearing white pearl-drop earrings, a smart charcoal-gray pantsuit, and suede peep-toe heels.

"I can't tell you how fortunate we are, Mr. Stokes," she said. "When we spoke on the phone, it didn't even occur to me that our offices had completely relocated since Stacy first started working at the resort. This entire *floor* wasn't even here. I believe the building only went up twelve stories at the time."

"But you were able to find Stacy's records in your computer system?"

"Only the recent ones. Going back a couple of years."

"I don't understand." Nick hesitated, recalling their brief conversation. "You told me—"

"Yes, that I'd located all of her files," she said. "They weren't in the system, though. That's the lucky part."

Nick waited as she opened a bottom drawer, leaned over to reach inside, and produced a thick stack of manila index folders.

"These and a few other batches of folders—I'm having my assistant bring them up to us right now—

cover an entire decade's worth of special-events reservations," she said. "They run almost from Stacy's first day on the job until our data-storage system went entirely paperless. That coincided with the hotel's last major overhaul. At that time, virtually every scrap of information in the computers more than five years old—relating to conference and party banquets, I mean—was deleted without backup."

Nick crossed his ankle over his knee. "Doesn't seem to make sense. They flush what's in the computers but hang on to records that take up all kinds of space?"

"That's just it," Karen said. "I gather there are corporate assessments showing how the names of patrons aren't relevant after so-and-so many years. You know, surveys on how they choose the places they hold their affairs, executive turnover rates for business clients, averages on the number of private bookers wishing to change banquet venues rather than return even after successful experiences . . ." Her voice dropped a notch. "But Stacy was the best. She stayed in touch with clients. Cultivated relationships with them. Bent over backward to make their events memorable. Sent cards on holidays, wedding anniversaries. She was full of get-up-and-go."

Nick tried to associate the person Karen was talking about with the broken, embittered woman he'd seen in the depressing gloom behind her blackout shades. It wasn't easy.

"These records—" he began.

"They were in a filing cabinet that didn't even belong where I found it."

"Which was?"

"At the rear of a basement storage area for our floral and catering supplies. It's massive, several rooms, closets galore," Karen said. "I'd forgotten all about the cabinet. Then it came to me that Stacy had it brought there when the hotel was renovated—and a short while after I was hired. She'd showed me around as part of my training." A pause. "The resort's lawyers were very quick to approve my showing you its contents once they reviewed it. Everyone here wants the person who kidnapped her caught."

Nick took a folder from the pile, saw that it was tabbed "Alderson Wedding/December 20, 2002," and spread it open. It was stuffed with paperwork for the affair—printed contracts, checklists, letters, and expense logs, plus Stacy Ebstein's hand-penciled floor layouts, seating arrangements, floral design sketches, price estimates, and scribbled notes.

"I told you over the phone that Stacy was meticulous," Karen said. "She took care of people the way she'd have wanted to be taken care of. That's probably the most important thing she impressed on me."

Nick closed the folder and put it back on the pile. He was thinking he could still make the press conference if he hurried, then get busy sorting through the files at the lab ASAP.

"You mentioned the rest of these were on the way," he said. "I don't mean to rush you. But I'd like to—"

Nick heard the wheels rolling up outside the office an instant before Karen nodded toward the door. He turned around in his chair and saw a young man standing in the hall with a large delivery cart, its upper basket filled with index folders, its bottom rack loaded with cardboard boxes.

It occurred to him that Hodges was going to go nuclear at the lab unless the evidence clerk serendipitously reappeared from wherever he might have scrammed.

"Andy can help you bring the files to your car," she said. "I'd only ask that you return them when you're finished."

Nick looked at her. "Sticking with tradition?"

"Something like that."

He nodded and stood. "You're a good friend to Stacy," he said. "I also want you to know how much I personally appreciate this."

Karen waved him off. "That's okay," she said, her eyes overbright with moisture as she rose to show him to the door. "Find the person who ruined an innocent woman's life, and I promise it will be thanks enough."

". . . and speaking on behalf of my office and the sheriff's department, I pledge to everyone in this town, residents and visitors, inked or not, pierced or otherwise, that your government and law-enforcement agencies have been galvanized by the recent spate of tattoo-related homicides," His Honor Fred Stancroft, former casino showroom manager and recently elected mayor of the city of Las Vegas, was saying from his podium. "As I said during my campaign, I am committed to lowering our violent-crime rate, whatever the particulars. Our skin belongs to us! And no—I repeat, *no*—bloodthirsty, maniacal tattoo killer or killer cult will deny us our basic right to safety and self-expression . . ."

Her hair blowing around her face, Catherine sat in the plaza outside city hall along with Jim Brass, a handful of LVPD officers, and fifteen or twenty reporters who'd been thrown out in the cold to hear Stancroft spout endlessly through his manicured Van Dyke beard, all of them looking irritated as they trembled in the brutal crosswinds between the building's tower and curved outer wing. Flanking Stancroft, meanwhile, was a coterie of aides and police officials, Ecklie among them, the undersheriff looking as if he wanted to drill himself into the pavement and stay out of sight until the mayor's rambling, disjointed statement, or perhaps that shivery Sunday in March, reached a merciful conclusion, whichever came first.

"I do not know the reason for the murderer's tattoo fixation," Stancroft went on. "I do not know whether these crimes are a vicious means of asserting power, sending a warped message, or possibly settling a feud. But to whoever may be orchestrating them, I want to be clear about my own message." Stancroft paused, sought out a television video operator hunched in front of him, and looked straight into the lens of the camera balanced on her shoulder. "We will take you down. We will bring you to trial and impose the maximum penalties the law permits. Tattoo violence is unacceptable, and rest assured, we will stem the tide. In a free and open society, you will be reminded that the colors on a man's skin are as irrelevant as the color *of* his skin . . ."

Catherine thought she saw Ecklie cringe at that. But maybe a wayward gust had just spun up beneath his overcoat. Tough call from her vantage.

She felt an elbow poke her side. Brass.

"Yeah?" she whispered.

"I've got a tip about politics," he said through the upturned collar of his coat. "Something this press conference establishes for a fact in my own head."

Catherine waited, looking at him out of the corner of her eye.

"When dicks like Stancroft can be voted into office," he said, "we've got serious goddamned problems."

Minutes after loading up his trunk with Stacy Ebstein's files, Nick was headed over to city hall on North Fourth Street when a voice crackled from the dashboard radio.

"CSI Stokes?"

He grabbed the mike. "Right, what's up?"

"This is Operator Conroy. You received a phone call about the Dorset case."

"'You' meaning the lab?"

"It was for you specifically, sir," Conroy said. *"The person had seen your name in a newspaper article. I gathered it indicated you're the primary investigator."*

Nick grunted and braked for a stoplight at the East Ogden intersection. Williams had probably passed his name along to a reporter.

"What'd he say?"

"She, sir," the operator said. *"Her name was—I hope I'm not mangling it—Beshlesko. Spelled B-e-s—"*

"That her first name?"

"No, sorry. The first's Anabelle."

"Annabelle Beshlesko. Rolls right off the tongue."

"You see what I meant, sir. A tricky one. She said I could call her Miss Annabelle."

"Uh-huh."

"Claimed to have some information about the murder but wouldn't give it to me or speak with anybody besides you. I assume because—"

"I know." Nick inwardly vowed to get back at Williams. "I'm the supposed primary."

"Yes, sir." The PCO paused. *"The woman insisted on talking to you in person, sir. She's on West Charleston."*

Nick asked for her exact location and frowned even before punching it into his GPS unit. "Okay, thanks. Out."

He racked his mike. Miss Annabelle was easily fifteen miles away. In fact, he'd have to stay on North Fourth and shoot onto the highway to get there.

The light changed, and Nick drove through the intersection. City hall was just a block up ahead on his right. He considered phoning Catherine to tell her about his radio call but knew she'd have her phone off at the press conference. Besides, what would it accomplish? And how much longer would the mayor jabber on, anyway? Well, now that he thought about it, the question reminded him of a joke somebody once told him. "How long can a horse run? Till it *stops*."

Be that as it may, he'd been on a hot streak. And meant to ride that streak till *it* stopped.

As Nick reached city hall, he saw the news vans with their satellite uplink dishes parked outside under some trees. It made him feel the slightest bit guilty for not joining Cath. Of course, she had Brass to commiserate with her. No point in all three of them sharing the misery.

He bore left driving by the vans, went on beneath the freeway overpass, then took the ramp for I-95 North out toward West Charleston. *Miss Annabelle, here I come.*

Nick reached the address he'd gotten from the PCO to find it belonged to Miss Annabelle's Psychic Readings, a tiny storefront squeezed between a discount drugstore and a pet groomer in a shabby

strip mall that resembled one of a trillion in outer
Vegas, its window decorated with a palmistry chart,
tarot cards, some neon planets and crescent moons
and stars, and a hokey, crackling blue-plasma-light
crystal ball that likewise made it anything but a
standout among spiritualist joints the world over.

He cut the engine and smiled a little ruefully as
he gazed out his windshield at the shop. A woman
was bent there in the recessed entryway picking
windblown fast-food wrappers up off the ground,
wearing a babushka around her head, a shawl
over her mouth, enormous dark sunglasses, and a
shapeless no-color peasant dress.

"Miss Annabelle, I presume," Nick muttered to
himself. Then he shook his head, thinking there
might be bigger wastes of time than attending press
conferences after all. Hoping, in fact, that she'd
climb aboard a broom and fly off toward the Be-
larusian forest or someplace equally remote before
he wound up wasting even more time than had
already been lost to the haunted winds driving out
to this part of town.

He exited the car and walked to the shop. Speaking of the wind, it had gotten downright blustery
out, the chill gusts plucking at the bill of his black
ball cap with the CSI patch displayed in front just
in case anybody mistook him for a shortstop on
the New York Yankees. Besides probably having
blown the trash up to her door, the wind was also
snapping and flapping the presumptive Miss Anna-

belle's dress around her small, scrawny body, giving Nick the sudden thought that she might not even need a magic broom to whisk her away to parts mysterious and ghostly.

"Miss Annabelle?" he said from a few steps in front of her, leaning over to snag a burger wrapper that had skittered away from her grasping fingers

The woman reached a hand out as he straightened and took the crumpled waxed paper into it. "Thank you," she said, speaking with a strong eastern European accent. *Da'ank you.* "You are Mr. Stokes, yes?"

He nodded, seeing her up close now. Looking at the portions of her face that the sunglasses, kerchief, and scarf hadn't hidden. And realizing at once that he hadn't wasted a moment heading out here.

"Come with me into the *ofisa,*" she said. "We must talk."

Nick could not have imagined a greater understatement if he'd tried.

"H'llo, crime lab. Greg Sanders speaking."

"Mr. Sanders," said the voice on the phone, "this is Hastings Watney, *Flash Ink*'s publisher and editor in chief."

Greg pulled himself up out of his habitual investigator's slouch at the multipurpose workstation he occasionally called his desk, holding the receiver closer to his ear. He'd left more voice messages than he could count at the magazine's main office number and shot off a similarly profuse barrage of e-mails to Watney's corporate address, explaining that he was a criminalist with the Vegas police and that he looked forward to somebody getting in touch with him before the weekend was over, all the while expecting there wouldn't be a soul who read or listened to anything he'd sent till Monday morning.

"I really appreciate you getting right back to me," he said. "As you know from my message—"

"Which one? The first, second, or thirty-seventh?"

"Ah, yeah," Greg said. "I did leave a few. But I'm sure you realize we have something to discuss."

"Why's that, bro?"

"Well, if you've heard what's happening here in Las Vegas . . ."

"We do get national news feeds here in Frisco," Watney said curtly. "Shame your town has a problem involving people with tattoos. I just don't see what it has to do with my magazine—"

"And Toronto," Greg interrupted.

"What?"

"There's also a problem up in Toronto."

"Toronto? I don't know anything about that."

"At least three people were killed north of the border after participating in last year's *Flash Ink* tattoo competition. They're all registered users of your social-media site."

"Hang on a second . . . I can't believe . . . are you *serious*?"

"This definitely isn't my idea of a practical joke," Greg said.

"I didn't say you were j—"

"Then take my word for it," Greg said. "Also, we've had three murders within the last twenty-four hours whose victims were your subscribers . . . and *Flash Ink: Las Vegas* contestants."

"Are you talking about that judge? Because I heard them talk about his body mods on TV and think I'd remember him."

"We consider his death a separate case. I can't be specific about it with you right now," Greg said. "But add the three deaths in Canada to what we've got on our hands, and that's a half-dozen known homicides linked to your website and reality show."

"It isn't my show," Watney said.

"What do you mean?"

"I mean, if you think we can have a give-and-take without specifics, cool. That's how cops work. On the other hand, I'm no cop. And I want it up-front that the show's a separate and distinct entity from the e-zine. We license our name to a production company with certain terms written into our contract. Creative input, approvals, but the contest format's their deal."

Greg took a breath, considered underscoring that he wasn't a cop, and decided it would probably fall on deaf ears. He'd identified himself as a criminalist in every one of his messages to Watney, and that was beside the point right now, anyway. "Mr.

Watney, let's start over," he said. "If you'll excuse my saying so, you sound kind of defensive—"

"Damn right, bro. The tattoo community gets enough horseshit pinned on it. You throw around hints my subscribers are offing each other like raged-out Neanderthals, it isn't appreciated."

"We aren't pinning anything on your community or the website," Greg said. "What we believe is that the killer might be trawling its photo galleries for his victims. And if you don't mind, we'd like to get in and see who's poked around certain areas."

"Get in?"

"Access your system logs."

"You're kidding me, right?"

"I already told you I wasn't," Greg said. "We're trying to find whoever's responsible for the killings."

"And trample all over our members' rights to confidentiality," Watney said. "Maybe you don't get it. *Flash Ink*'s into body-evo culture and techniques, but we're mainly about lifestyle advocacy."

"Yeah," Greg said. "And I'm thinking murder tops the list for putting a cramp in someone's lifestyle."

"Like I said, you don't get it. Not everywhere's New York, California, or Vegas. We got subscribers all over the place. They're either treated like they belong in Geekville or hide their mods because they worry their friends, families, and bosses might *start* treating them that way. They join the site, they can be themselves, network with people who won't tell them what to do with their own bodies. We blow that trust, we're done—"

"Your magazine's known for pushing the envelope," Greg cut in. "It was banned by a government oversight committee in Germany. If it features adult content—nudity, anything considered mutilating or sadomasochistic—and even if some of those people you're talking about are minors who subscribed without proof of age, you could be in violation of antiporn legislation."

"You want to bring out the hammer, fine. We've got lawyers for that."

"Bet they can recite the Constitution backward and forward."

"The Bill of Rights, too, man."

"Eyes closed, I'm sure," Greg said. "They work pro bono?"

"Huh?"

"Guys that smart don't have sale tags hanging off their designer suits," Greg said. "But they've usually got whopping hourly rates and expenses, and that's before they tack on court fees."

"So you're telling me what, exactly?"

"That I'm trying to stop a killer," Greg said. "And that it might be worth your while to cooperate before you lose any more of your subscriber base to him."

Silence at Watney's end of the line. Then a long expulsion of breath. "Okay, fine, I'll see what I can do, " he said. "Where you want to start?"

Greg pumped his fist in the air, thinking Archie was going to love this.

"With you putting me in touch with your custodian of records," he said.

"So, to reiterate, while ours is a city of fabulous dreams, a city where freedom and creativity reign, we are also a city that is serious about law and order. A city where serial murderers will not be tolerated for any reason!" Stancroft emphatically boomed into his mike.

Her lips numb from the icy wind, the tip of her nose stinging, Catherine sat among the mayor's captive audience, wondering exactly what city in the United States he supposed had found a *right* reason to give serial killers a pass.

"I realize some may be offended by tattoos and other bodily markings based on moral or religious views," he said. "But as we approach the Easter holiday, we must remember that ink only goes skin deep and that we are all God's children *under* the skin. In this time of rebirth, this season of new beginnings, I know the bloodthirsty homicidal lunatic prowling our streets, boulevards, and family attractions will be brought to a place of atonement and that he must soon answer for his massacre of the innocents . . ."

Catherine checked her wristwatch. After going at it for about twenty minutes, it sounded as if Stancroft finally might be bringing things to a wrap—and Nick was still a no-show. Even if he arrived that very moment, he'd probably escaped the worst of it, lucky him.

Her envy aside, she hoped he'd made some progress on the Tattoo Man case. Because it seemed to her that besides enhancing his reputation as a fool and mangling religious metaphors, Stancroft's idiotic rant about bloody massacres and whatnot was bound to stir up the very commotion he wanted to avoid once it was snipped into sensationalistic audio bites and hit the airwaves in time for the Monday morning commute.

She frowned, shoving her hands into her pockets. How had it gotten so miserably cold and windy out so *fast*?

"This a Sunday sermon or a press conference?" Brass whispered to her.

She gave him a sidewise glance and lowered her head so the cameras wouldn't catch her response. "Don't ask me, Jim," she said. "I can't stand sitting through either of 'em."

Lighted by muted stained-glass lamps and scented candles and separated from its back room by velvet drapes that dropped in heavy folds behind strings of hanging beads, Miss Annabelle's *ofisa*, as she referred to her fortune-telling shop, was small and squarish, with a table and wicker chairs on a maroon Oriental rug in the middle of the floor. The storefront display window and curtained-off rear accounted for two sides of the space, with a large

Egyptian zodiac circle occupying a third, and cubbyhole shelves holding various religious icons and mystical charms on the wall opposite.

Seated across from Nick at the table, Miss Annabelle had removed her sunglasses and shawl but left her kerchief on. Her face was tattooed with three sets of pale gray hands, their long, bony fingers tapering to inhuman claws. One pair appeared to be folded across her eyes. Depending on the tilt of her head, Nick was able to glimpse the outspread hands covering her ears. The third pair looked as if they were clasped over her mouth and chin.

See no evil, hear no evil, speak no evil.

With a single major exception, the story she'd told so far was much the same as the accounts given by Tattoo Man's other known victims. She'd left the *ofisa* after closing time one night about six months ago and was about to enter her parked car when someone came up behind her. She'd felt a hard, stunning blow to the back of her head, then another sensation she compared to a bee sting, before losing consciousness.

After that, her memory was ragged—full of dangling threads and wide-open holes. She recalled a buzzing noise of the sort Stacy Ebstein had described in her statements to detectives. Like Ebstein and Noble, she remembered suddenly awakening in a room with mirrored walls and the *gajo* standing behind her in a hood or a mask, speaking to her in the softest of voices.

"Gajo?" Nick asked.

"Someone who is not Romani," she said. "Like yourself."

Feeling vaguely disparaged, Nick nodded and motioned for her to continue. After briefly coming to in the room, she'd blacked out again for an unknown period, only to regain her senses late one night in an abandoned lot on the west side of town. She recalled having wandered the neighborhood for a while before finding a pay phone and placing a collect call to a member of her *famiglia*—her extended family—the members of which had been frantically searching everywhere for her for almost an entire week and who'd driven over to pick her up at once and . . . then gotten their first look at her unbelievably changed appearance.

Nick held up a hand to interrupt her. Similar story to the rest, with one glaring exception. He wanted the point clarified, though he had a feeling he knew what she'd tell him.

"Ma'am, why didn't you contact the police about any of this?"

She looked at Nick as if he'd asked how come she hadn't used her signal watch to summon Superman from his Fortress of Solitude.

"We take care of our own," she said simply. *"Gajo* law is not our law."

"Then why call me today? After all this time?"

"A man was killed."

"Judge Dorset, you mean."

She gave a nod. "When this happens, I cannot be silent."

Nick decided there was nothing to gain by pressing her to elaborate. He had more basic and critical questions that needed asking—though, again, he didn't figure they'd get him much mileage. "Do you have any idea why someone would do this to you? Or who it might be?"

"Maybe," she said slowly. "I think maybe so."

Nick opened his mouth. "You do?" Closed it again. Then he waited in silence a moment, watching her eyes grow distant with recollection.

"Ten years ago," she said, "a young boy was taken from his father. Dumas . . ."

Kyle Dumas? Nick thought, consciously willing his jaw not to drop again. While sloughing through Mitchell Noble's files, he had noticed the boy's name several times, indexed along with cross-references to the photos of his father holding his body, the Dorset court docket log, and the attached newspaper stories. "Go on," he said. "Please."

"In this time, my *ofisa* is not here."

"It was in a different location then?"

"Yes."

"And where was that?"

"Shhtoort Avenue," she said.

Shtoor—? "Stewart Avenue?" Nick said, wrestling with her pronunciation.

"Yes."

"Near the Starglow?"

"It is one mile away," she replied, nodding. "Maybe less."

Nick was remembering every detail he could about the Dumas case, reminding himself not to share too many of them with Miss Annabelle. He did not want to color her recollections with anything he might have read.

"How is what happened to you connected to the boy's kidnapping?" he asked.

"They say the boy is with his father, yes? That the father leaves him in store to take car out of parking lot . . ."

Close, Nick thought. It hadn't actually been a store but rather the Desert Game video arcade on Main and Fremont, right past the mall. Frank Dumas, the father, had taken him there on a Sunday afternoon, leaving his car around the corner in the municipal garage.

"Back then, I live in apartment over *ofisa*," Miss Annabelle was saying. "There is market near to it, I often go to buy things . . ."

"Hanson's Grocery?" Nick said.

"Yes."

Nick knew the area. The grocery was on South Main northwest of the Starglow and video arcade, like Miss Annabelle's old parlor. But it was even closer to them, probably an eighth of a mile away, tops.

"Tell me about the day Kyle Dumas was abducted," he said.

She looked at him, but her eyes seemed distant. "I go to market, shop for many groceries, walk back to *ofisa* with wagon. When I cross street, I see white truck . . . no, not truck . . . eh . . ." She paused, groping for the right word, shaking her head in frustration.

"A van?" Nick said.

"Yes, van," she said. "It make turn in front of me, drive too fast. Man is driving, and there is little boy in back." She made a pushing gesture with her hands. "I can see boy doing this by the window. And he is crying."

"You're sure about all that?"

"Yes." Her voice trembled slightly. "I can re-member like it is this minute. Wagon comes close to sidewalk . . . tires make loud noise . . . how you say?"

"They were screeching?"

"Yes. Like that. I pull wagon back, almost fall, look inside . . . and there is the boy."

"Was there anything written on the side of the van? A company name?"

Miss Annabelle shook her head.

Nick looked at her. "Nothing?" he said. "You're positive?"

She shook her head again. "This is also what police ask me. It is next day, I think. They come to every store in neighborhood with pictures of boy. Come to my *ofisa*. And I say to them the same thing."

"That you recognized Kyle Dumas."

"Yes."

"But that the van you saw had no writing on its side."

"Yes."

"What about the driver? Did they show you photographs of the man they believed was responsible for taking Kyle?"

"Later, yes."

"So they paid you more than just a single visit?"

"Many," she said. "The first time, it is a police officer. After another week, two weeks, detectives. They come again. And then again. When they show me pictures of a van, I say it is different from the one I see. When they show me the man in their pictures, I tell them he is *not* who was with the boy."

"And their pictures of the vehicle . . ."

"It is white, yes. But with writing on door, *Leez-terndoostral.*"

Nick thought a moment. "Would that be two words? Lester Industrial?"

"Yes . . . is it."

He nodded, his thoughts again returning to Noble's archive disc. According to the material Nick had reviewed—sacrificing a night of red-hot Tex-Mex food and music in the process—the Lester Industrial Equipment Supplies Company was where the only real suspect in the kidnapping, Ronald Clarkson, had worked as a repair and deliveryman.

Prosecutors had insisted Clarkson pulled Kyle into the van, sped off, then killed him before dumping his corpse.

"Ma'am," Nick said, "I appreciate you going through all this and think I have an idea why you've done it. But I need to hear it in your own words. How does it all connect to what happened to you?"

Miss Annabelle favored him with a pained, humorless smile. "To me," she said. "And the judge, eh?"

Nick waited. Maybe it was that he was running on empty, but that smile seemed to give an illusion of elasticity to the tattooed hands around her mouth, as if their clawed fingers were extending to keep her from speaking.

He suppressed a chill as Miss Annabelle rose to her feet, went over to the chest across the room, and opened it, extracting a hardboard portfolio bound in pebbled cowhide leather. When she carried it to the table, she did not return to her chair but instead set it down in front of Nick and stood beside him, leafing through it.

He recognized many of the newspaper photos and articles inside from Noble's files, saw some that hadn't been on the disc. All of them related to the Dumas murder.

Miss Annabelle turned a page, briefly looked over an article, flipped to another page. And finally came to the photo Mitchell Noble had sold to the *Globe News*. Frank Dumas crouched in a sagebrush barren, cradling the battered, lifeless body of his son in his arms.

"You *gajos*, you say Gypsies are liars," she said. "But ten years ago, I tell the truth to your police. I would not help the killer of a child walk free. I would not see the wrong man punished for such a terrible crime. The judge, too, would not allow this to be." She tapped the photo's plastic cover sheet. "Now see what *he* does. To us."

You, Dorset, Mitchell Noble, and Stacy Ebstein. "You really think it's him? The boy's father?"

The woman looked down over his shoulder. "The present is just this moment and so has only a moment's weight. But the past is all the moments that have come before. If we carry their weight, it can break us."

Nick supposed he agreed, though that led to another question or two he felt it was incumbent on him to pose, even if he could guess at their answers. "Why would he do it, though? What's he trying to accomplish?"

She smiled again, the thin gray hands seeming to extend themselves across her mouth. Nick suddenly thought of the Silly Putty he'd played with as a kid, pressing a wad over newsprint cartoons and photos to transfer the image onto it, then stretching the stuff to distort the image. It was not a pleasant association under the circumstances.

"This is the nightmare he cannot change," Miss Annabelle said, giving the photo another tap. And putting a fingertip to her face, she added, "This is the dream he makes."

*   *   *

After leaving the church in Miriam shortly before the conclusion of services, he had walked back to the railway depot outside town, again giving himself time to appreciate the high-country scenery. The mass had left him energized, and he believed his legs could have taken him twice, perhaps three times, as far as the station. He imagined himself walking without limitations, over and around mountains, down into gaping rifts in the earth, and up their arid, wrinkled sides onto lonely desert flats. And then walking on, nothing to stop him, no calling him back, his heels kicking up gravel and dust, striding over the horizon to dissipate like a cloud of fine, powdery sand over some hazy blue-and-dun vanishing point.

He was almost saddened when he reached the station. It had been enjoyable letting his mind roam, but now there was a great deal to do. He knew this would be his last trip to Miriam. He would stay overnight, drive into town for the boy, and then head east, toward Las Vegas.

It struck him that he had seen the last of the city, too. That when tomorrow came, he would cut loose what was behind and ahead of him, his past and future. At the altar he had prepared to release the boy's spirit, his existence would crystallize to an eternal Now.

Lamb of God, who take away the sins of the world, grant us peace.

On the road outside the parking area to his right,

he glanced over his opposite shoulder toward the trading post, noticed that the "Open" sign was in the door. He'd brought the knife he meant to use in his trunk, but seeing the trading post earlier had made him think to honor his sacrifice with the purity of unblooded steel.

He turned and went inside.

"G'mornin'—and congratulations!"

He looked over at the sales counter near the entrance. Grinning affably at him from behind it was a tall, husky man in a flannel work shirt with tousled red hair and a fiery beard.

"Am I a winner?" he asked the bearded man.

"You betcha," the shopkeeper said. "First person through the door on Sunday gets ten percent off his purchases. And that's on top of any other discounts."

He gave the shopkeeper a pleasant smile. "I didn't see the sign."

"That's 'cause I just made the policy up, my friend, so do me a favor and keep quiet about it!"

The shopkeeper laughed now, and he laughed along with him, the sound issuing from his throat like an old recording of someone who had since died.

"I'm Lee Rayburn, keeper of the post," the bearded man said, coming down the counter to where he stood. He thrust out a hand. "I take it you're here on a day trip?"

"A little longer, I hope," he said as they shook. "I came out for some hunting."

Rayburn pulled a slight face. "Oh . . . no kiddin'."

"You sound surprised."

"Maybe a little," Rayburn said. "Most times, we get people out here in the fall for elk and prong-horn season. This part o' year, there's just fur bearers. Plus, I thought I saw you come in from town like you was takin' in the sights."

He regarded Rayburn a moment, visualizing him with a brown mane and the curved horns of a pronghorn buck.

"Actually, I went to mass," he said. "The beautiful church overlooking the valley."

Rayburn nodded. "Our Lady of Guidance."

"That's it . . . there was a full congregation."

"Always is up on Easter," Rayburn said. "But now you're gonna make me feel guilty about not attendin'."

"Ah, but a man's reach should exceed his grasp, or what's a heaven for?" he said, prompting a slightly curious look from Rayburn. "An old quote, don't mind me. Back to the hunting . . . I'm here for the small game and thought I would buy a new knife. A quality blade."

"Particular, huh? Think I've got somethin' might be just the thing for you."

He smiled and nodded. Molded silicone antlers, flat with the forward-pointing tine, subtle pigments for a bony appearance. And then a wide black band running up the middle of the face.

Rayburn came around the counter and led the

way back past shelves of Native American trinkets, Western art and needlework, saddlery, wildlife taxidermy, outdoor clothing, and other locally manufactured items. The showcase containing his assorted knives was at the rear of the shop under wall racks of archery equipment, shotguns, and rifles. He stepped behind it, got his key ring out of his pocket, and unlocked the rear sliding panel.

"If you don't mind spendin' a bit extra, this Bowie's quality can't be beat." Rayburn reached inside and set a knife on top of the case. "Guy who made it's a pal of mine from out near Dayton. Go ahead 'n' check out the feel."

He gripped the knife and lifted it off the case. The handle was a dark, stained wood, its pins and pommel heavy brass. "It's solid . . . nicely balanced," he said, turning his wrist to examine it. "Very well constructed."

"Ain't no wall hanger, for sure," Rayburn said. "The blade's hand-forged—with a hammer 'n' anvil, you know? Ten inches of virgin steel."

He looked at Rayburn. "Is that true?"

"Guaranteed," the trading post owner said. "I don't like to give the hard sell. But even decent commercial knives nowadays use cheap, recycled steel. My friend has his shipped from Japan. Can't get purer. They say it's so strong a bullet shot from a gun won't chip it. Called tamaha-somethin'-or-other."

"Tamahagane. Jewel steel. I've heard of it."

Rayburn looked impressed. "Well," he said. "Guess I can just keep my mouth shut, then."

He turned it in his fist once more, eyes on the blade. "Yes," he said under his breath. "It should be pure."

"Excuse me?"

Looking up at the shopkeeper, he carefully passed the knife back over the counter to him.

"I'll take it," he said.

"Hey, Arch, ready for some great news?" Greg asked, swerving into his lab.

Archie pushed out his lips and expelled a breath to make the noise you got by flapping them. He was thinking Greg's line was a perfect setup for dumping a fresh ton of work on his lap. "I'm a sponge," he said. "Spill it out, I'll soak it up."

"Ray really should hear this, too." Greg glanced around as if he might be camouflaged against the cubicle walls. "You see him anywhere?"

Archie shrugged. "He told me he'd be taking a nap in the morgue."

Greg looked at him questioningly.

"In that morgue *closet* he used for an office once upon a time," Archie clarified. "At least, I think it's where he meant. He still keeps a cot in there."

"Hope you're right," Greg said. "I'd hate to see him shoved into cold storage by mistake."

Archie waited in silence. A few moments earlier, he'd logged off the LVPD, Department of Transportation, and Las Vegas government video databases, having downloaded dozens of compressed files from traffic-monitoring and red-light cameras that had been operative in the downtown area ten years ago—specifically on the date Nick had requested. If Greg's appearance didn't put a crimp in things, and he was afraid it might, he planned on leaving the office for a coffee fix before he started the complicated task of putting together a mosaic for Nick's desired time span.

"All right, check it out," Greg said. "I spoke to the custodian of records at *Flash Ink*, got the internal codes for accessing the log-in and browser histories of its members."

Archie looked at him. "That is good news," he said.

"The word I used was *great*," Greg said. "Why the reined enthusiasm?"

"Because the site has ten thousand registered users," Archie said. "And because we have to keep our fingers crossed that our Internet stalker prowled his victims' galleries often enough for him to stick out in the crowd."

Greg gave him a look. "Ever go browsing in a specialty shop, Arch?"

"Sure. What's the specialty?"

"Dunno. High-end designer computer geekware. Props from classic Hollywood space operas. You tell me," Greg said. "This isn't impulse shopping. The merch is too rare. It's stuff you really, really want that's also really, really hard to find—and even harder to get your hands on. If you could plunk down a wad of cash, back a truck up to the place, and empty it out, you would. But there's no way that's possible . . ."

"So you have to choose between things," Archie said, nodding. "Seriously look at them."

"More than once. Maybe look at them a bunch of times before making your decision."

Archie had kept nodding his head. "I see what you mean," he said. "All right, listen. Far as your great news . . . if you give me those codes, I can take a little break from what I've been doing for Nick. Try to—" He suddenly broke off, his eyes flicking past Greg to the entryway behind him.

Greg turned just as Nick plunged through the door from the hall, grinding to an abrupt halt in the bare nick of time to avoid a collision, then stepping in front of him with nary a word of acknowledgment. "Archie. What's happening? How's it coming with those traffic videos?"

Archie was thinking it was high time he grew an extra pair of arms. Or should he just skip ahead to cloning himself? Maybe he could find the requisite innovative biotech at that specialty shop Greg had mentioned. "I've got everything available from the day you wanted," he said. "It'll take some time to—"

Nick shook his head to interrupt him. "C'mon, man," he said. "Let's get it done *now*."

*   *   *

"Cath, you're back," Nick said. "Where've you been?"

Catherine entered Archie's lab, a Styrofoam coffee cup in her hand. "Home," she said. "I make an appearance every so often to see if Lindsey'll recognize me."

"How'd it go?"

"I showed up," she said with a prickly look. "That started us off on the right foot. And incidentally, I don't recall noticing your presence at the press conference."

Nick cleared his throat. "I meant to call, got sidetracked like you wouldn't believe." He motioned toward Archie and his console. "You're going to have to see what we did here."

Catherine peeled the tab back from the coffee's lid. The computer monitor showed a black-and-white photomap with color directional symbols above a zoom bar on the upper left. A digital time stamp at the upper right-hand corner of the screen read, "4/19 2:55 P.M." She peered at the image. "Looks like a traffic cam shot from downtown," she said. "Not a recent one, judging from those oil guzzlers on the road."

"It's ten years old," Nick said. "Main and Fremont Streets. Right outside the covered mall at the intersection where Fremont divides the north and south sides of Main Street."

"And its significance is . . . ?"

"April nineteenth is the day a nine-year-old boy

named Kyle Dumas was abducted from the Desert Game video arcade," he said. "It isn't in the picture because the cameras were positioned to monitor two-way traffic along Main, and the arcade's at the end of Fremont. Under the canopy—"

"Where there's obviously no traffic," Catherine said.

Archie was nodding. "We tried to get security-camera images from hotels and casinos inside the mall but came up blank. It was too long ago, and those places have all cleaned house," he said. "Then I had the idea of checking police and government databases for their traffic and stoplight camera archives . . . and got lucky."

She frowned with interest. "Good thing *they* never get around to cleaning house."

"A real good thing. Less than a week later, on Easter Sunday, some hikers find Kyle's body in Red Rock Canyon. COD is a broken neck."

Catherine's lip ticced slightly. "Was he molested?"

"No," Nick said. "The day Kyle's kidnapped, his dad takes him along while he runs some errands. Frank Dumas is a single parent. His wife died in an accident when Kyle was still an infant. He's an artist for a graphic-design outfit at his day job but also sells his prints, paintings, and sculptures in galleries. Has a decent following for his work, too."

"Does the work include tattoos?"

"Not that we know—but give me a minute,"

Nick said. "Frank's on a heavy-duty shopping run. Art supplies, Easter decorations, groceries for their holiday dinner . . . he's trying to cram it all into his day off. He promises the kid he'll take him to the arcade as a reward for dragging him everywhere in town, brings him there when he's done, spends maybe an hour there with him. Then figures it's time to get home and heads out to get his car out of the indoor parking garage one block over and across the street. On the east side of Carson and South Main."

"That's next door to the Starglow Hotel."

"Check."

"Where Stacy Ebstein worked, isn't it?"

"Check again," Nick said. "We'll get to her in a while. But for now, I want to stick to Frank Dumas and his son."

Catherine nodded. "So Kyle's left *unattended*?" she said sharply.

"Yeah, Cath. A mistake. But he still has some tokens for those games, and he's pleading with Dad to let him finish. I know you've been there."

She pouched her cheeks, expelled a breath. "Suppose I have," she said. "Kids can lay it on thick."

"Plus the two of them are loaded down with packages from all this shopping they've done."

Catherine looked thoughtful as she considered that. "One thing . . . if I'm not mistaken, Desert Game runs the whole length of the block from Fremont to Carson Street."

"Right, you can see that on our map." Nick pointed it out. "There's a front entrance under the canopy, a rear entrance facing Carson."

"Doesn't the Carson Street entrance lead right to an outdoor parking area? On the same side of the street as the arcade?"

"Uh-huh."

"Wonder why Frank didn't leave his car there instead of *across* Main Street. It's closer, more convenient . . ."

"I'm guessing the lot was filled up. It's where all your mall visitors and employees leave their vehicles and where trucks pull in for pickups and deliveries. Those service areas use up big heaps of space."

Catherine was nodding. "Sounds logical. This *is* just before Bunny Day. Busy, busy."

"Right," Nick said. "Anyway, right up on three o'clock, when the image you're seeing was taken, Frank tells his son to finish up whatever game he's playing and keep an eye on their bags. He figures it'll only take a couple of minutes to hustle across the street for the car, pull into the service area right out back of the arcade, and hurry in to pick up Kyle. Warns him not to leave the place in the meantime."

"And of course, Kyle pays no attention to him."

"He actually does, Cath—until something happens to make him stop," Nick said. "Archie, center and zoom in on the crosswalk outside the mall."

He nodded, clicked his mouse to drag the map, then clicked again to move in for a close-up.

"Tighter, Arch, on the guy with the beard," Nick said. "That's it. Now, circle him."

Catherine grunted. The bearded man in the crosswalk heading toward the opposite side of Main appeared to be of average height and weight and had on a denim jacket and jeans. "Frank Dumas?"

"You got it," Nick said. "Remember, this is at a couple of minutes to three. Now, let's move ahead to three-oh-one. The garage's exit."

Archie clicked and dragged. And then Catherine was looking at an image of a two-car smashup in front of the exit ramp on Carson Street, the traffic on Main visibly clotted around the vehicles. "Frank got stuck in the garage," she said.

"Couldn't get out because of the accident," Nick said. "He was in a row of cars on the ramp for more than twenty minutes till the tow trucks came."

"And meanwhile, back at the arcade, Kyle's getting worried."

"He's used up his tokens, can't figure out where his dad went," Nick said, nodding. "Then, sometime after three o'clock and before three-fifteen, he goes outside the rear entrance for a look."

"The rear because that's where his dad went out . . ."

"Being closest to Carson, right," Nick said.

The creases on Catherine's forehead deepened

as she stared at the screen. "It's another blind spot. Your map doesn't show either entrance to the arcade."

"True," Nick said. "But it shows enough of what was going on around it to help us. See, Archie and I started out looking for one thing and found it . . . and then found something else besides. So if I can just get back to Kyle Dumas. . . ."

He steps out Desert Game's rear entrance, wondering why his father hasn't returned yet, his young face cinched with the anxious concern of a young boy who isn't quite as mature and independent as he'd fancied. He's somehow managed to bring along all the bags he'd been entrusted to watch, hanging the ones with handles over his arms and wrists, half carrying, half pulling the rest across the floor of the arcade onto the pavement.

Kyle becomes aware of the commotion the moment he hits the street. He looks to his right, toward South Main Street and the garage entrance, where horns are honking in the growing logjam caused by the accident. There are rubberneckers peering out the windows of their vehicles, pedestrian gawkers, and then suddenly the wail of police sirens. Soon those patrol cars come screaming up with their roof bars flashing, and the tow trucks that had been monitoring their emergency radio calls are converging on the scene like bees, spinning off more glaring dashes of light. And still Kyle's father is nowhere to be found.

Standing outside the arcade, his anxiousness swells to greater trepidation and eventually to full-blown fear. His father told him he would be back in a couple of minutes, and now he's been gone much longer. It is uncertain whether the boy is even aware how much time has passed—in his increasing panic, the ten or fifteen minutes since then might feel like half an hour or more. He's likely lost track. What's beyond doubt, however, is that his father's absence has stretched on well beyond his expectations and that there are squad cars and tow trucks right in front of the garage where his father parked and that he's been left here to wait, left alone, and is feeling small, confused, and helpless.

It is precisely at this vulnerable moment, amid all the confusion on the street, that the stranger approaches Kyle from his white van.

"Hold it, Nick, what van?" Catherine asked with a slight shake of her head.

Nick looked at her. "That's just it," he said. "A white van owned by an outfit called Lester Industrial Equipment is pulled up to the arcade in one of those loading and delivery areas near the back entrance. We know it's been there at least an hour because witnesses see it and Lester Industrial has records. The driver's a guy name of Ronald Clarkson, and he's been working on Desert Game's air circulation system—"

Perhaps the driver of the van says something to turn Kyle's attention momentarily from the scene of the car accident, voicing a comment that lures him or a question that distracts him. Or possibly he steals up on him without a sound. He might approach from behind, from one side, from in front of him. No one remembers him lingering near the boy. No one sees him make the snatch.

What is undeniable is that it happens quickly—almost in the blink of an eye. The driver seizes the boy, forces him into the rear of the van, and locks him in as he screams out for help.

The witnesses—and the problem is that there are very few, just a handful of shoppers getting in and out of their cars and a gift-shop employee returning from a break— are in accord remembering the boy's cries, the slam of a vehicle's door or hatch suddenly aborting them, and then looking around to see the white Lester Industrial van career out of the parking lot, its engine revving as it peels right onto Main Street, bearing north, slowing just long enough to squeeze through the worsening bottleneck caused by the accident—which is thickest on the far side of the street, where the collision occurred—and then head on past it. . . .

"Bring us to three-seventeen, Arch. Corner of Fremont and Main," Nick said.

Archie glided his mouse over its pad. The Lester Industrial Equipment van could clearly be seen in the intersection as it bore toward North Main with the Starglow to the left and the pedestrian mall to the right.

"Okay, great. Now, pan so we can get a look at that woman at the curb. The one about to cross the street outside the mall."

Archie clicked and dragged.

"That's her right there," Nick said. "Zoom in on

her a little more . . . a little more . . . let's keep it right there. We're losing some definition."

"It's Stacy Ebstein," Catherine observed. She'd moved closer to the screen for a good look at the pretty brunette with a shopping bag in her hand. "The van went speeding past her."

"Cut right in *front* of her, Cath," Nick said. "Notice the driver's blowing through a red light."

"Did she give some sort of witness statement?"

Nick shook his head no.

"Then—" Catherine blinked. "Wait, those photos of Stacy's tattooed face. The *clock* . . ."

"Its hands point to three-fifteen," Nick said. "I figured that meant something from the beginning but at first didn't know what. Then I found a photo and some articles about the abduction in Mike Noble's archives, saw that it took place across from the Starglow Hotel, and decided we'd better find out exactly when it happened—and where Stacy was at that date and time."

"So you went to get hold of Stacy's records at the Starglow . . ."

"And they told us she was busy setting up a corporate dinner," Nick said. "That afternoon, she ran out of the hotel on an errand—it was to pick up some last-minute frills for the banquet—and was hurrying back when the van crossed her path."

"Did you get that from Mitchell Noble's files?"

Nick shook his head again.

"Then how'd you know? If she never mentioned

it to the police or detectives and didn't tell you and Sidle anything about it . . . ?"

"There's a fourth Tattoo Man victim," Nick said. "Miss Annabelle, a Gypsy psychic. My tongue's too dog-tired to pronounce her last name without tripping over itself right now. She never reported her kidnapping to the police."

Catherine was staring at him. "How'd you get a line on her?"

"I didn't. She contacted *us*," Nick said. "Miss A's my reason for missing the press conference. I needed to head over to her place, hear her part of story. And she had plenty to add that I didn't know." He paused. "She's also got a whole album full of newspaper articles on the Dumas case. I found a piece written maybe a month after the abduction about the lack of police witnesses. A columnist for the paper interviewed everybody around, spoke with someone identified as an event planner at the Starglow."

"No name?"

"The columnist said she asked to stay anonymous. Not that it would've been hard for anybody to figure out who she was. Stacy Ebstein was the only one there with that job title."

"What'd she have to say?"

"Not much. She remembered a white van almost running her over. After hearing about Kyle Dumas on the news, she guessed it must've been the getaway vehicle. But she was in too much of a hurry to notice anything else about it."

"Then why'd this writer bother quoting her?"

"In a way, I think it made his whole point in a nutshell," Nick said. "A child's grabbed in plain sight. Middle of the afternoon, one of the busiest sections of town. He's asking how nobody sees it happen. And Stacy kind of represents your average person. Blinders on, rushing around—"

"Caught up in trying to beat the clock," Catherine said. "Like the clock on Stacy Ebstein's face. Our writer wasn't alone using her to illustrate a point, Nick."

They looked at each other for a long moment.

"Your mind reader—" she began.

"Psychic," Nick said.

"Whatever." Catherine frowned. "You told me she had new information."

He nodded. "Archie, take us to three twenty-six. Main and Carson. Wait to go in tight."

On his screen, the traffic along Main was now spaced apart in normal patterns, the road seemingly open and clear. Although a police car was still parked between the Starglow and the indoor garage, the two cars involved in the accident had been removed, leaving shards of broken glass as the only evidence of their impact.

"Didn't take long to get the mess cleaned up," Catherine said. "A half hour or so, huh?"

"And keep in mind this is eleven minutes after we saw the Lester van take off," Nick said. "Arch, drag and zoom to the outdoor parking-lot exit."

Again the lot itself was a mass of black pixels.

But Catherine could see the lowered curb where vehicles would exit onto Main Street, and leaving it in the frame, angling south—

Her upper and lower molars met. "Another white van."

"No writing, no markings. Just moseys out of there when everything's quieted down," Nick said. "Okay, Arch. Now, show us the front tag."

He went in on it. It was a California license plate, plain white like the van, the state's name written in red script above the blue tag numbers.

"That's either stolen or a fake. I ran a check with the California DMV, and no van was ever registered with it, white or otherwise," Nick said. "If we follow this one south on Main and match the time stamps to the traffic-cam images, we'll see that it travels along nice 'n' easy till it's left the police car and the mall way behind. But when the driver reaches Stewart Avenue a few minutes later . . ."

Archie had already jumped ahead, the stamp on his frozen screen image reading, "Stewart/N. 1st Street. 3:31 P.M."

Turned off Main now, the white van was heading southeast on the corner of Stewart, a woman in a peasant dress also visible in the frame.

"That's Miss Annabelle pushing her shopping cart," Nick said. "You can't tell from the still shot, but the driver's burning rubber around that corner. We can play you the full video footage, and you'd see."

"Where's he headed?"

"The video tracks the van almost to Eastern Avenue before we finally lose it."

"Lousy neighborhood, no traffic cams."

"That's how it goes," Nick said. "The time stamps on the video we've *got* tell us he was doing almost seventy miles an hour on city streets. I'd bet he turned onto Eastern, took it to the highway. From there, it's anybody's guess whether he went straight to Red Rock Canyon or detoured somewhere."

"And Miss Annabelle . . . what did she see that tells us the driver's anything but a speed demon?"

Nick looked at her. "She saw the boy," he said. "Through a rear window. He was hysterical, banging his hands against it. But when she told detectives about it, nobody paid attention."

She stared at him. "Nick . . . *why*?"

"Your guess is as good as mine. But we're talking a long time ago . . . things were different. This was before Grissom headed the CSI unit. Even before Brass had the job. He was just working his way up as a detective after transferring from Jersey . . ."

"And there's the white Lester van outside the arcade."

"And its driver, Ronald Clarkson, who had the opportunity to hunt out Kyle in the arcade. Clarkson had a prior claim of sexual harassment against him. It was deemed totally wrongful—the woman even apologized. But you know how it goes."

Catherine nodded. "Hard to live down that sort of accusation."

"Like it's hard for people to believe a Gypsy, especially when they've locked in on a suspect," Nick said. "The detectives who spoke to her never even filed her statement, but she eventually got in touch with the *Vegas Metro* reporter doing his series. The judge alludes to her statement in his ruling summary, but he's indirect . . . I'm guessing because Clarkson's lawyers didn't hear about it in time to include it in their motions."

"Were there reprimands?"

Nick shrugged. "If not, it's never too late," he said. "Luckily for Clarkson, Judge Dorset never saw enough evidence against him to have the case go to trial."

"And Clarkson . . . why was he speeding from the scene?"

"Easy," Nick said. "He had another appointment."

"That was confirmed by . . . ?"

"His boss and the client. When he saw a chance to shoot through the jam-up on Main, he took it, figuring he'd be stuck there otherwise," Nick said. "The driver of the plain white van had everybody deked. Maybe he saw the Lester van and figured it might help confuse things. Or maybe he didn't and just sat there in the parking lot waiting for things to quiet down before he gunned out. Probably had the boy subdued in back . . ."

Catherine closed her eyes, massaged her brow

with her fingertips. She could see it all too vividly.

The killer holds Kyle Dumas in the van's rear section, covering his mouth to mute his scream from passersby, restraining him there in back. Taking his time, waiting for the majority of police officers to leave the scene, then climbing into the front of the van and slowly driving away. Whether he used brute force to hold the boy or had him bound, Kyle somehow gains enough freedom of movement to begin pounding on the van's windows before it reaches Miss Annabelle at the corner of Stewart, but by then, it is too late. His captor is already speeding on toward the highway.

Her eyes opened. "After they found the body in Red Rock, what did the trace evidence show? Besides that he was unmolested?"

"Not much," Nick said. "No fingerprints. No hair. Fiber transfers were inconclusive. To make matters worse, his father got there before the body was removed. The news stringers pick up a four-one-nine over the police band, and next thing you know, Dumas hears about a dead boy in Red Rock on his television or radio. Shoots over in his car before the uniforms arrive, sees his son in the ditch, then pushes his way down and picks up the body. It winds up as a front-page headline photo."

Catherine looked at him. "I'm guessing the shutterbug's Mitchell Noble."

Nick slowly nodded his head. "It was submitted to Dorset by Clarkson's lawyers in a motion to exclude evidence—such as there might've been—on grounds of contamination."

"With good reason, too." Catherine sat there looking thoughtful. "Our tattooer gives the judge who dismissed the case a king's crown, monocle, and kisses on his ass. Gives a clock to the woman who didn't see anything because she happened to be rushing to work. Gives a camera to Noble, who takes a picture that helped get the case dismissed . . ."

"And gives a see-no-evil mask to Miss Annabelle, who threw more cold water on the prosecution," Nick said.

Silence. Catherine's eyes were on him. "Do you know when anybody last saw Frank Dumas?"

"Not for sure. But the house he lived in with Kyle is his most current address, and public records show he sold it."

"Sold it *when*, Nicky?"

Nick was silent for a very long time, his gaze meeting hers. "Ten years ago," he said. "Give or take."

10

Out on the ridge, the coyote's baying cries of pain had diminished to feeble bleats and whimpers toward evening and then finally ceased altogether.

Fatigued, Bockem was grateful for the silence as he prepared to tap out a simple five-letter message on his notebook computer. He had labored on his newest gallery items throughout the afternoon, as might have been expected with art created on their large scale. But when evening had fallen outside the cabin, he had happily found himself past the most delicate, time-consuming stages—one of the pelts tumbling in the drum as its companion piece drained off fluids in a dish-drying rack over the sink. After showering, he had gone into the bedroom and plugged the laptop into a cable connection at a small writing desk.

Ever his father's son, Bockem considered himself as much an enthusiast as an astute dealer and so had decided to follow his inclination to mount and auction off the pieces together. In his connoisseur's

heart, he felt that separating them, even option-
ally, would be a shame for aesthetic reasons, while
Bockem the shrewd entrepreneur was willing to
gamble that they would draw higher or equal value
as a diptych. There was no conflict within him.

He had been taught long ago that it was always
preferable to service the high-end patron rather
than pander to the low. His was an elite group, a
secret fellowship of sorts. More than a handful of
them shared an obsession that had been passed on
from a previous generation and that, like his own,
was in and of the blood.

Chenard, for example. Although Bockem had
been purposefully blunt with him, he appreciated
his pedigree and his passion. While it went unspo-
ken between them, the frisson they felt on discov-
ering an extraordinary work was without question
one and the same.

Now, Bockem opened his Web browser, navi-
gated to a popular social-networking website, and
logged on with his user name and password. Its
millions of daily users would send brief, text-based
personal-status updates to its readers, or subscribers. Although the great majority chose for their
messages to be publicly viewable, Bockem had
opted for a locked account whose posts could be
read only by members he approved.

Bockem had just twelve approved readers, and
the update he was about to send could not have
been more basic. There was no reason to use cryp-

tic language or codes, since the content was hardly important. For all real purposes, the sending and receipt of his post constituted its entire message.

Vaguely aware of the *slap-slap-slap* of the skin against the sides of the drum, Bockem typed in his update and clicked the onscreen "Share" button. Then he sat back in his chair and relaxed, knowing the message had been instantaneously delivered to his subscribers.

"Chirp," it read.

Basic.

"If we wish to understand the human capacity for acts of atrocious violence, we must be willing to recognize it within ourselves," Ray Langston said. "Only then can we begin our transformation."

He looked out over the university's lecture room and was glad to see it filled with young, interested faces. He'd worried about a light turnout. This was the first academic talk he'd given since the publication of his book on the psychopathology of serial murderers, and its sales had hardly broken records.

"Our antlers mark us as a species. Their removal is at best partial and temporary," Langston went on, looking at a young man with a large, sweeping pair in the front row. He tapped his own head and felt the bandages over his stumps. "The koi are relentless as they swim upstream, so hiding from our feelings is useless. Questions are welcome."

An orange young woman toward the rear shyly

raised her hand, and he pointed to her with his fingerprint brush.

"Beep," she said in a quiet tone.

"Excuse me?" Langston said.

"Beep," she repeated, gills pulsating.

"Beep-beep!" added the antlered young man.

Langston moved around his lectern toward the edge of the stage, cupped a hand behind his ear. "I'm not sure I understand—"

But now the entire audience had joined in, including a girl with a spur of cheekbone protruding from ragged flaps of skin. "Beepbeepbeepbeep—"

His head pillowed in his folded arms, Langston awakened from his doze with a jerk. He saw his ringing cell phone on the cot near his elbow and groped for it. "Hello?"

"Is this Dr. Langston? With the police lab?"

"Speaking," Langston said. He rubbed the crust from his eyes. "May I ask who's . . . ?"

"Cody Vaega," the caller said. "My partner, Mick Aztec, told me you had some questions."

Langston straightened. "Yes," he said. "I thought you were out of town for the weekend."

"I was," Vaega said. "I'm over at the terminal. At McCarran, you know. Just got in from Dallas."

"Right, that's where he told me—"

"Caught a late flight out. Sunday nights are the joint. No crowds, cheap. Anyway, you want to talk?"

Langston glanced at his wristwatch to orient

himself. It was almost eight P.M. "Yes . . . when can we do it?"

"That's why I called. Right now works best for me. Ain't gonna have much time the rest of the week—got to catch up with business."

"I understand," Langston said. "Would you like me to meet you at the airport?"

"S'all right. I know where you are. It's on my way home," Vaega said. "You gonna handle the taxi fare?"

Langston nodded, the phone to his ear. "I've got it covered," he said.

When he heard the incoming e-mail tone on his PDA, Chenard was in the glass atrium behind his home, sipping Ceylon green tea as he looked out past the shore over a lake shimmering red in the sunset. He set down his teacup, lifted the device from the antique cane table beside his armrest, glanced at its display, and produced a soft trill of excitement.

The message was a notification that he'd received an update—and Chenard had no need to waste a second contemplating who might have posted it. The user account, of course, was "Bart12." It was the only account he followed. Or would possibly care to follow.

He opened the e-mail, read its one-word message, and felt a charge of excitement kick through his body. Forty-eight hours now. Just two days until the auction.

Chenard recalled what Bockem had told him, sounding conciliatory at the end of their last, somewhat tense conversation: "If my plans hold, there will be more than a single additional offering."

Teased by those words, Chenard had been unable to keep from wondering what the mentioned offerings might be. And as he did whenever an auction was about to come up, he'd compulsively gone back to the *Flash Ink* website, browsing the appropriate galleries again and again, becoming wishfully thrilled by the possibilities.

Then, late Sunday morning, Chenard learned which pieces Bockem had gotten hold of. It hadn't taken much deduction. A scan of the Las Vegas newspapers online had run a breaking report of the murders in Floyd Lamb Park. Although details were initially sparse and no photographs of the scene were yet available, the eyewitness who'd discovered the victims had given his story to a member of the press. Two bodies alongside each other under a tree, a man and a woman, the male Asian. The disclosure that both of them were partially skinned had set the media abuzz with understandable speculation.

Again, however, Chenard hadn't needed to engage in guesswork. Throughout the rest of the day, and long into a night in which his eagerness had denied him any sleep, he had delved repeatedly into *Flash Ink* on his handheld device, no longer looking among pieces that might become available but touring the photo galleries containing those he *knew* Bockem had acquired for his imminent sale.

The PDA in one hand now, Chenard reached for his tea with the other, sipped, and delicately replaced his cup in its saucer. The orange light of sundown washed the orchids lining the atrium in woven bamboo baskets, gently tinging the colors of their blooms—blush cymbidiums, mauve Vartuglands, creamy white moths. What a glorious evening it was!

Two days. Two more days.

Chenard trilled again, like a cat eyeing a nest of pink infant squirrels. Then, fingers moist and tingling around his handheld, he returned his attention to *Flash Ink*.

Greg Sanders clacked at his computer keyboard with a vengeance. Hours after Nick had barnstormed into Archie's office and practically shoved him aside, he continued to fume at being treated like a twentyish lab tech with spiky hair pretending to be all about overactive hormones and punk rock. That bit was done for him long ago.

Past the need for attention, Greg wasn't the insecure adolescent who'd once hated being smart because it just seemed to get him pushed face-first into walls. Grissom had instilled pride in his intelligence and inspired him to utilize it with confidence. This was the Las Vegas Crime Lab, not high school. And he was a CSI-3.

No, Greg was hardly pleased with Nick tonight. Or with Archie for deferring to him instead of having insisted that he wait his turn. But although Greg's specialty was DNA, he knew his way around computers. If people were going to cut into line around here, he could simply step off and go it alone.

The *Flash Ink* user log passwords typed in, access to its databases acquired, he opened his tracker program, typed some more, jabbed the "Enter" key with authority to complete his query, and then sat back with his arms crossed. What he was doing was more time-intensive than difficult.

In front of him now, Internet service providers and address protocols flashed on a grid chart, the network packets revealing their information in alphanumeric sequences, compiling more data with each hop of his trace.

Ten thousand *Flash Ink* members sounded intimidating. But Greg only sought the usage habits of some of them, and the questions he needed answered were fundamental. Who had visited the photo galleries of Laurel Whitsen, Daichi Sato, and Lynda Griffith? And the galleries of the Canadian victims? How often had their visits come, how long had they lasted, and had they participated in chats?

Message-board posts might or might not prove important, and reading through them could be protracted and laborious. But determining whose messages were significant would greatly winnow down the numbers.

Frequency and percentages. Simple arithmetic. And the software would do the cooking for him, making him feel almost lazy.

Definitely not worth waiting in line for, Greg thought.

"I want you to know up front, this don't feel right," Cody Vaega said.

"What doesn't?" Langston said.

"Me talking to cops."

"We aren't cops," Sara said.

"Isn't this here laboratory next door to police headquarters?"

"Yes."

"And," Vaega said, gesturing toward the hard-card ID clipped to her breast pocket, "aren't those the words 'Las Vegas Police Department' on your name tag there?"

"Correct."

"And a gold LVPD badge printed behind your name, right?"

"Correct."

"A gun holster on your side there?"

"An empty one, yes."

Vaega shrugged. "Well, you total it up, and it means . . ."

"We're scientists who deal in criminal investigations and deputies of the LVPD licensed to carry firearms," Langston said. "It's an appreciable distinction."

Vaega looked at him. Wearing a black leather biker jacket over a black sweatshirt and jeans, he was a barrel-chested, thick-necked, dark-complected man of twenty-five or thirty, his long black hair pulled up in a tight Sumo-style knot, the intertwined black tribal patterns covering his face in monochromatic accord with his clothes and hair. And while the rings and studs in his nose, lips, eyebrows, ears, and tongue *weren't* black but metallic and might therefore have been considered aesthetic departures—or even distractions—from his overall body motif, Langston's personal opinion was that they, in fact, provided some well-placed and necessary accents.

"Look, I'm here to help," Vaega said. "I'm *not* telling you I didn't know what to expect. But I'm just sayin' I don't usually . . ."

"Trust the police," Sara said. "And that you aren't too fond of talking to anybody associated with them, even if we're only trying to stop your people from getting killed."

He leaned backward. "What you mean *my*—"

"She just means people in the tattoo community," Langston said, wanting to take him off the defensive. He was glad there'd been an available conference room, with its potted plants and relatively comfortable chairs to help put Vaega at ease. This was not, after all, an interrogation. But everyone at the lab, including Sara, was frazzled from overwork and fatigue. "I can't tell you enough how much we appreciate your coming in here after a long flight from Texas."

Vaega looked into his face. "No problem, man. I just want us to be straight."

Langston nodded. "Cody—it *is* okay if I call you by your first name, by the way?"

"Yeah, please, man."

"Cody, I'm sure you know there've been several recent instances where people were abducted, drugged for a period of time, and involuntarily tattooed. In two cases, there was what might be considered extreme facial modification. A couple of nights ago—"

"I heard about the judge who died."

"From Mick Aztec?"

"Yeah. But even before," Vaega said. "There was talk down in Houston. About that and then those skinnings."

"At present, we view them as separate investigations," Langston said. "You might hear differently on the news tomorrow morning. But I'm giving it to you from our perspective here at the lab."

"Which is telling you something that could give us burn marks if it leaves these four walls," Sara said. "Just FYI."

Vaega gave a nod. "Reason I'm here is body art is supposed to be a beautiful thing," he said. "For me, it's about kindness and respect and making people what they want to be. Whoever's doing this, he's turning it inside out. Making it about *him*."

"And he's killed someone," she said.

"Like we just talked about a second ago, right," he replied, a note of exasperation in his voice.

Langston looked at Sidle, then Vaega. "I think it might be best to show you some photos now," he said, reaching for a folder on the table between them. "Then ask a question or two about epithelial samples. They're taken from—"

"The outer layer of skin, I know," Vaega said.

Langston smiled at him, nodding as he produced close-ups of Dorset's lip tattoos and Noble's face.

Vaega shuffled through the photos. "These lips . . ."

"Were tattooed on the judge's body where the sun doesn't shine," Sidle said.

He sat studying them. "Wow," he said under his breath. "This is *vivid*."

"What's that?" Langston said.

"The red. The photo ain't enhanced, right? Color saturation boosted, anything like that?"

"No."

"Wow."

"Cody, is this important?"

"Yeah, sorry," Vaega said, glancing up at Langston. "Red's the hardest color to find in a pure, high-quality ink."

"The shade, you mean?"

"No, like, chemically."

Langston shook his head to show he still wasn't following.

"Most commercial red dyes are naphtha-based," Vaega said.

"The petroleum derivative?"

"Same as they use in acrylic paint, high-octane gas, plastics . . . that's why you get so many allergic reactions to red ink," Vaega said. "Look at *my* inks. Red's the only nonorganic I use. You know the color wheel, right?"

"Goes back to Isaac Newton."

"Right, right. Even before that apple conked his head, made him forget colors, waste his time with useless shit like gravity."

Langston grinned. So did Vaega.

"Red's your primary for purple, pink, magenta down the blue end of the color spectrum," Vaega went on after a moment. "Gives you oranges and yellow-oranges at the other end."

"How about black? Would you use it for that?"

"For accents, yeah. If you really have a fine touch."

"Mick Aztec told me the colors that the Tattoo Man uses are distinctive," Langston said. "You've seen the photos of his victims online?"

Vaega hesitated.

"Something wrong?"

"No, no."

"Oh," Langston said. "Because I know *he* saw them. And that, putting aside everything that surrounds the work, it's created a buzz in the tattoo community."

"Definitely, definitely."

"So you know the photos we mean," Sara said. "The guy with the camera head. The woman whose face got turned into a clock straight out of a Salvador Dalí wet dream . . ."

"I seen 'em," Vaega said. "And you want some free advice, you can do without the 'tude."

"I wasn't—"

"We're talkin' some serious shit, you don't gotta be *scoffin'*," Vaega said, shifting his attention to Langston. "I always used to tell him, you mass-produce an organic red ink, it's gonna rock the market."

"Him?" Langston asked. "Who's 'him'?"

Vaega started to say something, appeared to waver again, sat there in silence.

"Have you ever heard of hematite?" Sara asked.

More silence.

Langston began, "Cody—"

"Sounds like some kinda stone," he said. "That right?"

"It's an unusually red iron oxide," Sara said.

"Yeah?"

"Yeah," she said. "Found in Red Rock Canyon."

Vaega glanced at her briefly but didn't respond.

"Cody," Langston said. "Tell us who you were talking about a second ago."

Vaega remained silent.

Langston reached for the folder and pulled out several more snapshots, these taken of Dorset's body in the trailer depot where it was found in the nether hours between Friday night and Saturday morning. He set the photos down on the table in front of Vaega, who did not lower his gaze to look at them but kept it fixed on a blank spot on the wall across the room.

"Go on," Langston said. "You need to see them."

More hesitation. At last, his eyes went down to the exposures. "Serious shit," he said.

"I think that's why you came here tonight," Langston said. "That the photos are just reminders."

Vaega's head slumped, moving slowly from side to side. Then came back up. "Tell you somethin',", he said. "Travelin' around, I learned there's three types of tattoo artists. You got the ones like to party . . . outgoin', you know. Then the laid-back brothers—I kinda fit in there. And then you got the scary dudes, the ones you don't want to mess with. But I never met a tattoo artist isn't all about emotion, inside and out, like it's vibratin' right off the skin . . . never in my life. And sometimes emotions, they take you places you better off not goin'."

Langston nodded, encouraging him to continue.

"Brother goes rogue, the whole community's harassed. Next thing you know, we're cited for colorin' with crayons," he said. "Ain't right, he takes us down with him."

Langston nodded again.

"About five years ago, I met a guy at an expo out in Reno," Vaega said. "Quiet like me, but superintense, an' still learnin' the trade. You can tell he's got some history, forgot more comes to color than most people ever know. First vegan artist I met, says he won't kill no innocents."

"Does he have a name?"

"I hear people callin' him the Master. So that's what I call him, too."

"Because of his expertise with color."

"Color, design . . . the whole deal."

"And he mixes his own ink?"

"Has it down to a science," Vaega said. "Understandin' what to use for pigments, how to extract and mix them, that's jus' part of it. You got to have the right carriers, sterilize the inks . . . it takes knowledge."

"You stay in touch with him after the show?" Sara asked.

"Oh, yeah. I pick his brain about color, he asks questions about technique. How to calibrate the machine—"

"Say that again?"

"*Tattoo* machine, gun, whatever . . ."

"So he can develop a light touch," Langston said. "Work with the healing cycle."

Vaega looked at him. "I can see m'boy Aztec liked you."

Langston nodded, smiling slightly.

"The Master, he learned fast," Vaega said. "I wasn't the only one he was talkin' to."

"This is in Reno?"

"Like I said, that's where we *met*—I seen him in

different places on the road," Vaega said. "Couple years after Reno, he's elite. People from all over are seekin' him out. Has a private studio. No name, no ads, nothin'. Everythin's by appointment." A shrug. "Then, you know, maybe six months back, I stop seein' him around. But word is, he's still here. It's like, you'll be hanging out, and somebody or other'll say, 'I had me a Master sightin'.' "

"Wait." Langston's brow furrowed. " 'Still here,' meaning Vegas?"

Vaega paused. Took a very deep breath. And nodded. "North side," he said. "The Master's got a warehouse out by Poppy Lane."

It was twenty past eight when Catherine received Langston's phone call in Archie Johnson's lab, where she and Nick had just finished reviewing decade-old traffic-cam composites. Less than one minute later, she phoned Brass, who contacted Ecklie with an immediate request for manpower, which included several patrol cars and a Zebra tactical unit.

A swift title search revealed the warehouse near Poppy Lane was owned by Casa de Coral Ltd. after having been purchased from a small, family-owned moving-and-storage outfit that had packed up and left the location seven years earlier.

Brass and Catherine figured they would have time enough to worry about the intricacies of the property sale. Their immediate concern was bringing in a psychotic killer.

It took Ecklie less than twenty minutes to rouse a judge for a search warrant. By then, the various units had assembled at headquarters, and Catherine, Nick, Langston, and Sara had gotten their assault vests and sidearms out of their lockers.

Sirens muted, flashers off, the LVPD vehicles were soon speeding north.

The warehouse was a square, flat cinder-block structure on a dead-end street behind a chain-link fence, a row of broken streetlamps running up to it, the night there black as slate, the lights of the police cars disclosing graffiti-splashed walls and sudden, skittering movement amid the trash bags heaped along the sidewalk. This was not the beckoning Vegas of neon and wishful sins; this was a neglected, impoverished hellhole, where the sins were desperate and violent and got you fifteen to twenty assuming leniency for good behavior and overcrowded cell blocks.

The six-man Z unit pulled up in the lead, silently exiting their van. Clad in black coveralls, they slipped toward the fence like shadows cut out of the surrounding darkness, thermal night-vision goggles attached to their helmets on flip-up mounts, Sig556 rifles at the ready. Right behind them, Brass and the CSIs grabbed their own NVGs, leaving their unmarked cars as the unis formed a hasty perimeter.

One of the tac cops jogged around the left side of the place, another went to the right, a third scouted the rear. All three returned without seeing anyone. There were no lights on inside or outside. No guard dogs beyond the fencing. No alarm wiring. The warehouse looked unoccupied.

Brass and the Zebra commander exchanged nods at the gate, and a chain cutter was brought out. A tac cop clipped its links, the chain slackening in his gloved hand like a dead metal snake, and then the group was moving through the gate toward the warehouse.

There were very few windows, and all were barred. They would enter through the front.

Another gate now, this over the entrance—a rusty pull-down, padlocked to its metal frame. The tac produced a second pair of cutters. Moments later, Nick helped him bring up the security gate with a rattle.

Now the Z unit again took the lead, a pair of tacs at the door, three more crouched to one side, Brass and the CSIs on the other wearing NVG headsets.

A whispered countdown, and they hit the door with the ram. It flung inward into pitch blackness, and they made their entry, a practiced crossover maneuver, the Z commander cutting to the right of the door, another tac buttonhooking to the left, the rest storming into the center of the room and coming back-to-back, Sig assault rifles sweeping their sectors of fire.

"This is the LVPD!" Brass said. "We have a warrant to search the premises! Is anyone here?"

Silence. They all sensed vacancy.

The group moved from one large, lightless room to another, goggles down, making rapid adjustments to their diopters and monocular front lenses as the warehouse's interior sharpened out in shades of gray. It was unfurnished, its walls bare. They went down the hallways, passed through unused storage areas, found only emptiness on emptiness at every turn.

And then they stopped short at an interior door. Metal. A wide sectional overhead on a galvanized steel track, with an electronic keypad lock.

"Goddamn," Brass muttered with a glance at the Z commander.

He slid out of the way, waited down the hall with the CSIs as the tacs took breaching charges from their gear bags, peeled off the foil, and molded the triangular slices of plastique around the door enclosure. One of them linked the saddle charges with det cord, attached a longer length of cord to a handheld timer, winding it out as he and the entire group backed toward the CSIs.

"Give it thirty," said the Z commander.

The tac turned the timer's dial.

A half minute later, there was an explosive *flump*, the groan of contorting steel, a crash as the door frame was torn from the wall, the overhead twisting and falling. Their thermal goggles automatically compensating for the glare of the blast, the team waited as a train of smoke churned up the hall and then hustled into the room.

Catherine paused inside the entry, looked around. "Found the light switch," she said. "I'm hitting it."

Her hand went to the switch, and banks of overhead fluorescents came on.

Goggles flipped up, the CSIs, tacs, and Brass stood in a gallery of nightmares. Colored pencil drawings lined the walls—the sketches alternating with photos of Stacy Ebstein, Mitchell Noble, Annabelle Beshlesko, and Quentin Dorset at various stages of their modification and healing processes.

The words graffitied on the wall above Ebstein's drawn and photographic images said, "The Tick Tock Woman." Over Noble . . .

"The Camera Man," Catherine mouthed. Her eyes went to Dorset's images. "The King," she read. And then she looked at Beshlesko's. "Sanzaru . . ."

"The three monkeys of Asian folklore," Langston said beside her. "See no evil, hear no evil, speak no evil."

Catherine's gaze went to a fifth collection of drawings—these not accompanied by photographs. Meanwhile, across the immense room, Sara stood looking around at a massage table, medical utility carts, intravenous solution bags on upright metal stands, and counters and shelves busy with neatly organized inks and equipment—the whole area surrounded by gooseneck standing lamps.

"Looks like we found our man's studio," she said. "I—"

"*Jesus Christ!*" This from one of the tacs who'd

roved to the left side of the storage space, kicking open a locked door that was as black as the night outside.

Catherine, Nick, and Langston hurried through. The area was small—possibly converted from a stockroom. There was a chain-and-pulley assembly in the middle of the ceiling. More IV stands in one corner. Dried bloodstains on the concrete floor. They saw their own shocked expressions multiplied by floor-to-ceiling mirrored walls.

"Doc," Nick said, "what is this, some kind of torture chamber?"

Langston had noticed a metal toolbox on a table at one end of the room. He unlatched it, raised the lid, and saw the deep-water fishing hooks in sealed glassine envelopes.

"He's into suspension," he said.

"What?"

Langston reached inside for an envelope, opened it, showed her a hook. "He pierces his skin and hangs to achieve a meditative or ecstatic experience. It's unusual for it to be done without assistance."

Catherine gestured around them. "He does a lot that's unusual, wouldn't you say?"

Langston looked at her. "Suspension is an ancient practice. With Hindu sects, Native Americans, other tribal cultures. The endorphin boost from the pain induces altered states, visions . . ."

Catherine, struck with a thought, hitched in a

breath. She looked at Nick and Langston. "I have to show you two something."

They moved past the tacs into the storeroom. Seeing Brass, Catherine gestured for him to join them.

She stopped at the fifth gallery exhibit. Its sketches showed a lamb with a knife or sword over it, a red-and-white cruciform banner on the blade's handle. Langston stared at the spray-painted words on the wall above.

"The Paschal Lamb," he read aloud.

"And no photos to go along with the art," Catherine said.

Nick was shaking his head. "That crazy son of a bitch is out to add something to his Easter basket."

Brass looked at the CSIs, his eyes moving from one to the next before they settled on Nick, a grave scowl weighting his features.

"You mean some*one*," he said.

11

Early mass at Our Lady of Guidance was held at eight o'clock in the morning from Monday through Friday, and Father Molanez, in his gentle implacability, had persuaded the headmaster at the school next door to allow the full choir to join his altar boys for services throughout the forty days of Lent. This had required some assurances to ease the grumblings of certain jittery lay teachers, so to lubricate the wheels of his agreement, the father had agreed that his weekday services would feature a somewhat abbreviated homily and a condensed program of hymns and psalms.

He would, of course, have to include the reflective Attende Domine and its deeply penitential bookend, the Parce Domine. He had promised himself he would only add the uplifting Jesu Dulcis Memoria if a sizable crowd filled the pews—say, five or more congregants. Now that the Passiontide had come, he'd been tempted to slip in the poetic if somewhat obscure Pange Lingua Gloriosi Proelium of Saint Venantius Fortunatus, but for the time being, he had reserved the Medieval hymn for weekend services.

And then, of course, there was the essential and much-loved Agnus Dei, into which Jake Clarkson would so earnestly pour his soul to the delight of parishioners.

Watching Jake dash up the aisle in his cassock now, the priest could not help but smile fondly. True, this morning's turnout was a tad thin, with just four congregants having shown up for prayer. But he was inwardly resigned to quiet Mondays. It was as if worshippers considered Sunday attendance a heavy dinner that provided two full days of spiritual nourishment, treating the next as optional dessert.

Still, Father Molanez thought, for those who were present—small handful though they might be—the morning had brightened the instant Jake began his sprint from the sanctuary to the narthex. And for him, the looks on their faces made all of his dickering with the headmaster and his instructors worthwhile.

Pacing himself to give the boy a chance to reach the choir loft, the father, relishing the show-stopping moment as usual, waited until Jake scooted out the doors before he began to prepare for communion. Only then, as the doors swung shut behind him, did he slowly—slooooowly—turn toward the sacraments.

*   *   *

He had left his car in the church's parking area at seven-thirty A.M., shortly after watching Jake Clarkson hurry up the lawn from the school bus to the vestry's outer door. Pulling alongside the church—he'd had almost every space in the lot to choose from—he had popped his trunk, gone around for the heavy moving blanket he'd brought from the warehouse, and lowered the trunk lid without latching it shut.

He had then walked around to the front of the church, climbed the steps, entered the narthex, and stolen a quick glance around. With no one in sight, he had pushed open the polished oak door to the choir loft and slipped through.

Behind it was a wooden landing from which a creaky staircase rose along a brick structural support wall to the loft. Running down from where he stood, another flight of stairs bent around to the church's basement. Leaning over the rail, he'd seen a space where a corner of the support wall created a blind spot for anyone coming in from the narthex. He had stepped down off the landing and flattened himself into that convenient niche, the folded moving quilt tucked under his arm.

Afterward, he had waited in silence, standing there for perhaps fifteen minutes, hearing the footsteps and noisy laughter of the choirboys as they made their way up to the balcony.

When the service began, he had listened carefully to the priest and the beautiful Lenten hymns of the mass, able to hear it all clearly as he prepared to act. The Agnus Dei would be sung once the congregation, such as it was today, began sharing in the Eucharist. His plan was to return to the landing shortly before the sermon concluded. And wait.

A pause now in the priest's delivery and the vocals above him. He flexed the stiffness from his arms, reached into his pocket for his auto injector, and removed its cap.

Another minute or so went by before he heard the boy push past the double doors between the church and the nave. He wetted his lips, ready to launch back onto the stairs from his hiding place

Then the door swung in. He waited for the boy to appear on the landing, sprang from around the corner of the support wall, and came up quickly behind him, clapping a hand over his mouth while pulling him close to his body. The boy somehow managed to twist his head halfway around, his pink-cheeked face briefly turning just enough to allow him a glimpse of the man who'd surprised him from the murky dimness below the stairs. Having been filled with excitement as he'd raced to join the choir group, his eyes suddenly turned fearful, giving his attacker a split second's pause, almost making him lament what had to be done, before he jabbed the spring-loaded auto injector against the boy's neck, waiting ten seconds for its dose of pentobarbital to be fired through the soft, thin flesh.

He did not strike the boy to ensure that he was fully out. He could not have brought himself to do it. At any rate, the tranq was powerful enough to make him droop instantly, his mouth lolling open.

Holding the small body against him with one arm, keeping it erect, he shook open the moving blanket, draped it loosely over the unconscious boy, and slung him over his shoulder.

A second later, he pushed out into the narthex, left the church through its arched entryway, and hurried down and around to his car, depositing the boy's limp, covered body in the trunk before slamming it shut.

He drove slowly along until he turned from the church grounds onto the road and only then accelerated a bit. As he did, it occurred to him that if the boy's father had done the same when he'd abducted Kyle all those long years ago, his flight might well have gone unnoticed, resulting in his identity forever remaining a mystery. But instead, he had sped from the scene and attracted attention . . . leaving all those who had seen and done nothing to suffer the necessary punishments for having let him go free.

His hand clenched around the telephone receiver, Father Molanez waited as the operator for the Douglas County sheriff's office transferred him to a deputy. The silence in his earpiece was maddening, although only three or four seconds had passed since he'd been put on hold.

Jake Clarkson had vanished. Impossibly vanished. One moment, the priest had been standing at the altar, looking toward the back of the church, expecting Jake's face to join those of the other choirboys. The next, he'd wondered what was taking him so long to reach them. And then the restless, puzzled stirring had begun in the pews and up in the loft.

Vanished, Father Molanez told himself again. From the church. From under his supposedly attentive care. It was almost too much for him to comprehend.

His first confused thought when the boy didn't appear in the balcony was that he'd bumped into an acquaintance in the narthex. Perhaps a late arrival to services. It hadn't been very sensible, of course. The boy had a keen sense of responsibility and would not delay the communion.

The explanation that followed in Molanez's mind seemed more plausible. Jake's father had showed up. He'd forgotten to pack Jake's lunch or noticed his homework on the table—something of that nature—and then had hurried over with it on his way to work.

But even that idea only half made sense. Ronald Clarkson would have had no reason to interrupt services to drop off whatever he might have found.

Even if he'd arrived just as his son was dashing upstairs, he would have taken communion and quietly given it to him afterward. Either that, or, if he was in a hurry, left it in the narthex or in a rear pew. Or with Jake's homeroom teacher at school.

No, it wasn't that Jake had met his father or anyone else. Heaven forbid, then, might he have slipped on the stairs and gotten hurt? Surely, the boys up in the loft would have heard that. But what else could have happened? There was a restroom in the vestry—Jake might have had some sort of emergency, perhaps been taken ill, and rushed out to the side door rather than embarrass himself by doubling back through the church.

That, at least, seemed a rational possibility.

All of this had passed through Father Molanez's mind in a matter of seconds before he begged patience of his little group of congregants, hurried down the hall to the vestry, and knocked on the restroom door, lightly, then with greater urgency, calling Jake's name when there was no response.

When he returned to the nave, the congregation had instantly read the alarm on his face. It had not taken long for them to start looking everywhere for the boy, even as Molanez called the school to ascertain that none of Jake's teachers or classmates had seen him there.

They had not.

And now he was on the phone with the sheriff's office. Being transferred. Waiting through the unbearable, seemingly interminable silence for someone to—

"Hello, this is Deputy Vasquez," a voice said. "Do I understand correctly that there's a missing child?"

Father Molanez's throat almost clamped shut around his monosyllabic answer. "Yes," he said.

"Okay, I want to see exactly where we stand," Catherine said, thinking with dour amusement that it almost seemed a loaded statement, given that everyone at the conference table looked utterly discombobulated, their weariness evident from their raccoon-ringed eyes, scrambled and beaten hair, and wrinkled clothes. Catherine herself was willing to bet her own body chemistry now consisted of ninety percent coffee, and judging from everyone's breath—not to put too fine a point on things—she wasn't alone.

"Nick?" she said. "How about you start off with Frank Dumas?"

Nick nodded. "I think your using his name tells us a lot," he said, running a hand over his stubbled cheek. "Everything we know points to him being Tattoo Man. We've got various lines of evidence that tie the victims to the murder of his son. In his eyes, every one of them would have had a role in Ronald Clarkson's exoneration."

"And you're positive there was never another suspect."

"Never," Nick said. "It's a cold case."

Catherine thought for a moment. "Kyle Dumas's body is found ditched in Red Rock Canyon. The epithelials from Dorset and Noble tell us Tattoo Man uses homemade pigments made from minerals in Red Rock Canyon . . ."

"And then Cody Vaega confirms someone he knows as the Master does, too, and that producing it is no easy skill," Langston said. "Next, we raid the Master's warehouse and find photos of all of Tattoo Man's victims."

"Plus one," Sara said.

Catherine considered that and frowned. "It's one thing connecting Tattoo Man, or the Master, or whatever name you want to give him, to the murder of Kyle Dumas. But how do we know he's the boy's father and not someone else with an attachment to the case?"

"We don't conclusively," Nick said. "But there's plenty to suggest that he's our guy. Frank's a top graphic designer, moonlights as a fine artist. He sells his home and drops out of sight right around the time somebody buys the warehouse in Poppy Lane. Also, we need to go back to Mitchell Noble. He wasn't one of the perceived erroneous or non-witnesses. His only sin, if we want to think like the Tattoo Man, was that he took a photo of Frank Dumas holding his boy's corpse."

"A photo that Clarkson's defense attorney argued tainted virtually all of the trace evidence against him," Catherine said.

"Right."

Catherine lifted her coffee cup, saw it was drained, and frowned. "Okay, let's premise that Frank Dumas is acting out of payback, warped justice, again, pick your own term. That image of the lamb . . . what did you call it, Ray?"

"The Paschal Lamb," he said from across the table. "Literally, the sacrificial lamb at ancient Passover celebrations. It holds great symbolism for Jews and Christians."

"We have to believe it does for Dumas, too," Catherine said. "And that it'll have a meaning we don't want to contemplate for his next victim."

"Unless we find Dumas first," Sara said.

Everyone at the table thought in silence for a while.

"While we're grasping here, do we know Ronald Clarkson's current whereabouts?" Catherine asked.

"A little town called Miriam way out near the California border," Nick said. "I checked it out this morning. His number's unlisted, so I had to go through procedural hoops to get hold of it."

"You phone him yet?"

Nick nodded. "Got his machine, left a message to please return my call. This time of day, people are at work. Or on the way. I hope to hear back from him soon."

"We should quietly notify the local police out there. Just so they keep an eye on him," Catherine said.

"Uh-huh."

Catherine sighed and turned to Greg. "Okay,

let's move on. How'd you do poking around in the *Flash Ink* member logs?"

"I did more than poke," Greg said. He glanced about the table. "I think I came up with somebody we'd better talk to."

She looked at him sharply. "What's his name?"

"Pierre Chenard," Greg said. "Lives right nearby in one of those posh Summerlin villages."

Catherine didn't know why she felt disappointed. *Not Bockem? Follow the evidence, though.* It had been Grissom's mantra. "Tell us what you know, Greg."

"Since the murders—Laurel Whitsen and the couple in the park yesterday—there's been a huge uptick in traffic on the site. The victims' photo galleries in particular."

"Internet lookeeloos."

"Right," Greg said. "That's predictable. But the IP addresses I zoned in on were ones that frequented the galleries before *and* after the killings. I included the Canadian murders, too."

Langston was nodding. "Serial killers will often trawl for their catches and then admire them."

"Like trophy hunters," Catherine said.

Greg nodded some more, looking contemplative. "This wasn't about fancy evolution equations for me. My computational method wasn't too different from what market researchers use to find a celeb's likability index. Or what any website would use to monitor its success rate pulling in targeted visitors. I narrowed down the number of unique and repeat

IPs that hit the galleries, then factored in chronological proximity to the murders. And then sat back while the software went through successive iterations."

"And this Chenard . . ."

"Is way over the top, visiting the victims' galleries over and over again," Greg said. "I'm talking compulsive. Besides that, he repeatedly hit them *before* the stories hit the news, and I got him on there in real time for maybe two hours last night."

"How'd you match the IP address to his name?"

Greg grinned. "The clown logs on with his smart phone, uses Wi-Fi on open networks," he said. "I just traced the IP back to his mobile account. And I'll be able to pull even more on him from the cellular provider and *Flash Ink*'s user database once we get a warrant."

"*Flash Ink* wouldn't give you voluntary access to his personal info?"

"Not without a warrant," Greg said. "Can't blame them, either. They have privacy guarantees for membership and need to protect themselves against lawsuits."

"Then let's request those warrants and see if we can get a search-and-seizure for his home while we're at it," Catherine said. "With Stancroft laying on the pressure, I think we can probably get instant approval—"

Her cell phone beeped. She held up a hand, pulled it out, and listened without saying a word.

And then listened some more, deep lines materializing around her mouth like parentheses. Finally, she put down the phone and looked at the waiting faces around the table.

"There's an AMBER Alert out," she said. "Issued in Douglas County. A boy named Jake Clarkson disappeared from a church in Miriam."

Four pairs of eyes widened into stares.

"I think at least one of us needs to head out there," Nick said after a pause. "Damn, it must be three, four hundred miles away—"

"Red Rock Canyon isn't," Sara said.

They all looked at her.

"I have a hunch," she said. "We walk out this door, go twenty miles, and we can stop."

"Okay, we're set for takeoff," said the Bureau of Land Management ranger from behind the controls of the Bell 206. A whipcord-thin guy named Ken Granderson, he glanced over at Catherine in the cockpit beside him, shifted halfway around toward his other passengers. "You two strapped in back there?"

Nick and Sara nodded from the rear, hearing his voice in their headsets over the whine of the chopper's engine. It was now a little past three o'clock in the afternoon, twenty minutes after he'd met the CSIs outside the visitor center at the east end of the Red Rock Canyon conservation area. From there, he'd driven them out to the helipad in a spot he'd called Calico Hill that was maybe a mile away.

"I'm gonna guess your man would need six hours minimum to get here from Miriam," he said. "That's assuming he did a good seventy-five, eighty out in those open stretches of the interstate."

"So if he's here, he hasn't been for long," Catherine said.

Granderson nodded. "My guess is he'd take Charleston into the valley—it's the easiest way from the north. Problem is that once he's in, he's in. Could be anywhere."

"And we don't know what sort of car we're looking for. Or if it's even a car or some other sort of vehicle."

Granderson considered that, his hands on the sticks. "Couple of things we do know," he said. "It's early in the year for tourists, so there won't be a lot of them."

"And?"

"We won't find him by staying here," he said, and brought the bird up.

"We ought to have the mayor stick his schnoz into every case," Greg said, glancing over at Langston from the Mustang's passenger seat. "It's like he's got judges all around town waiting on standby to authorize warrants."

Ray grinned as they left the gate behind and made the turn curving toward the lakeside estate of Pierre Chenard. They went up between rows of towering palms and swung past ornamental gardens into a circular drive. A silver Bentley was parked outside, a black Mercedes SUV behind it.

"And here we felt lucky getting the Mustang out of req," Langston said, pulling in.

They exited the car, strode along the tiled front walk to the door, and rang the bell. A servant in a blue blazer, red necktie, and tan trousers promptly appeared, and they showed him their identification.

"Mr. Chenard is expecting you," he said. "Please come with me."

He led them through expansive rooms filled with antique furniture and crystal vases to a warm, sun-washed atrium facing the man-made lake out back. As they approached, the man they assumed was Chenard rose off a high-backed cane chair to meet them. Short and corpulent, he had on a Panama hat, an eggshell suit over a light blue shirt, and brown crepe-soled loafers.

"Gentlemen," he said, motioning them toward chairs. "Please make yourselves comfortable. Daniel here can bring us some refreshments."

The CSIs remained standing. "No, thank you," Langston said.

"Are you certain? We have coffee or tea prepared—"

"Mr. Chenard, I assume you know we've come with a warrant to search your premises," Langston said, getting it out of his jacket pocket. "You may want to look over the papers."

He shook his head slightly, keeping his hands at

his sides. "My attorney is on his way to take care of that. I contacted him on short notice, so he'll be arriving in a bit. Which is why I thought we could wait arriving in the meantime. Perhaps discuss the reason for your visit."

"Do you have your cell phone handy?" Greg said.

Chenard shot him a look. "Why do you ask?"

"Because we need you to turn it over to us, sir."

"I'm not sure I understand."

"This is a search-and-seizure warrant," Langston said. "That's why I urged you to read it. We don't have to wait for your attorney. We have a half-dozen patrol cars outside the gate and can have officers turning this place inside out before he's decided which pair of shoes to wear for his visit. But we thought you might prefer that we handle this discreetly."

Chenard's upper lip twitched a little. "Handle what? I have nothing to hide."

"Then you should have no problem with the cell phone," Langston said. "We'll also want to take a look around the house."

"I still don't know what all this is about."

"Then let me make it clear. You are under suspicion for the murders of Laurel Whitsen, Daichi Sato, and Lynda Griffith. We've come to collect potential evidence. And it's in your best interest to cooperate."

"This is ridiculous." Chenard's features had blanched. "I would never harm, let alone kill, anyone. Moreover, I don't know those people."

"Then you must have an awfully bad memory," Greg said.

Chenard looked at him. "Again, I'm bewildered. And frankly haven't any notion where you're going with these accusations."

"*Flash Ink*," Greg said, and saw the remaining color leach from Chenard's cheeks. "For openers, anyway."

"You see the depression down there to the left?" Granderson asked, pointing out the chopper's windscreen.

Catherine nodded, saw the thick carpet of sage-brush along its sides and bottom. "Is that where the Dumas boy was found?"

"You've got it," he said. "I wasn't here back then, but I checked out that newspaper photo you e-mailed, then did some reading up. On average throughout the state, all those plants reach full flower in the summer. But the canyon as a whole's unusual as far as temperature and sun, and it's especially true of this area. Another week or two, and they'll be blooming like in the picture."

She narrowed her gaze, the image of the man with the boy in his arms superimposing itself over the empty gully below. After a moment, she looked over her shoulder at Sara. It was her hunch that had brought them to the canyon, and Catherine was going to ride it.

"You suppose that's where Dumas would bring Jake Clarkson?"

Sara sat very still. Although her eyes were on Catherine, they seemed to be looking inward. "No," she said after a long moment. "It's loaded with negative vibes."

"He kidnapped the boy," Catherine said. "He doesn't have anything good planned."

Sara shook her head. "I don't think he'd see it that way," she said. "Whatever he's done or intends to do . . . I think he believes it's right."

Catherine silently absorbed that, trying to follow her thought process. "If there's anything here with a positive significance for Dumas, what would it be?"

"*Affirmative* would be a better word," Sara said. "I'm not playing semantics. But it's something that gives him a reason to go on."

"His art," Nick said. "I mean, something that's associated with it."

"The minerals," Sara said. "The ones he uses for his pigments. They'd make Dumas feel in touch with his dead son. Closer to him."

Nick and Catherine looked at her as understanding dawned on their faces.

An instant later, she leaned slightly forward, tilting her head toward Granderson. "Is there someplace where the hematite and Caetano tuff are mixed in heavy concentration?"

The ranger nodded. "Keystone Thrust," he said. "Slopes aren't too awful and . . ." His sentence faded as he worked the cyclic and collective and the chopper banked sharply north.

"What is it?" Catherine said.

"There's an overlook," he said. "One where you can park a car and then climb down pretty easy."

"What's on the other side here?" Brass asked Chenard. Bookended by a pair of LVPD unis, he was standing in front of a heavy paneled oak door in Chenard's basement, or underground art gallery, whichever term one chose to describe the climate-controlled space with its rows of framed paintings.

"A private study," Chenard said. He was sweating heavily despite the low temperature. "It contains items of personal sentiment."

Brass tried the handle. "It's locked," he said. "Open it."

"I do feel compelled to wait for my attorney," Chenard said. "In spite of having a difficult time with this situation, I've gone out of my way to be helpful."

"I'm glad you're coping," Brass said. "But now you'll either have to open the door or get out of our way so we can break it down."

Chenard flinched as he turned toward Langston. "You told me this would be handled with discretion. That the police would wait outside the gate."

Langston was thinking he hadn't said precisely as much but was not about to enter into a dispute. "And you told me you had nothing to hide," he replied instead. "I suggest you listen to the detective."

Chenard produced a handkerchief from his lapel

pocket, unfolded it, and dabbed a glistening spot of perspiration off his brow. Then he gave a resigned shake of his head, reached into the jacket for a fob with a single key attached to it, and slid it into the lock.

He stepped back as Brass, the two cops, and the CSIs moved past him into the room.

Greg's eyes widened in horror and revulsion the instant he followed Langston through from the outer gallery. "Oh," he said, a hand going up to his temple. "Oh, man."

There were more than a half-dozen acrylic frames on the walls containing tattooed human skins. A large pinkish heart with a radiant blue-and-yellow eye in the middle. A feathered serpent coiling through gemstone-colored constellations of stars. A concupiscent male face composed of countless tiny flowers, with shriveled brown protuberances discernible as human nipples on the skin itself . . .

Greg looked around the room, his expression of sick disgust mirrored on the face of everyone who'd come into it with him. And then his eyes abruptly froze on one in particular.

Below the framed tattoo of a nude woman with graceful angelic wings, a brass wall plaque read, "KZ Buchenwald, Block Two, Germany, ap-1943."

Greg snapped his head around toward Chenard, who had remained outside the entrance. "How?" he said. "How could you . . ."

"I'm only a connoisseur, a buyer," Chenard said,

the handkerchief in his hand again. "But I can give you the one who sold them to me."

Its rotors whopping, the chopper reached the heaving bluff Granderson had called Keystone Thrust, then climbed almost vertically alongside its rock face to fly over its flattened summit.

Catherine looked down at an unattended Honda sedan parked on the overlook and motioned out her window.

"Only car in sight," she said. "How do we find out if it's our man?"

"I'll widen my circle," Granderson said. He nodded toward a small compartment beneath the instrument panel. "The binoculars are in there."

She reached inside as he glided out over the edge of the rocky platform, then brought the lenses up to her eyes.

As he made his second looping run around the cliffs, breath hissed through her front teeth. "I see him!" She gesticulated to her right and passed the binocs back to Nick and Sara. "He's got the boy."

Catherine stared out the windscreen, following his progress with her unaided eyes. He was down at the bottom of the gully, struggling across a wash to the opposite slope, Jake Clarkson's limp form over his shoulder. The boy was gagged and trussed like an animal, his arms and legs bound with cord. As the Bell chopper flew above him, the fleeing man craned his head back long enough to get a look at it, then continued stumbling on foot toward the far side of the wash.

"If we go back to the overlook, try to climb down from there, there's no chance we can catch up to him," Nick said.

Granderson filled his chest with air. "You want to hang on to your seats, I can try bringing her down here in the arroyo," he said. "It ought to be level enough in the wash for me to get my skids . . ."

"Do it," Catherine said.

And then she felt her stomach lurch as Granderson made a sheer, rapid descent, the bird shuddering as it dove in low over the ground, shedding a hundred fifty feet of altitude in what felt like a heartbeat.

Catherine looked out the windscreen. The fleeing man was still well ahead of them, rushing toward a cut in the gully's wall that hadn't been visible from above. But she thought they at least had a chance to catch up. *If—*

"You've gotta land this thing now!" she exclaimed

Granderson grunted. "All right, this is where it gets bumpy."

He gripped the sticks hard. A moment later, the bird made a touchdown that jarred Catherine's spine, the backwash of its blades kicking up a cloud of sand and gravel.

She sucked in a breath and unclipped her safety harness. In the rear of the aircraft, Nick and Sara were doing the same.

"Just wait a few seconds so the blades can slow," Granderson said. "Keep your heads tucked."

Catherine gave it exactly one second and jumped out her door, crouched beneath the flapping rotors, Nick and Sara close on her heels. Ahead of them, their quarry had almost reached the notch in the slope.

"Frank Dumas!" Nick shouted, jogging behind at a fast clip. "Las Vegas police! Stop where you are!"

The man barely held up. But Catherine had seen the slightest hitch in his step as she kept running, running, running, arms pumping at her sides.

He continued on, stumbling a little under the awkward burden of the boy's weight. And then he plunged into the notch.

Nick had drawn his duty weapon, an H&K .45-caliber pistol, and he put on the speed now, moving alongside Catherine and then slightly in front. She and Sara had pulled their own pistols but let him take the lead. Texas boy, best shot, legs all hard muscle, he had a better chance of eating up the ground that separated them from their man before it was too late. Assuming, God help all of them, that already wasn't the case.

A blurry yard, then another few feet, and the CSIs were inside the cut.

They drew to a halt. The boy was on a flat red stone the shape of a large anvil. Semiconscious— they could see him moving his head groggily from side to side. Standing over him, his abductor was gripping a Bowie knife in both hands, holding it over the boy's throat.

"Mr. Dumas," Nick said. Twenty, thirty feet away from him. Decent range. His firearm held out. "You don't want to hurt the boy."

The man turned his head in Nick's direction. The knife was poised over the boy's jugular.

"God demands balance," he said. "A pure sacrifice."

"No," Sara said, stepping up from behind Nick. "No, listen to me. God didn't want your son to die. He doesn't want another man's son—"

"This boy's spirit will be given unto him," Dumas said. "Be cleansed and sanctified at this altar. And Kyle's soul will be reborn in the flesh. Returned to us. Balance . . ."

Sara was shaking her head. "Kyle's at rest," she said slowly. "He's someplace better than here. You can't bring him back, nobody can, so why don't you put down the knife?"

He looked at her. Their eyes locked.

"Please, Mr. Dumas," she said. "Drop the knife. We understand your loss and don't want to hurt you."

He shook his head. "I don't have long to live," he said. "It's lung cancer."

"Then we can get you medical care."

"You *don't* understand," Dumas said. "The cancer is God's message to me. A gift of Awakening. So that I would know it was time to act. And what had to be done."

"No," Sara said. "I'm telling you, Mr. Dumas. You are making a terrible mistake."

He started to say something, appeared to reconsider, and instead shut his mouth. Looked from the boy to Sara, then back down at the boy. Finally, he shook his head and lowered the Bowie knife to the boy's throat.

Nick pulled the trigger of his gun once, knowing that was all it would take. Dumas staggered backward, blood splashing from his chest, hitting the ground with the knife still in his slackening grip.

His weapon against his thigh now, Nick ran over to him, knelt to check his pulse, turning toward Catherine and Sara as they untied the boy, carefully lifted him from the stone, and set him on the ground.

He shook his head, holstered the pistol. "Gone," he said.

Sara looked over at him and met his gaze, the cords she'd helped remove from Jake Clarkson's wrists dangling from her hand.

"If there really is a better place than this . . . I'd like to think he's with his son," she said. "But heaven help us, I'm not even sure he deserves it."

12

"I WANT TO MAKE sure we're all clear about this," Brass said. Along with CSI Willows, he was in Interrogation Room B at headquarters, addressing Pierre Chenard's defense lawyer, a middle-aged guy named David Billson who was decked out in maybe two thousand dollars' worth of tailored Armani fabric. "Your client here is insisting he is not the person who's been murdering contestants— and would-be contestants—who appeared on the *Flash Ink* television show but a collector of unusual tattoos."

"A connoisseur of exceptional body art and human skin rarities," Chenard broke in from where he sat beside Billson. "However repetitious that might sound, I prefer not to be mischaracterized. Also, as my attorney has indicated, you may address me directly, Captain."

Brass stared across the table at him. "I appreciate that," he said. "As I understand it, Mr. Chenard, you claim that you weren't trawling the *Flash Ink* website for potential victims but were checking out merchandise—"

"Browsing for modern *masterpieces*," Chenard said. "A bit compulsively at times, I admit. But I dive into my passions with abandon."

"Which you say explains the frequency of your visits to the galleries."

"Correct."

"And so—again, I want to make sure there's no mistake—you are asserting that you were a buyer and not the seller."

"Yes."

"And that you belong to some sort of secret auction group that bids on these human skins online."

"A very select group of body-art connoisseurs with members around the world," Chenard said. "Although I don't know the identities of the other bidders."

"Because you all use screen names," Brass said.

"That, too, is indeed correct," Chenard said. "Mine being Virgo because it is my astrological sign."

Willows looked at him. "Mr. Chenard, you've said you do know the name of the seller. The individual who assembled the group and has been murdering people for their tattoos—"

"One moment, Ms. Willows," Billson said, raising a hand. "Before my client responds, I'd like to ascertain that his offer to cooperate fully with your investigation will be rewarded with a recommendation of leniency."

"We've already told you it will," Brass said.

"I understand. But, like you, I want to be absolutely certain of things."

Brass grunted and pointed at the video camera on the ceiling. "As you know, Counselor, this entire conversation's being recorded. A deal is a deal, so you can settle down."

Billson glowered but left it at that.

"About the auctioneer," Catherine said, picking up where she'd left off. "You are confirming that his name is Bockem."

"William Bockem, yes," he said. "We have ties going back many years."

Catherine was thinking Gris would be ecstatic when he heard about this. "Because your family has bought art from *his* family."

"Yes. When both lived in Europe," Chenard said. He frowned. "Although you should be aware I've never gotten any sort of discount or special treatment because of that relationship, much to my chagrin."

"Pity." Brass sighed. "Okay, how about we cut to the chase? According to you, Bockem is preparing to auction off the skins he took from Laurel Whitsen and the other two *Flash Ink: Las Vegas* contestants, Diachi Sato and Lynda Griffith. That right?"

"Yes. Tomorrow, in fact. I meant to bid on all three pieces," Chenard said. "*Took* is such a nasty word, however. Might we use the term *harvested* instead? It's far more refined and indicative of how I view their appropriation."

"I don't care how you view it," Brass said testily. "What I do care about is our deal. And to repeat its specifics for the benefit of you, your counsel, and those goddamn cameras over our heads, it is that you are going to bid on those pieces of dead human beings tomorrow, and you are going to make sure you're the winner. And when Bockem comes to deliver them to that beautiful home of yours, I will be waiting there to bust his sick, ghoulish ass. Are we in agreement here, Chenard?"

Chenard glanced at Billson, received a nod, and then returned his attention to Brass, crossing his arms over his chest. "Your crude vocabulary aside, Detective, I believe we are," he said.

Two cases, two killers. Catherine had been right all along . . . but she was by no means feeling celebratory.

Ten minutes after leaving Brass to finish up with Chenard and his attorney at headquarters, she was next door at the morgue with Nick and Sara, where the CSIs had been summoned to hear the results of Doc Robbins's preliminary autopsy on Frank Dumas, a.k.a. Tattoo Man.

Like every other aspect of the probe, it had yielded anything but predictable results and compounded tragedy atop senseless tragedy. Dumas had not only been mistaken about his son's killer— a maniac who was never arrested for the crime and who, for all anyone knew, was still at large somewhere these many years later—but he'd let his vengeful impulses destroy his sanity and then turned them upon innocent people when he'd thought his own life was nearing its end.

Which, Robbins was explaining over Dumas's Y-sectioned remains, had been yet another instance of him being terribly wrong.

"It's hard to fathom," Nick said. "You're *positive* he didn't have cancer?"

"I didn't find any sign of it," he said, leaning on his cane. "Certainly, there was no malignancy in his lungs, as he apparently believed."

"Just a tree," Sara said.

"A *sapling*," Robbins clarified. He set the towel in his hand down on the stainless-steel morgue counter and unfolded it to reveal the three-inch-long evergreen specimen wrapped inside. "It's an anomalous occurrence—but not a singular one. There was a similar instance in Russia several years back. A patient shows up at a hospital or clinic coughing up blood. The doctors see a large shadow on his MRIs and decide he has a metastasized tumor in his lung. But when they open him up, they find a tree. With roots, branches, and leaf buds."

Standing beside Nick, Catherine shook her head. "It's a strange one from start to finish, isn't it?" she said.

"Yeah," Nick said. "About three years after his son's death, Dumas quits his job as a commercial artist and sells his house. He uses the money he's saved up from his job and freelance gigs—and the profits from selling his home—to buy the warehouse on Poppy Lane."

"And then he goes underground," Sara said. "Travels the country, learns the tattoo trade, earns a rep as a master of the art."

"Even though there isn't a single tattoo on his body," Robbins said. "I found fresh wounds from a recent suspension and older scars from previous ones. But that's it. There's no deliberate scarification, no ink anywhere."

"Pretty unusual in itself," Sara said. "Especially when you consider he'd achieved what amounts to cult status in the tattoo community."

Nick looked at her. "The bottom line is that Dumas was good at what he did. Great, I guess. And he shared what he learned along the way with other artists."

Silence momentarily pressed against the tiled walls of the room. "I wonder whether his plan for the kidnapping spree started taking shape right after his son's death or maybe the dismissal of the case against Clarkson," Catherine said. "If it was growing inside him all this time just like that tree. And if learning the tattoo trade was an intentional part of it."

"That's possible," Nick said. "Keeping his body an ink-free zone also would've made him harder for his victims to identify. Nothing to cover up . . . could be it was deliberate."

"The guy who sold him the Bowie knife up in Miriam said he would've never guessed Dumas was a sociopath," Sara added. "He was buying it for a human sacrifice—the sacrifice of a *child*, no less—and having a friendly conversation with him the entire time. It's almost as if he was disguised in his own skin."

There was another silence in the room, this one longer than the first.

"His belief that he had a terminal disease and was nearing the end was the final psychotic trigger for his mission . . . or at least made him decide its time had come," Catherine said. "But I don't understand why he didn't have himself checked out by a doctor."

Robbins shrugged. "He might've done so initially and not followed through, like that Russian man," he said. "Remember what I told you about the *feldscherer* in medieval Europe? In our country, there's one thing most freelance artists live without, and professional tattooers are statistically the fastest-growing subgroup to deal with the problem. The costs are prohibitive even for those who do well enough to support themselves in a fairly comfortable manner."

Catherine looked at him, comprehension dawning over her features. "Dumas was a tattoo artist," she said after a moment. "He had no health insurance."

"Mr. Chenard, I'm quite pleased to deliver these to you," William Bockem said. "They are works of the first order."

Across the table from him in his atrium, Chenard deeply inhaled the perfume of his cultivated orchids, savoring it perhaps for the final time as he took the skins in their tubes and brown paper wrappings. "I'm sure the other bidders were disappointed," he said.

Bockem gave a dismissive shrug. "While I admit I was surprised you won the entire lot, your bids came in higher than theirs," he said. "Fine art should go to those who desire it most. As you know, it is something I learned from my father and that he learned from his."

Chenard nodded, his hands on the tubes. How he wished he could take them with him.

"Well, I'd best be off now," Bockem said. He reached down beside his chair and lifted the attaché case full of bills Chenard had given him. "May we continue our business into the future."

Chenard looked at him. "That would be my wish."

"I believe the next competition is in New York City," Bockem said, rising. "There's quite a thriving creative community there, and I have no doubt I'll obtain some wonderful pieces—"

Bockem started, his eyebrows lifting. He'd been facing the French doors leading from the house and noticed a sudden, rustling movement through the reflected sunlight on their glass panels.

He had time enough to give Chenard a brief quizzical glance before the doors were flung open and a bullish man in a dark blue suit stepped through, followed by several others in police uniforms.

"Detective Jim Brass, LVPD homicide," he said. "Enjoyed listening to your conversation, but if I were in your shoes, I wouldn't make any travel reservations for the Big Apple for a while."

Ray Langston turned his car into the parking lot, pulled into an empty slot, got out, and strode up to the tattoo studio.

"Hi, Doc," Raven Lunar said from behind her front counter, facing the door as he walked in. "You're a little early, aren't you?"

"I'm not used to days off," he said with a shrug. "They play tricks with my timing."

She smiled. "That's okay. It'll give us a chance to go over the sketches. They're all based on your design."

Langston took a moment to admire the paper *koinbori* hanging from the ceiling. "Are they down here?" he said. "The sketches, that is . . ."

She shook her head. "I kept them in the private studio. I figured you'd want to get a look at them. Before I show them to my clients, that is."

"I do . . . and thank you."

Raven's smile grew larger and brighter. "They're going to be beautiful," she said. "I really wish the world knew of your talent."

Langston flashed a grin at least as warm as hers. "A little secret here and there never hurt anyone," he said, and started upstairs.

About the Author

JEROME PREISLER has written almost thirty books of fiction and nonfiction. He is the author of the *Tom Clancy Power Play*s series published by Berkley Books, all of which have been top-of-the-list *New York Times* bestsellers, have sold millions of copies worldwide, and have been translated into many languages. These include *Politika*, *Ruthless.com*, *Shadow Watch*, *Bio-Strike*, *Cold War*, *Cutting Edge*, *Zero Hour*, and *Wild Card*. Jerome's previous novel in the *CSI: Crime Scene Investigation* series, *Nevada Rose*, was published by Pocket Star Books in 2008.

Jerome is the co-author (with Ken Sewell) of the narrative history *All Hands Down: The True Story of the Soviet Attack on the USS Scorpion*, currently available in paperback from Pocket Star. His next work of nonfiction about the most extraordinary submarine battle of WW II will be published by Berkley in 2012.

Jerome and his wife, Suzanne Preisler, have collaborated on several pseudonymously written comedic mysteries, including *A Brisket, A Casket*, the first in a new series to be published by Kensington Books.

Jerome is now in his sixth year of writing baseball commentary and analysis for YesNetwork.com, the official website of the New York Yankees Entertainment & Sports Network. His newest regular column for YES, Yankees Ink, was launched after the Yankees' 2009 World Championship season and is among the site's most popular features.

He may be reached at Preisler@JeromePreisler.com.